Stephanie: The Savage Land

Among the fires and street-fights of revolution, at the battle-front in the Crimea, and during the terrible days of the Siege of Paris, Stephanie has experienced danger, terror and excitement. In her relationships with her lovers and during her two short but happy marriages, she has shown herself to be as passionately loving as any man could wish. Now she has achieved what she has always longed and fought for—marriage to René de Guinchamp, her first lover.

But life never stands still for Stephanie. She can never be the submissive wife whom René wants, and frustrated by the conditions of their life together, she travels to visit her properties in New Caledonia, France's new Pacific possession. In Yann Kerdelec she finds a man with all the qualities which René lacks, and in the freedom of colonial life an outlet for her ambition. Yet none of her past experiences has prepared her for the peril she is to find herself in—as a hostage in the hands of rebellious natives, the savage Kanakas who have never accepted French domination.

Stephanie's story began in

STEPHANIE: THE PASSIONS OF SPRING
STEPHANIE: THE SNOWS OF SEBASTOPOL
STEPHANIE: THE EMPEROR'S AGENT
STEPHANIE: ALL FOR MY LOVE

and will be continued in

STEPHANIE: THE PRICE OF FREEDOM

Stephanie
The Savage Land

MARCELINE GOBINEAU

Translated from the French by
Jocasta Innes

ALLAN WINGATE · LONDON
A Howard & Wyndham Company
1976

Published in France by Éditions de Trévise, Paris,
under the title *Stephanie: Le Prix de la Liberté* (part I)

Printed in Great Britain by
Fletcher & Son Ltd, Norwich
for the Publishers, Allan Wingate Ltd,
44 Hill Street, London W1X 8LB
Bound by Richard Clay (The Chaucer Press) Ltd,
Bungay, Suffolk

ISBN 85523 121 1

Chapter One

Stephanie swept out of the drawing-room in a furious flurry of silks, ruffles and lace, and slammed the door violently behind her.

Trembling with anger, she went into her study and a second door slammed. Another episode in the contest of wills which had begun with her marriage to René.

Why wouldn't he see that she wasn't the sort of woman to be satisfied with a life of pretty clothes, parties, gossip and idiotic social conventions? He went on and on about their social position, and the things that could or couldn't be done because people in their set would *talk* ... let them! She didn't give a damn for the opinions or criticisms of all those useless creatures who knew nothing of life beyond their own worldly, shallow, ornamental existence. She wanted to *live* her life, to gulp it down in great greedy draughts, seeking its meaning whenever it might be found, experiencing its variety, its unforeseen twists and turns, its dangers ...

Yes, she missed the spice of danger, though she wouldn't admit it to herself. However, her role in the Dytteville Company's concerns, anxiety over her ships at sea, pride in snatching new markets from competitors, the thrill of drawing up plans, backing her hunches, all helped to make up for it. And now René wanted to take it all away from her!

Stephanie gave the bell pull three sharp tugs to summon Aimé, and went on pacing the room with long, impatient strides, striking her open palm with her clenched fist. Her fury refused to subside. This time he had gone too far! 'If one has the honour of being Madame Guinchamp . . .' Honour indeed! What honour, whose honour? Where would he be now if his mother had not shrewdly bartered his good looks for Agnes's fortune? Living on an officer's pay. No money, no social position, no Guinchamps mansion, nothing!

She despised him, but it didn't stop her loving him. After all, he hadn't changed, he had always been the same. She remembered saying to Pompette, who made no secret of her low opinion of him, 'I know what you think of him, but I can't help myself, I just love him the way he is!' And she had loved him with reckless passion, followed him at the risk of her life, and finally married him so that she might have him beside her night after night, for the joy of seeing him smile and walk, of hearing him murmur her name in that deep, sensual voice of his. When he said 'Stephanie' in that special tone of voice it was as if his lips were brushing her skin, his snobbery and vanity were forgotten as she lay, shivering and burning for his love. To be a lover, that was his role in life!

"Come in," she cried, as Aimé knocked three times on the door. This was their secret code—she gave three pulls at the bell to call him, he knocked three times to announce his presence.

Ever since her first quarrel with René, when she had told him she was pregnant and he had immediately made this a pretext to try and change her life and force her to give up her outside interests, Stephanie had found herself drawing closer to Aimé. Their old intimacy returned. She could tell Aimé anything because he knew her better than she knew herself. They had been born in the same part of the country, brought up together, and the soil, the climate of their native region were part of the mysterious bond between them. René was begging, demanding that she give up her 'shopkeeping' right up to the moment of her confinement. Ever since the birth of Diane, a girl instead of the boy she had longed for, he had been stubbornly repeating the same old tale: "When are you going to stop running about manufacturers' offices and showrooms, haggling over prices and contracts with shopkeepers and furniture makers?"

"Never, and that's final!" she had announced, banging the doors behind her.

"Madame wanted to see me?"

She saw at once that Aimé had the long, disapproving face on. Now that he and Stephanie were back on their old footing, that disapproving face and the accusing silences had returned, as had her own temper and blunt, outspoken way of talking.

"He's started all over again!"

"Not started, Madame—he never stopped!"

She gave him a black look. "Is he never going to stop hounding me!"

"Not while Madame refuses to give way."

"You mean ..."

"That in his own eyes, Monsieur has a good case."

"So you agree with him!" she stormed.

"Let us say I see his point."

"As if that made any difference to him!"

"I believe it does, though," he replied with the exasperating calm which always goaded her to fury.

"You do it on purpose, to infuriate me!"

And it was true that he goaded her deliberately, knowing that it was best for her anger to erupt and expend itself. Sympathy and understanding were reserved for the moment when she began to weary, and would listen. None of this made any difference in the end, but at least she and René would be lovers again for a few days. That was how these scenes always ended. Only to recommence, or rather, to resume shortly afterwards.

"Can you see me leading a life of idleness?"

"Certainly not. That would not suit Madame at all. She was always one for sliding down the banisters."

"The ... what?"

Stephanie had no idea what he was talking about. As often happened, Aimé's oblique way of putting things left her completely baffled.

"Ever since she was a small child, Madame showed a preference for such activities as sliding down banisters, jumping flights of steps, climbing trees, scrambling up rocks . . ."

He always took her back to her childhood, or to the Crimea and Pompette and Tuboisquoi, when he wanted to soften her and change her mood. Sometimes he would invoke Amelie too, because after her return from the Crimea, when she was in disgrace, a social outcast, a common cantinière, Amelie had taken her under her wing and reintroduced her to polite society.

"So . . .?" Stephanie demanded.

"Madame has a vigorous personality: it is bound to seek one outlet or another."

"What other?"

"Madame Hortense . . ."

Stephanie had always resolved to be more like her mother, though in fact there was scarcely any resemblance between them. When Aimé brought her mother's name up, Stephanie knew he was giving her a lesson in womanly decorum. Hortense never lost her temper. Her voice and manner were gentle, controlled, but so decided that no one dared argue with her, and she got her way without any shouting or banging of doors. Stephanie knew the recital of Hortense's virtues by heart, and she was in no mood to hear it again.

"My mother always got what she wanted—my father never refused her anything, as you well know."

"As Madame well knows Monsieur de Guinchamp and Monsieur de Boisnaudouin are two very different people."

He could always reduce her to silence with remarks like these. Their hidden meaning, which she could or would not argue with, was, 'Your marriage was a mistake.'

Another mistake had been agreeing to live in the Guinchamp mansion. It was *his* home, not theirs. She should have bought a house for them to live in, or had one built. At the time, though, she had been ready to agree to anything . . . hadn't she loved him for twenty years? And now, at long last, they were getting married!

"He seems to forget that I was Madame Dytteville before I ever became Madame de Guinchamp," she began, eager to defend herself. "I have responsibilities, after all. I have four children. If I didn't look after their inheritance, and invest it well, the money would dwindle away."

"Not if it is invested in land, and property, Madame; investments like those take care of themselves. But that is not what annoys Monsieur. He has property of his own."

"Only because his wife died!" she cried in a sudden fury.

Aimé's level gaze probed hers, challenging her conscience. Stephanie regretted her contemptible remark. Her eyes evaded his guiltily but she tried to excuse herself by laying the blame on René for angering her, Aimé for being so unsympathetic. They were all getting at her, she told herself, no wonder she lost her temper occasionally.

"A great misfortune. Yet Madame did all she could to save Madame Agnes's life," he answered in a careful, neutral tone.

She gazed at him for a moment before murmuring, with slow emphasis: "*We* did all we could, Aimé, that's the truth. Don't forget Noemie. If we hadn't all done what we could the child wouldn't be alive now."

They fell silent, remembering Agnes's appalling sufferings in childbirth, the desperate cold, the carriage they chopped up for firewood, the rum, and the baby's first cry. René's son! He was two years old now. He was called René after his father, the last wish of the woman who had died to give him life. From her he inherited his gentle nature and light blue-grey eyes, though in general he took after his father with his dark hair, shapely mouth and clear-cut features. He, and his two sisters Catherine and Juliette, of whom Stephanie was not overfond, all lived with her, whereas her own children still lived, as they had always done, with their Dytteville grandparents. She had never broken the promise she made to her mother-in-law on her return from the Crimea. After André died, and Stephanie was ill for so long, Françoise took little Maurice and Valentine de Bourdeilles to live with her own two grandchildren. Afterwards Stephanie abided by Aimé's advice, when he told her to leave the children as they were.

"They are happy where they are. In Madame's world adults and children lead separate lives in any case. Madame Dytteville treats them all as if they were her own flesh and blood."

A long separation followed, during the siege and the Commune, and by the time they returned, Stephanie had accepted the fact that the children's real home was with the Dyttevilles. She sometimes thought hers must be too, because she felt so much more comfortable and at ease there than in the Guinchamp mansion. If only René ...

But he would never understand. Now her anger had cooled, she realised she should not have asked him to come to the meeting that afternoon.

She glanced at Aimé. He didn't approve either, and she was as powerless against him as against her husband. Aimé was a tower of common sense, René a tower of convention. She never succeeded in dislodging so much as a pebble when she hurled herself against them; all she did was break her nails.

In a last bid for his sympathy, she assumed a martyred air, and murmured sorrowfully: "If you knew what he said to me! The cruel things he said ... it's not fair, I don't deserve it!"

Aimé's face went blank as a stone, but she could tell what he was thinking: 'There you go again, thinking up excuses for yourself—you know you don't believe them!' What an infuriating man he was! He was always forcing her to attend to that still, small voice inside her.

"He had the nerve to tell me that there are some people Madame de Guinchamp does not receive in her home. Or only very occasionally, in return for an invitation."

"Monsieur must have been referring to the Vaudières."

He was right, as usual. Instead of bridling defensively,

however, Stephanie went on playing the part of a helpless woman crushed by events.

"He's an old friend of mine. He's a banker, and we have done business together for years—René knows that."

"Just as you know Monsieur dislikes him."

This time she returned his fire.

"I want that Chesnay property near Versailles, and I shall have it!" she cried, her voice sharpening. "'I sniff something in the wind,' as Pompette used to say. It's an excellent investment, but I must act quickly. I can't arrange a meeting at the Rue Vivienne offices because of my father-in-law, who hates taking risks, and because of Hippolyte, who takes weeks to make up his mind. So I asked Vaudières and two advisors to come here—what's so dreadful about that?"

"Nothing. And Madame has no doubt asked Monsieur to come and pass the time of day with people he detests."

Naturally! She knew quite well that Antonin Vaudières and the others would feel flattered by a few friendly words from M. de Guinchamp, and therefore readier to agree to her terms. Twice before René had agreed to 'put in an appearance' to smooth the passage of her business deals, vowing each time that this must be the last. This time he had dug his heels in.

"I warned you! You know how much I dislike these occasions. In future you must not count on my presence. You must take your business dealings somewhere else. I won't have this sort of thing conducted under my own roof. There are plenty of offices and back rooms and tawdry business premises in this corrupt city we live in. If one has the honour to be . . ."

That was the phrase that stung! The honour of the Guinchamps! Had he been thinking of the family honour when his mother went chasing after the Lomanais marriage dowry?

"It is not much to ask," she said coldly. "A few handshakes, a couple of 'How are yous?', a smile or two and a couple of turns round the drawing-room and everyone is happy."

"Madame will forgive me if I decline to discuss the matter further. Madame is right, Monsieur is right, everyone is right, but the North Pole and the South Pole will never come together. Rest assured that I shall provide everything necessary for her meeting with these gentlemen. They will have all they need—paper, pencils, refreshments, coffee, tea, cakes. I shall see to it myself and I trust Madame will find nothing to complain of."

When Aimé disapproved, he adopted this mulish tone. It infuriated her, but she dared not let fly. She knew she was beaten. As he left the room she was already admitting that he might have a point—she should never have arranged for the meeting to take place here. She had chosen to have it here because it would be convenient, and private. And perhaps to dazzle Vaudières and his colleagues a little. But she had never intended to cross swords with René over it. What a fuss about nothing! He might do something to help her for once ... five minutes of his precious time, it wasn't as if she had asked for the moon ... she *was* his wife! When she thought of all the sacrifices she had made for him—she would like to see another woman do what she had done, signing on as an army cantinière, taking appalling risks, making every sacrifice simply to be with him. What other woman would have abandoned her children to march beside a donkey cart, serving the troops, enduring the horrors of Dobruja, Alma, the Sandbag Battery where she had saved his life, thanks to ...

Ah, Boris! His memory haunted her. Theirs had been a love without cloud or blemish, a dream of love! Throughout the Great Exhibition, Boris had taken a real interest in her work. He had even planned to return to France to draw up a report, working and making enquiries under her guidance. Boris understood her, loved her—but then there had been the war, the Siege, Agnes's death, René a widower at last ... and she had married René.

Prince and Princess Biotsky had sent formal congratulations ... and then she had received a marvellous letter from 'him', a letter she would treasure till her dying day ...

> '... I understand. I cannot offer to share my name, my fortune or my life with you, but I love you and always shall ... you are mine, my wife, closer to me in my heart than you can ever be as Madame de Guinchamp in Paris. I shall not return to France, it would be demanding too much of myself. I cherish you in my heart, my eyes, my soul ... be happy, my unforgettable Stephania, my own Stephania ...' The letter ended with a reference to René. 'I saved this man's life on the battlefield, for your sake and now you are his wife ... God's will be done! I ask only one thing of Him, my beloved, that we shall be reunited again in Him for all eternity, that is my only prayer!'

She ran her hands over her face. What was the good of dreaming, remembering? Boris had his own life to lead, she had hers, a life she had deliberately chosen. But for the past few months this life of hers had been tottering on the brink of collapse and failure, and René's obstinacy only made her more bitter. Why was he so unfair, so ... narrow-minded? Why couldn't he try to understand, or admit that he was wrong? Why was he so helplessly enslaved by pride and vanity and social convention? Stephanie sighed resentfully. But her disappointments never lasted long, she was too resilient, too active. 'The banisters,' Aimé had reminded her. She saw herself sliding down the polished wood, reaching the foot of the stairs, in a moment she would jump down and ... René *must* put in an appearance at the meeting! She promised herself this, willing it to happen with all her strength. But it would be for the very last time, she promised herself that too ...

She sat down for the midday meal in a mood to win the

day. As she rang for coffee she decided the moment had come to be charming, persuasive, gentle. She was about to speak when René cut in first, leaving her open-mouthed.

"You must excuse me . . ."

He used the formal 'vous', a form of address he liked and she hated though she accepted that it was the correct thing when they were at social gatherings together. But not here . . .

". . . I arranged to have coffee with the Resmonts. Achille suggested it, knowing you had important business to see to."

"*You* must have told him!" she said reproachfully.

"You told me of your plans and I made other arrangements. The last thing I want to do is interfere with your precious freedom. Naturally these gentlemen must be made to feel quite at home here. But be so good as to warn me if you decide to ask them to dinner."

He had flung down the gauntlet. This was war! She dropped her napkin, struck the table top with her fist and stood up, gazing at him with darkened, glittering eyes . . . René meanwhile, as if he had noticed nothing, was half-way to the door.

"René!"

He took no notice. He opened the door, passed through and closed it behind him, all with the same tranquil indifference. He was deaf, and blind! But he wasn't running away from the situation, she knew him too well to suppose that. This sudden departure of his meant that he had taken up his position, entrenched himself, and that nothing she could do or say would make him budge.

She was fuming with annoyance and frustration. She began nibbling jerkily at her thumb nails.

"I won't give in . . . I can't . . . he must be made to see things my way . . . I want . . ."

She wasn't at all sure just what it was she did want, or what it was he must be made to see, in fact she was torn this way and that, caught in a sea of conflicting emotions.

She felt angry, lost, betrayed, humiliated. She wanted to save what had been a grand passion. At the same time she did not want to alter her way of life. But the two things were clearly irreconcilable. They did nothing but clash, she and René, from morning to night, over petty things as often as major issues.

'If only ... but I'll have to think it over later. He makes me so angry I can't think clearly! Vaudières is expecting to see him, looking forward to it! I shall have to think of something, make other arrangements. But I'm going to get that property at Chesnay, whether he likes it or not!'

Stephanie's business meeting had gone off even more successfully than she had expected, but it left a bitter aftertaste in her mouth. That evening René was charming and attentive, but instead of asking whether she had had a good day, as he usually did, in his courteous, well-bred way, he merely wanted to know whether he should refuse the invitation to the Comtesse de Lozançaise's ball, as usual.

Keeping her jealous agitation well under control, Stephanie smiled charmingly and answered that she would *adore* to go. René bowed and thanked her appreciatively. He was delighted by her attitude ...

'I've done my bit,' she thought. 'I'm only doing it to please him, he must see that. But if I accept an invitation from that woman, he should be prepared to put in an appearance when I ask him to!'

She hated the Comtesse de Lozançaise even more than he detested Vaudières. This ravishing blonde—— 'the finest bosom and pair of shoulders in Paris' according to the men—was the widow of M. de Wensborg and had been René's mistress when Agnes was alive. Stephanie hated her because of the way she spoke and behaved with René whenever they met. Her voice fairly throbbed with intimacy as she gazed at him with those huge brown eyes, lips parted invitingly, bosom heaving itself half out of her low-cut gowns. 'I love you,' she seemed to be saying with those sultry eyes of hers, 'I can't forget you, I am yours whenever you want me, my body yearns for yours, for your caresses, for you!'

One night after leaving a gathering where 'that creature' had been present, Stephanie had made a terrible scene. René merely smiled—it was old history now, a pleasant memory but nothing more, she was behaving absurdly, it was ridiculous for her to get excited and jealous like this, she was the only woman in the world for him, she was his wife, his love, his life. He was irresistible when he wanted to be, and Stephanie had ended by believing him, though she refused to go to any more of the Comtesse's balls. The Comtesse appeared reluctant to admit defeat, however, and the invitations continued to arrive regularly each month. She had only accepted this time as a return for having entertained Vaudières and his advisors, as proof of good faith.

'We'll go to this ball to please you but I hope you'll be as anxious to please me when the time comes ...'

Alas, things were never quite the same between them from then on. The humiliating concessions they had made to each other—his leaving his own house while she received her business associates, her agreeing to go to the Comtesse's ball—seemed to have destroyed something: on the surface, nothing seemed to have changed, but a growing coldness made itself felt in their silences, in the way they avoided each other's eyes, in the reserved tone in which they spoke. The harmony of their hearts and spirits was passing into a minor key, and sometimes came perilously close to a discordant false note. Their life together was turning into a sort of luxurious, padded hell, full of barbed exchanges masquerading as polite conversation. Some comment from René on a particularly exclusive and elegant salon he had attended, frequented by people of impeccable breeding and social standing, would provoke a sharp remark from her about tiresome snobs with nothing better to do than dress up and go to parties. If she chanced to mention a successful business enterprise, or a rival firm, René would counter-attack with a scathing condemnation of vulgar tradesmen who betrayed their gutter origins by continuing to dabble in filth.

Day by day, week after week, Stephanie struggled against a mounting inner anguish and disarray. She longed to take a holiday from René, a separation which would send her back all eagerness to his arms. The atmosphere of the Guinchamp mansion, with its chilly elegance and formality, was becoming unbearable to her. She found herself loathing the very things which made it so splendid and luxurious—the collection of fine paintings, the magnificent furniture, exquisite knick-knacks, chandeliers, carpets. Compared with the free-and-easy gaiety of her life as a cantinière, or the tender passion she had known as Boris's captive in the cell in Sebastopol, it was like living in a museum. Boris had re-created the atmosphere of Sebastopol when they came together again in Paris. Suddenly everything about the Guinchamp mansion, everything René valued because it aroused the envy and admiration of his friends, was hateful to her, hostile even. She went out as much as she could, dreading to have to return in the evening. There was an abundance of life at the Dyttevilles' mansion, rich and elegant though it was. One felt alive there: if only she could spend her nights there!

She couldn't go on like this, life was becoming impossible. Something must happen soon, they must have it out with each other and make a new start. Miserably, she went over and over all the points at issue between them and it was like probing a fresh wound. Then the letter came. A letter from Yves Kerdelec. A complete stranger to whom she had written for information about New Caledonia, and to enquire why the nickel mines there were showing such poor returns. Her letter had been full of questions, and now here, after a year's delay, were the answers!

'New Caledonia is a new country and modernising it

will be a long, costly business. The mines are poorly equipped and inefficiently run; there is a shortage of skilled European labour. The natives are gentle and good natured, but hopelessly indolent. I am tired, and unwell. In a few years time my son will take over from me . . . I shall be discussing this further with Monsieur Georges Dytteville . . .'

Everything, in short, was going on much as before. There was no reason to make changes, still less any strong desire to do so. This letter, with its resigned acceptance of the situation, drove Stephanie quite wild with irritation. This wasn't the way to run a business! It needed someone to . . . to *go* there and ginger them up, get them on their toes, see what needed doing, what modernisations should be made—there was no time to lose . . .

'I'm not the one who should go out there, Hippolyte's the obvious person to go . . . the trouble is, he's timid, cautious, terrified of taking a chance. Old Kerdelec will get round him easily enough. Hippolyte hates taking on new responsibilities or making decisions. I know what his reports will be like already . . . nothing but insuperable problems and hopelessly inaccessible sites, with—perhaps . . . I don't know . . . we shall have to think it over. They won't tell us a thing we don't know already! And *I* shall know nothing more.'

It was gradually becoming clear to her, though she hadn't as yet put the notion into words, that the one person who could handle the situation properly was Stephanie herself. She fought against the idea to begin with because, well, because she was reluctant to leave her children, or René, for too long; because she was forty, and that was rather late in life to begin taking to the high seas . . . altogether, it was a crazy scheme.

Yet on the other hand, it would be too late in a few years time. New Caledonia was a new country and the wealth of its nickel deposits had been common knowledge for many years now. A whole new industry was growing up there ... growth, life, new horizons, space—a change of air! Her children would manage without her for a year, or fifteen months ... She must see the place with her own eyes, give orders, launch new schemes. When she got back she would engage young, vigorous, people, the sort of people they needed. With her knowledge of the terrain she could buy machinery, equipment ...

'I shall have to think it over; if it is absolutely necessary, if there really isn't anyone else who could take charge ... then perhaps ... and who knows, when I get back, René and I ...'

Chapter Two

When she got back René and she might ... not that Stephanie had great faith in happy endings, but this might be her one chance of rescuing and reviving a love fast sliding into complete deadlock. Everything was wrong between them, even their wildly passionate love-making was distasteful to her now that it was haunted by memories of their latest quarrel, and the certainty that there must soon be another. Then there was the long nightmare of mealtimes during which they eyed each other covertly, like enemies. She could not stand it much longer, his oppressive presence which implicitly condemned her. René was so convinced that he was in the right; he waited, like a judge, for her surrender, for her to yield at last to the prestige of her name and the realisation that a Guinchamp could have nothing to do with brokers, tradesmen and manufacturers. She had her rebellious moments, as on the occasion when she received Vaudières and his advisors. But more often than not she suppressed these flashes of independence for fear that René would shut the door in her visitors' faces, after telling them with frigid courtesy that his wife was out and that he would be obliged if they took their business elsewhere in future!

Their marriage was ... a mistake! She saw this clearly now. He wanted to lock their love into a secret compartment, apart from their daily lives together. All they had ever had in common was a love of love itself, love in its springtide and its summer. They had nothing to say to each other now that he despised her greatest pleasure in life and she despised his whole reason for living. *The honour to be Madame de Guinchamp* indeed! What pretentious nonsense. Had she not been Madame Dytteville and Madame de Bourdeilles before that? She had been widowed twice, and she had had her choice of suitors. Men of nobler birth than René had laid their titles and fortunes at her feet and begged her to do them the honour of accepting them in marriage. *She* would have been conferring the honour, not the other way round. But 'honour' seemed to be René's favourite word, though when you came down to brass tacks he didn't have much to boast about. His own father had frittered away his wife's fortune and reduced the family to penury. As for him! If it hadn't been for Agnes! No, she was 'up to here' with his honour ... as the Zouaves used to say when she ladled out their soup.

She was depressed, fed up, weary of it all and she began to cast about for a solution which would not shock people too much, a polite formula which would permit a temporary separation. She did not want complete rupture between them, if only for the sake of the children, her own and his. There was little René, who seemed as much her own son as Agnes's. She had snatched him up and willed him to survive so that René might have the heir he craved. She had only succeeded in giving him a daughter, Diane! Everything seemed to have turned to ashes between them, even their child. The little girl was going to be the image of her father, she could tell that already. She 'sniffed it in the wind'. Strange how often Pompette's favourite expression came to mind when she was anxious or annoyed ...

No drama, then, no scandal. She would be 'reasonable', to quote her mother's favourite word. She was not going to play the part of the wicked woman abandoning home and children, a pariah for people to point at in horror. No 'thoroughly Parisian scandal' for her. Impetuous and wilful as she was by nature, common sense forbade her to do anything reckless or extreme. 'Up to here, up to here!' she kept repeating to herself. She had been beginning to despair of a solution to her life when the letter arrived from Yves Kerdelec, and its mention of nickel had roused some answering echo in her, as if nickel were somehow the key word, as if the answer lay there. To tell the truth it was not the metal itself, which was of little interest, but because New Caledonia was where the mines were. A journey, a long journey! Peace, calm; what a blessing! Not to see him for months on end! She wouldn't count the months either, she would wait and see ... but first she must arrange for her departure.

Stephanie had no illusions. René would never agree to such a lunatic, impractical, harebrained journey. New Caledonia was at the other end of the world, an almost unexplored island. It was also the penal colony where men had been deported after the defeat of the Commune. She would have a bitter struggle to get her way, but now at least she had a purpose in going, something to aim for, and she was ready to try any means in her power. Should she try the soft, diplomatic approach, or a bold, forthright one? Ought she to deliver an ultimatum? And, if so, what should be the terms? Long ago, at the time of Napoleon III's marriage to Eugenie de Montijo, she had presented René with a clear-cut choice: 'Your mother or me!' He had chosen his mother, and although she was dead now Stephanie felt she was still fighting the two of them because the mother's teaching was still very much alive in the son. 'You are a Guinchamp, you are handsome, you have a right to the best!' René was still living out his mother's fantasies, and he had fashioned an inflexible and foolish code of behaviour out of what was really nothing but appalling, absurd vanity. That was the man he was, and had always been, and knowing this, she had married him!

The days went by. Stephanie dared not talk to René; she was afraid of his reaction. He had made her fearful and timid, full of wild impulses to which she dared not give way. Then one day she watched him come in and take his place at the table, his face glowing with pleasure and self-satisfaction.

"We have a soldier at last, my dear! Now we'll see some changes made."

He was referring to the recent election of MacMahon, Duke of Magenta and Marshal of France, to the Presidency of the Republic. She could have deflated René with one word. After all, it was the army, caught totally unprepared, who had allowed the Germans to invade France, and it had been a civilian, Thiers, an insignificant little fellow, who had got rid of them again. She restrained herself however, and merely observed in falsely honeyed tones, "You think that will be an improvement, then?"

"I shall be promoted to colonel in a few months time."

His unabashed vanity touched her—she had loved him for it once—and disgusted her too, because it was so childish. Disillusioned, weary, she could find nothing to say but: "Well?"

His eyes flashed. She didn't seem to understand what it meant. Why, to be a colonel . . .

"My dear, it means I have a good chance of being made a general in a few years time! That's a point worth your consideration I would have thought. You're too unworldly. You don't suppose, with my private means, that I'd have entered the army if I had not been ambitious?"

And now he was calling her 'vous'—the formal, affected mode of address he used when he wanted to wound her. Instantly, she was on the defensive, bristling like a hedgehog before a snake.

"Oh, you!" she hissed, calling him 'vous' in return, "you've got ambitions, we all know about them! They are more important than anything else in the world, aren't they? Well, I'd just like you to know that I've got a few of my own! I'm alive, you know, I'm still here and you can't simply pretend I don't exist!"

He started and frowned. What did she mean taking this tone with him? He already seemed to feel MacMahon's reflected glory streaming down upon him in the shape of glittering medals and golden orders encrusted with precious stones. It made her feel sick, he was so puffed up with self-conceit.

"And what might that mean?" he asked with lofty condescension.

She guessed that he was about to employ that most crushing of arguments, which she found so idiotic: 'If one has the honour to be Madame de Guinchamp . . .' Oh, what was the point of handling this conceited fool with kid gloves? How could she let herself be frightened of him?

"You want to know what that means? Well, I'll tell you, my good man, it means you're in for a nasty shock. Perhaps a knock on the head will shake some sense into you. What it means, *my dear*, is that I'm off to the East Indies shortly on business."

He blinked, speechless. But it was no use his trying to pretend he hadn't heard because she had enunciated each syllable clearly and composedly.

"You must be mad!"

The half-stifled exclamation conveyed as much contempt as disbelief. Things like this didn't happen. His wife had gone off her head. Her behaviour set him throbbing with rage. Holding her fork with her little finger crooked, she answered in mincingly affected tones, calculated to enrage him.

"Mad, did you say? On the contrary, my dear, I have never been more clear-headed. I am no more mad now than I was when I first went after . . . *you*." She still used the formal pronoun. "If I hadn't saved *your* life at the Sandbag Battery, *you* wouldn't be here now prattling about your prospects, and even though I may have the honour to be your wife, I must repeat that I am not mad in the least and that I shall go to the East Indies!"

She emphasised the '*yous*' with a particularly provoking shrug and flick of the wrist. She knew what his answer would be before he even opened his mouth.

"My position . . ."

Nothing existed for him beyond society, and his position in it! She felt the old Phanie surge up in her, gay, battling, vital, and, if need be, brutally outspoken.

"Oh yes, I know, you lecture at the Staff College, you are a member of the War Council ... but I'm here too, you know, I've got my own life to lead while you're busy with your stuffed shirts! I loved you once, passionately, for yourself, not for your medals or your decorations. That shocks you, doesn't it? Well, I couldn't care less! You've smashed and destroyed it all, everything there was between us, and so I'm going to set myself free now. You understand, I'm off! I've got to breathe, and live—you can still be alive at forty, you know! I'm not a demure old lady yet; I haven't lost my figure have I? A couple of inches in twenty years, that isn't much, is it? You should know, you hold me, you make love to me. You want to embalm me like a mummy—well, I'm going to *live*! The Colonel's lady, Madame la Générale! Pah! I couldn't care less, I tell you. You live your boring life and let me lead mine which I enjoy!"

Her utter incomprehension left him aghast.

"My life is yours too. You simply don't understand, a general's wife ..."

"You're running ahead a bit, aren't you? You aren't even a colonel yet."

"Now that the Comte de MacMahon is President of the Republic, I am sure ... we have always been on the best of terms ..."

"MacMahon! I saw him on the tower at Sebastopol! He pulled off his decorations and pinned them on Pompette because he felt then that she deserved them as much as he did. And she did, she deserved all that and more!"

"A cantinière?"

The word came thinly, disdainfully. Stephanie froze, glaring at him. He flushed and mumbled hastily, "I'm sorry, I wasn't thinking, I didn't mean ... forgive me ..."

He hadn't meant it, of course, but that only made it worse. The contemptuous expression had slipped out almost against his will. He had forgotten that she had become a cantinière for his sake. She would never, *never* forget the way he had said it!

"No. I won't forgive you, never, you haven't the right, you . . ."

"Please, please, I beg you, forgive me," he interrupted, "surely you must see that your whole attitude and the violent things you have been saying have hurt me, and upset me . . . I didn't know what I was saying . . ."

She hated him so much for that slip of the tongue that she had regained a frightening, implacable calm.

"However angry or spiteful you may be, you've no right to spit on us cantinières. It's an honour and a glory for me to have been one. When you spit on Pompette you are spitting on me. She taught me the job—if it hadn't been for her I wouldn't have known how to save your life! But for her, and Boris . . ."

"Please! I have no wish to hear about your lover!"

"Why not, since we are talking so frankly to each other," she exclaimed with feigned candour. "He saved your life by snatching at the sword which would have killed you; you may not like to be reminded of it, but it's true. You talk to me of your hopes and ambitions, all I'm saying is that if it weren't for three people—Pompette, Boris and me—you wouldn't even be here now!"

He pushed back his plate, set both elbows on the table and glared at her. She braved his stare, ready for anything.

"Very well, then, suppose we talk about your hopes and ambitions. I trust your earlier remarks were no more than bravado. A married woman, and my wife in particular, doesn't go traipsing off across the world for no good reason . . ."

"I do have a reason, several in fact. There's my property in New Caledonia . . ."

"It will get by perfectly well without you."

"You aren't serious?"

"Quite serious. I am your husband, and I have certain rights."

She knew this, and she knew what they consisted of.

She had been giving a great deal of thought to the situation, looking for a solution which would not give rise to gossip or scandal. She was ready to make compromises for the sake of appearances. But one thing she was not going to stand for—and that was to have him brandish his 'rights' in her face!

"I shall forbid you to go," he snapped. "I won't allow my wife to ..."

"You'll *have* to allow it," she interrupted, getting to her feet.

He was on his feet too, making a great effort at self-control. His face changed, softened, grew tender, charming and sad. He was trying to win her round, resorting to the successful seducer's bag of tricks; he seemed to grow younger under her eyes, become the dazzling young man of their first meeting, at Amelie's wedding.

"Stephanie ..." he murmured.

How beautifully he said it! His lips were slightly parted, and he was staring at her mouth as if defying her not to remember, not to long to feel his mouth close over hers, warm, moist, hungry. He really was a ladies' man! No one knew that better than herself.

"You ought to think over what I've just said, René," she said softly. The steadiness of her voice should have warned him. Her resolve was unshaken; she had decided to make this journey and make it she would!

He smiled tenderly, as if indulging her, but underneath she knew his brain would be racing, thinking of how to corner her. He'd get Achille and Amelie on his side, he might try to persuade Françoise Dytteville to send young Hippolyte instead of her. He would try and enlist Aimé's support—but Aimé was *her* man! He loved her. She had not forgotten the incident in the Place de l'Etoile, his body shielding hers, one arm flung round her in a protective—and revealing—embrace. And their mutual confusion when they stood up; Aimé ill at ease, while she dusted the dirt off his clothes. There was no question of it, Aimé would go with her! But René was quite capable of approaching MacMahon himself. Remembering how Stephanie had flung herself at the Empress Eugenie's feet once to further her own pet project—ambulances, medical care and supplies for war-wounded—he might well consider taking his problem to MacMahon and asking him for help and advice.

She thought of everything, just as she was sure he foresaw everything. They were thinking on exactly the same lines with the difference that he wanted to stop her going, and she was utterly determined to go. Their behaviour towards each other, during the coming weeks, would consist of nothing but open or covert attacks, and pretences. She was already planning her campaign. Just now he seemed to be relying on his prowess as a lover. His eyes were softening, darkening—she knew his next moves by heart. But how accomplished he was at the game, how expertly he used his eyes, face, gestures! 'What a swell!' as the Zouaves would have said.

"We'll see, Stephanie."

That caressing use of her name again ...

He took her in his arms and kissed her long and fiercely, masterfully, arousing her deliberately, watching for the little tremors and sighs which meant she was weakening. Passion was a contest where he would always reign supreme. She felt her body responding, her breathing quickened, but ... no matter what he did ...

"Till tonight," he murmured, lips brushing hers, voice warm and sensual, as if she were already lying there beneath him.

How sure of himself he was—and how mistaken!

"Tonight," she whispered, her eyes locked in his.

He trusted to passion to win her back and convince her that she would be lost and helpless without him. He was so vain, so sure of his powers that it was almost disarming, like a spoilt child who thinks he can have everything he wants because he knows no one can ever refuse him. After all, was it surprising? Life had treated him royally, he had love, wealth, everything he wanted—and now

MacMahon's election seemed to promise further delights: colonel, general, decorations, honours . . .

"Poor René," she sighed, when he had gone, "you shall have your night of love, and so shall I, but this time it won't get you anywhere!"

He was magnificent that night. He was determined to win her back, to dominate her and bend her to his will, and so he became the lover he had been before his departure for the Crimea, when he wanted to imprint himself on her unforgettably. But now she was the one who was leaving. He had no idea that she was taking her leave of him, that this night marked the end of a phase in her life and that she too wanted it to be sublime, perfect, a brief rapture with no aftermath, no coming down to earth. She gave herself with complete abandonment, knowing that for her a new life was about to begin. They both wanted it, what happened between them that night, they had both been thinking about it all day. All the vivid, reckless passion they had known together returned, burst into flame, and consumed them. But there was a difference . . . Their bodies might strain and clutch in passion but their essential selves remained aloof, apart. When the rapture was over and they lay in each other's arms, their eyes were wary and watchful. She played the submissive, ravished woman to his conquering male. But why, she was thinking, had he refused to allow her to lead a life apart from his? He wanted to own her, he kept reminding her that it was his home she lived in, he looked down on her relations, treating the Dyttevilles, whom she thought of as her family, with a polite condescension no less irritating because he was utterly unaware of it. He was not a bad man, nor a cruel one, he had been—still was—breathtakingly handsome, but when all was said and done he was a creature of appearances, shallow, worldly. Not that she regretted one moment of the great love which had dazzled and blinded her. It had come into being at Amelie's wedding, now the wheel had turned full circle and it was drawing to its close. Freedom! To be free of René!

She had never believed it possible. Yet she felt a lingering tenderness, deep down, for the love which had been her youth, twenty years of her life, a grand passion she would never forget. Now, and always, René would remain for her 'The one I loved so much.'

'The one I loved so much,' she thought, stroking his hair absently. His head rested on her breasts, she felt his warm regular breathing as he lay stretched across her, one arm round her waist, one leg between hers. She closed her eyes. She was not unhappy as her mind dwelt nostalgically over the past. But there, that was life for you!

Next morning, sure of his triumph, velvety-voiced, he murmured, "Stephanie ... you must have thought it over ..."

She hesitated, as if trying to decide what he was talking about.

"Thought what over, René?"

"But, well ... what you told me yesterday."

When she spoke her voice was smooth, gentle, just a little astonished. "I told you I was going. I haven't changed my mind."

His face hardened into an angry mask, and she saw his fingers curl, driving his nails into his palms. But he controlled his anger. Then, to gain time, he said in an almost conciliatory voice, "Nothing is decided yet. We shall see."

"My mind is made up!" she said sharply.

They stood looking defiantly into each other's eyes. She met his angry stare without flinching. Looking at her René recognised the stubborn streak which he never could prevail against. Stephanie was sorry she had spoken out so hastily. She must keep calm, she must explain.

"René," she said gently, "I beg you, please, don't let's have any more scenes like the one yesterday. I only want you to understand, to see that ..."

"I don't know what you are talking about."

"Let's not pretend, René, we both know how things are between us. We do nothing but argue and fight. I can't go on living like this. We must look at things differently. I hate having to tell you this, but let me go; then when I get back it will be easier to begin our life together on a new footing. I need to live the way I do, to work: you simply won't admit that. Well, I can't go on as we are, I'm suffocating, you are suffocating me, you're crushing the life out of me and I'm not the kind of woman who lets herself be crushed. Whatever you do, I'm leaving."

" 'Whatever you do.' What do you mean by that?"

"You talked about your rights, didn't you?"

"You are my wife!" he exclaimed, astonished. "I can forbid you to do certain things which might harm my position, or my career. You keep asking me to be more understanding. Surely you must understand, Stephanie, that I can't allow you to undertake a journey like this. It's quite impossible for you to go to the East Indies. Your usual good sense seems to have deserted you. I am opposing you for your own good, Stephanie, not because it gives me any satisfaction, and the last thing I want is to have to resort to ... extreme measures?"

He'd come out with it at last! He would use any means to stop her! He had tried passion, now he was trying gentleness, the veiled threat, while pretending to find it distasteful. She had tried to convince him by her total frankness, appealing to him, imploring him, but all he did was talk to her as if she were a naughty little girl. She should have remembered that the frank approach was the wrong one with a man like him. She would have to use shock tactics, frighten him, threaten him through his career, his social position. Adopting a completely different tone, calm but resolute, she said,

"For your own sake I hope you don't feel driven to use what you call extreme measures! Let's stop beating about the bush. You will have to get it into your head, once and for all, that I have made up my mind, that nothing will stop me and that if there's any scandal it will be your fault entirely. I am quite prepared to leave the matrimonial home, if need be, and if you put your lawyers on to me, I shall put mine on to you. I daresay the press would get to hear of it, but the idea of being splashed across the front pages doesn't worry me in the least. All I am doing is defending my right to live my own way. No," she went on, when he made as if to interrupt her, "no, let me finish. Having said this, I'll do anything to make it easier for you. This is the way to behave to avoid gossip. The story will be that *you* suggested I should take the East Indies trip because you saw I was worried, and you love me and want me to be happy. See how many lies I'm prepared to tell to bolster up your façade? Any gestures you require of me I shall of course make, and I shall take every opportunity to praise you for the good, kind man you are. I'll go into the smart world under your husbandly eye to take my leave of Paris. You see, you shall have the plum part. You can even arrange my departure any way you like. Meanwhile I shall be as grateful, obedient and wide-eyed about it all as you could possibly wish, the model of wifeliness. Unless ..."

"Unless?"

"Oh, never mind. You were wrong just now, it's not me who needs to think things over, it's you."

"But ..."

"No, no buts," she cut in, shaking her head vigorously. "I'm going to give you some good advice. Accept my suggestions, and accept them at once because I promise you that from the minute we sign our pact right up to the minute I leave, I shall be no better than putty in your hands, a little puppet whose strings you pull. But it will be worth it. Accept, then, and save your name!"

There was a long silence while he weighed up the pros and cons. Her appeal seemed to have got through. He knew very well that she would brush aside any arguments and objections he might make; experience had taught him that she always did the first thing that came into her head without worrying about the consequences. She had set off for the Crimea in conditions which still made him shudder, and again to Italy to find him and look after him: in those days she used to run after him, but now it was she who was running away! And last night ... he didn't understand what was going through her mind, but he realised that he did not have much choice.

Stephanie watched him quietly. It would be difficult for him to accept her ultimatum all at once, she had dealt him too crushing a blow for that, especially where his masculine pride was concerned. After that night of passion he must have been certain of his victory. Now he would be thinking about how he should play the role of understanding husband, and how to present his story at the Staff College and in the salons. That's what he would be worrying about—what people would say: why is the 'future' General de Guinchamp letting his wife set off halfway across the world? What would people think of him, what would their verdict be? She knew him well enough to be sure that he would handle the situation skilfully.

"Stephanie," he began, and this time the name seemed to be torn from him, "you must know that you are making me very unhappy."

"Am I? Yes, I'm sorry ... but we need to separate for a while for both our sakes. When I get back ..." She sketched a gesture which could have been interpreted as hopeful.

"You've made up your mind?"

"Absolutely."

"You are prepared to leave your home, give all this up just to see to your business interests? You seem to think of everything and everyone except me!"

Except him! That was a good one. He was already starting to twist the situation to his advantage. Well, she didn't care, he could do as he pleased, his world wasn't hers. But there was no sense answering, it would only prolong the argument and take them back over the same familiar ground. She turned and looked away.

He strode out of the room, shutting the door behind

him briskly. Stephanie stared after him, rubbing her hands.

"It's settled, I've won!"

Here she was again, leaving Paris from the Gare de Lyon, but how different this was! She remembered the first time, as a cantinière with Pompette and her Zouaves: the rush along the platforms, boarding the wagon with 'Canteen' scrawled in clumsy letters along one side, greedy hands feeling her, pinching her bottom. The second time she had been disguised as a poor widow intent on good works, with a Bible, rosary and birth certificate in the name of Stephanie Mourlon tucked into her shabby reticule. This was the third time and she felt thoroughly disgusted. René had taken her at her word, and played his part up to the hilt. Her head reeled at the memory of all the teas, dinners, dances, receptions—and now this ludicrous, sumptuous private coach to herself, a Second Empire showpiece if ever there was one with its caryatids supporting a gold-starred vaulted ceiling, its deeply padded and buttoned chairs sagging, like the curtains, under the weight of fringes, tassels and cords. It was magnificent in its stuffy way, a symphony of gold and green and yellow. And the flowers! They cascaded on to the platform from her private coach, bunches, baskets, great sheaves of blossom ... it all reminded her a bit of Saint Eugenie's feast day at Compiègne, when the flowers invaded every corner of the place, from reception rooms to the corridors, even the staircases. She had given him a free hand ... if only she had known what she was in for! However, she had sworn to play her part faithfully, and play it she would as far as Marseilles. He had decided to accompany her as far as the quayside where she was to board the Dytteville company ship, *Araucaria*. She had chosen the name herself seven years earlier on discovering that this hitherto unknown conifer had impressed all the naturalists travelling with Captain Cook in 1774, when, *en route* for New Zealand, they sighted a mountainous island—New Caledonia!

René had even gone to the lengths of announcing Madame de Guinchamp's time and place of departure in the social columns of all the newspapers. The platform was packed. All the Dyttevilles were there, hundreds of friends, with Amelie, Achille and Skittles in the forefront, then there were the fashionables who simply wanted to be seen, and the busybodies who had come along to stare and see if they could discover which Minister was on the train, and finally, at least a dozen photographers. 'He hasn't forgotten a thing, not one,' Stephanie thought. 'What can he have laid on at Marseilles?' she wondered anxiously as she smiled and charmed, divinely dressed, divinely lovely. The answer, when it came, had a breathtaking simplicity quite characteristic of her husband. He had arranged for her arrival to coincide with that of the War Minister on a tour of inspection.

So at Marseilles there were red carpets, banks of greenery, a welcoming delegation headed by the mayor, harbourmaster, the Captain of the *Araucaria* and assorted wives and mothers. All these good people were deeply moved by this appearance of Parisian celebrities in their midst—some of the most distinguished names the Republic could boast. Stephanie could not help admiring René, despite her mounting exasperation. He knew how to do things in style!

The *Araucaria*, under Captain Noel Plantain, was finally casting off from the quayside. Four whole days of receptions, bows, smiles, introductions, toasts, good wishes and clothes ... the number of times she had changed her gowns—at least three times a day! It wasn't till she stepped out of the train at Marseilles that she had realised why René kept insisting that she did not have a large enough wardrobe for ... such a long journey. But now, at last, it was all over! The last hawser had been cast off and now they were hauling it in as the stretch of water between ship and quay gradually widened. Stephanie stood at the stern, foolishly waving her hand with a handkerchief fluttering in it. It came home to her suddenly, not for the first time, what a reckless impulse had prompted this journey halfway across the world.

The nickel mine had been a pretext, Kerdelec's letter had been a pretext, the real reason was that she was still at heart the Boisnaudouin tomboy who recognised no rule but her own, no law except this mysterious instinct which was rapidly taking her away from France and René.

When the crowd on the quayside had dwindled to mere dots she turned, intending to go up forrard and enjoy the fresh sea wind blowing in her face. Her eyes met Aimé's. There was the faintest of smiles on his face but her own was frank and gay.

"Come!"

He followed her. They were facing out towards the open sea and the unknown, drinking in the immensity of sky and sea and the rushing sound of the waters churned up by the ship's giant screw propellers.

Chapter Three

That evening Stephanie had remarked, almost casually, to Aimé, "We'll have breakfast together in my cabin, like in the old days . . ."

'The old days!' That short phrase erased almost three years of married life. Aimé said nothing, but in the morning he brought in the breakfast tray, buttered her toast and sat down in the armchair which henceforth became his special chair.

"Ah, that was good!" she exclaimed. "The only thing missing was the newspapers. And, now, let's see to the trunks!"

Stephanie had decided to discard her fashionable gowns for simple, workaday clothes in which she would feel more comfortable and less conspicuous. Three special trunks had been sent on ahead to Marseilles, with Françoise's help, with instructions that they should on no account be taken into Madame's cabin till after the ship sailed. M. de Guinchamp must not even know of their existence. This secret wardrobe, consisting of plain, sensible dresses, laced-up boots and sturdy shoes for walking through bogs, woods and hills, added to her delicious sense of freedom —René's eyes had not so much as lighted on a stitch or a shoelace!

She and Aimé exchanged conspiratorial smiles as they unpacked and shook out one set of dresses and carefully folded and packed the other. Then they set about tidying and arranging their new quarters. These consisted of a state-room, dressing-room and drawing-room for herself, the whole suite decorated and beautifully furnished by Françoise and René, who had collaborated over this aspect of her journey. René wanted her to travel in the most refined comfort whereas Françoise knew how much space would be available. Aimé slept in a little cabin leading off the drawing-room. She could summon him by pulling on a specially embroidered bell pull, which René had had made, with their combined initials prettily entwined along its length. Soon all the elaborate flounced gowns, the ones which had dazzled the 'gentry' of Marseilles, were packed away.

"Well, that's done!" Stephanie cried triumphantly.

"Shall I wait for Madame?"

"I'll change out of this dressing gown into a dress, then I want to see round the ship and get to know the men."

She said 'men', not 'Zouaves', but Aimé was not deceived. She was overjoyed at being free again. From now on she was going to be independent and suit herself. That was obvious from the way she had decided that they must have their breakfasts together again. The officers and men could think what they liked. She was the boss, after all, and if this was the way she wanted to behave they would simply have to get used to it. At dinner the previous night, for instance, she had observed that there were only four places laid at the captain's table, one for herself, one for the captain and two for his young lieutenants. With a ravishing smile she turned to the captain.

"We shall need another place laid, I would like Monsieur Becave to eat at my table," she said in a voice at once gentle and insistent.

To set their minds—or imaginations—at rest, she added sweetly, "Monsieur Becave and I were brought up together ... his mother was my wet nurse. Since then we have scarcely been separated for a day, and he has my complete confidence ..."

She turned to him.

"You will sit facing me, Aimé."

She used the familiar 'tu' form of address as if it was the most natural thing in the world.

Now they left her state-room together. She couldn't help

smiling when she emerged on deck and noticed the captain's look of surprise at her severely practical dress, without so much as a ribbon, frill or furbelow to be seen.

"I'm no longer on show, Captain Plantain," she explained. "I want to be able to move about comfortably and freely for the remainder of the voyage."

Two months later, after a journey of unvarying monotony, Stephanie stood beside the captain on the bridge watching through binoculars as the distant silhouette of New Caledonia rose slowly above the horizon. At first, all that could be seen was a spiky backbone of land. But as the ship drew nearer, she was able to distinguish bare mountain peaks emerging from a dense green fleece of forest, where rounded hills alternated with green valleys, sometimes threaded by a silvery stream or waterfall. Then they were near enough to make out the coastline clearly, a strange, flat terrain where giant trees thrust up out of mirror-like pools and stretches of stagnant countryside with scarcely a building or human figure to be seen. These must be the marshes, she told herself. Girdling the whole island was a belt of tossing foam.

"Those are the reefs," the captain explained.

"Ah, yes, the coral," said Stephanie, who had learnt from Aimé that New Caledonia was encircled by coral reefs.

She had come upon him with his nose in a pile of travel books, and works of early explorers. He appeared to be learning the information off by heart.

"You'll have to tell me all about it," she had exclaimed. "I can't feel anything about a place till I'm standing on it with both feet." Even now she knew very little about the island except that there were no snakes or dangerous animals, that the climate was tropical for most of the year, with the sun directly overhead, and that the nights barely altered in length from one season to the next. She was impatient to be on the move again. One thing worried her —the monotonously predictable export figures shown by

Yves Kerdelec's annual reports. She had brought them to study on the voyage.

'I am sure he is honest but he must be hopelessly unenterprising,' she thought. 'No doubt the climate is to blame, as he says in his letter. I must be careful not to jump to conclusions about such a new, strange country. I shall go cautiously at first, find out all I can about the mines, crops, timber ... then I'll get things moving. I'll have a lot to teach them; after all I've been managing my own property, my pig farm and timber business, since I was little more than a child!'

Poised between past and future, with the dauntless spirit of a pioneer and the eager heart of a child, Stephanie stood gazing round in delight as the *Araucaria* slipped into the island's beautiful natural harbour. It was sheltered from high winds and heavy seas, as the captain pointed out, by the offshore Isle of Nou, and shipping could approach either from the east or the west. Now the town of Noumea itself was coming into sight, a flat cluster of buildings scattered over a flat stretch of land, with one hill rising like a rock wall in the background.

"That is Conneau Hill," the Captain remarked. "One day it will vanish entirely; they are using the soil to fill in the marshy coastal strip."

"Didn't you say that Noumea has very few hotels?"

"Few, and primitive, Madame Stephanie."

"Tell me more, Captain. It's all right, I'm not trying to frighten myself!"

"Well, the best is the Island Hotel. The most comfortable certainly. Then there is the Mount Ouen Toro, and the Boulari Hotel should be finished by now, I think ..."

"That one doesn't sound very promising," she said hurriedly, her face white. "I shall want to take a suite ... I don't know how long I shall be here, there are so many things I must see ..."

The words tumbled out carelessly—anything to keep herself from thinking, remembering ... Armand! The Boulari Straits: his ship had broken up on the Great

Barrier Reef just after passing through the Boulari Straits ... totally wrecked ... sharks ... it was too horrible to think about! She blinked rapidly, trying to force back the tears, and launched into a stream of chatter about the great variety of shipping massed in the harbour, sailing ships, sloops, fishing smacks, skiffs ...

"I shall go ashore in the first boat, Captain," she announced suddenly. "Please don't let anyone know who I am, or what my name is. I would like to get to know the people here before they know who I am. I want to form my own impressions of the town—and of the Company's agents here too! But I shall follow your advice, Captain Plantain, and engage a suite at the Island Hotel."

"You will find it in the Rue de l'Alma."

Alma. Her heart missed a beat. He threw out the name so casually, quite unaware of what it meant to her. Alma! Her first Crimean battle, the wild scramble up the cliffs, her dash with Pompette through whistling bullets and screaming shells ... later that night ... Aimé's head gripped fast between her knees as the field surgeon hacked off his shattered arm ...

"You will find a Rue de Sebastopol too ..."

That set her thinking about Boris ... Boris in faraway Russia dreaming of his Stephania, preferring to forget the existence of Mme de Guinchamp. What a strange welcome the island was giving her—a parade of ghosts from her past, Armand, the Crimea, Pompette, and now Boris, her last great love.

"And a Rue d'Austerlitz."

"What a triumphant list of victories!" she exclaimed lightly to hide her agitation. "I hope it is a good omen for my visit, Captain! And now, I hope you will give me the pleasure of dining with me tonight at the Island Hotel? Please bring these two gentlemen too," she added, turning towards the lieutenants with the faintest suggestion of a wink, a wink which implied that she counted on their acceptance, and that the prospect gave her great pleasure.

They bowed acceptance.

"There's just one thing, Madame, I feel I ought to tell you. That hotel ..."

She was a little disconcerted by the captain's uncharacteristic hesitancy, but she was quite determined not to let anyone put her off the island, or anything in it, before she had timc to form her own impressions. She interrupted him quickly:

"No, you mustn't tell me a thing, please! I want to see for myself," she said with gentle insistence.

The *Araucaria* had stopped moving. She could hear the rattle of the anchor chain. She moved towards the gangway.

"Madame, excuse me ..."

It was the captain again.

"Yes?"

She turned her most brilliant smile on him.

"It would give me such pleasure to escort you ashore on your first visit to New Caledonia!"

Really, his persistence was most odd! It put her on her guard. There must be something about the island, or the hotel, or perhaps the Kerdelecs themselves, which he did not wish her to encounter for the first time on her own.

'I expect he wants to let them know that the "boss" has arrived, I'm sure that's it,' she told herself.

"Now, remember your promise!" she exclaimed, pouting prettily. "My only request of you, Captain, is that you and these gentlemen should do me the honour of dining with me this evening ... and please continue to call me Madame Stephanie," she added, with a gay twirl of her hand. Then she said, with all Phanie's old gay assurance, "Don't worry about me! I'm quite capable of looking after myself ... besides, there's Aimé!"

The oarsmen gave a final spurt and the prow of their boat slid on to the glistening mud leaving the stern afloat. Noumea might be the principal city but it still lacked quays, docks or any proper facilities. A hundred yards or so distant, some sort of construction work was going on. Men, stripped to the waist, trundled barrow-loads of stones and boulders to the site, tipped the contents out and trundled away again to fetch another load.

"Well, we're here!" she cried to Aimé, as she leapt ashore, one hand resting on a sailor's shoulder to steady herself.

" I daresay it will be a fine place in a hundred years' time," he commented drily.

"Why not before?" she retorted. "Do you know what it reminds me of?" she asked, gazing at him with shining eyes.

He stared at her for a moment, eyes narrowed, then he said, "Gallipoli?"

"Exactly," she replied. "Everything half-finished ... so must to be done everywhere!"

"I wonder if Madame can guess what I'm thinking."

She pondered for a moment.

"No, I can't," she confessed. "I only hope you are as pleased to be here as I am. You can't think how delighted I am with it all!"

"That is crystal clear from the look on Madame's face. But there's another thing ..."

He left her in suspense for a moment, then in that slow, deliberate voice of his she so often found exasperating, he went on, "It's curious ... but Madame already seems to belong here!"

She did not answer. Aimé's remark so exactly summed up her own feelings. She paused for a moment to reflect why it should be that she suddenly felt almost drunk with joy. Then it came to her. She was free! Free to walk, laugh, live her own life in her own way. Free of René, and of her father-in-law, Georges Dytteville, ruling like some benevolent dictator over the offices in the Rue Vivienne! She turned an eager gaze on the town. There were a few two-storey buildings, but for the most part they were bungalows with wide verandahs and large gardens set back on either side of wide, straight streets intersecting at right angles like the new Paris boulevards created by Napoleon III and Haussmann. In the distance a broad expanse of open country with marshy pools which shone dully in the sun like mercury.

"That must be the one we want," said Stephanie, pointing to a building of some size. "The sailor said it was straight ahead, the largest two-storey building in sight. Well, I must say it's a lot better than I expected, this hotel ..."

"Seven windows far apart on the first floor," Aimé observed in his precise fashion, "which leads me to suppose that the bedroms are of a good size. There is a slight raise in the roof, from which I infer that there is a corridor down the middle with an identical set of rooms opening off each side."

"I declare, it's a palace!" Stephanie cried gaily, taking Aimé by the arm.

She did so impulsively, without thinking, but the gesture startled them both. They stood for a moment looking at their linked arms. They had not been so close since the days of the siege and the Commune. The smile Stephanie flashed at him was sisterly, conspiratorial, brilliant.

"Back to our old ways, Aimé," she cried. "It doesn't matter here. They'll see us walking about arm in arm and they won't think twice. Oh, how happy I feel!"

"Madame likes to be free."

"Just what I was telling myself," she said, pulling him along.

'Island Hotel ... Proprietor ... Vincent Cocfigue' was written up in large black letters along the freshly whitewashed wall above the terrace. The terrace ran the width of the building, and it was scattered with tables and chairs. At one of these tables a group of Europeans was drinking.

"Boulevards ... a café ... and," she gestured with her chin, "look there! What more could anyone want?"

Aimé glanced across to where five naval officers clustered round a blonde, fair-skinned creature in a gaudy dress fairly plastered with jewellery, most of which, like the curls piled on top of her head and spilling down her neck, appeared to be false. A ridiculous hat cascading with ribbons, flowers and feathers, completed the picture. The young woman herself was handsome, sensual, common looking. She laughed a little too loudly as she bestowed languishing glances on her five admirers, each one of whom was clearly hoping to enjoy her favours.

"Trade seems brisk ... in her case!"

"Noumea is a port as well as a capital," Aimé pointed out. "The female may be what you take her for ... or she might be the wife of one of those naval gentlemen."

"Suppose we find out for ourselves!" Stephanie suggested with a little laugh.

She took a last quick look round outside and then went in to the hotel, still arm in arm with Aimé.

The relative elegance of the reception hall surprised her. It might be a somewhat clumsy imitation of the style of a large European hotel, but it boasted a long, polished reception desk with pigeon-holes behind for mail and keys, cushioned wicker chairs, a profusion of unfamiliar green plants and flowers, and a bell which she had to ring several times.

"Madame, Sir ... can I help you?"

A dark man of around thirty, stoutish, and of medium height, had materialised and now stood bowing before her.

She suddenly regretted her severely simple travelling dress. It gave the wrong impression. To correct this, her voice, when she spoke to him, was a careful blend of formality and graciousness.

"Monsieur Cocfigue?"

"At your service, Madame."

"I should like to take a suite of rooms."

He gave a start of surprise.

"I shall need three rooms: a bedroom and drawing-room for myself and a third room, also a bedroom, for this gentleman here, who is my steward. They must be rooms with communicating doors, naturally ..."

"Whom do I have the honour ... ?"

But Stephanie, who was resolved that the Kerdelecs must be the first to know of her arrival, pretended not to hear.

"Can I see what you have?"

"I'm sorry ... but I'm afraid we have nothing at all to offer you of that description, Madame."

Aimé was enjoying himself. The proprietor didn't know what a serious mistake he had made there! Trying to fob her off with the excuse that there was nothing available! To a woman like Stephanie that left only one course open—to take her suite by storm as she had once scaled the Malakov tower in the Crimea.

He waited quietly for the first salvo in a bombardment which would annihilate the unhelpful M. Cocfigue. That unfortunate man found himself unable to get a word in edgeways. That was only the beginning. Stephanie interrupted, snatched up his excuses and brushed them aside almost before they were out of his mouth. "Oh, sailors ... sailors ... here one day, gone the next. I propose to stay six months ... a year perhaps! No adjoining rooms free, Monsieur? You cannot be serious! I am quite sure none of those gentlemen would object to moving ... would you like me to ask them? No communicating doors? You must allow me to have those put in at my own expense. I shall have them hung with drapes, which of course I will leave to you when I go."

The question of the price came up. Stephanie took a handful of silver from her purse and slapped it down on the desk. A month's payment in advance, she declared. By the time ten minutes had elapsed the proprietor was putty in her hands and she had got what she wanted.

"Stay and see to the trunks and bags," she told Aimé. "There are seventeen of them," she informed the proprietor casually but in such a way that he could hardly fail to recognise that she was a person to be reckoned with.

He bowed. As she had expected, the number of bags and trunks had impressed him. Her imperious manner overwhelmed him. It was the first time he had ever had a lady step into his hotel with seventeen trunks demanding three rooms with communicating doors.

"Did you arrive on the *Araucaria*?" he asked, trying to start a conversation.

"Yes," she said. She wanted to avoid further explanations. "Where are the Dytteville Company's offices?" she asked next.

Vincent Cocfigue looked momentarily taken aback. "If it's to do with timber or the mines, I should have to give the agents warning of your arrival," he began craftily, hoping to find out more about this eccentric client with a grand disregard for money. "They don't very often come in to the agency here."

This was not the sort of thing Stephanie hoped to hear, but she did not flinch. No doubt they were out prospecting . . . in the forests somewhere, down the mines. She hurried on,

"No, no, just tell me where I can find them."

"At home, in their village, with their tribe."

Tribe? That really did seem to be going a bit far! Stephanie's face was a study as she struggled to digest this news.

"Tribe?" she repeated flatly.

"Well, in a manner of speaking, Madame," said Vincent, his self-command quite restored. "They own . . . many houses . . . and . . . er . . . servants. I can let them know that a lady wishes to see them and they will be here in no time—they are charming people, greatly respected here."

'Greatly respected? Well, that's something,' thought Stephanie. 'All the same I'd like to see the shareholders' faces when they hear the Dytteville Company's representatives have gone native. This is something I *must* see.

Right away!'

"Is Madame perhaps a relative?"

"No, a friend of the family. I want to see them as soon as possible. I've got good news for them. Do you think you could show me the way to the ... er, village?"

The hotelier coughed, then with smiling stubbornness, repeated for at least the third time, "Let me send for them, Madame."

The man was trying to hide something from her, she was sure. And what about the captain's curious insistence on accompanying her ashore? She had stumbled on a mystery, it seemed. Being Stephanie she was determined to find out more. She decided to make an ally of Monsieur Cocfigue. Summoning up all her charm and persuasiveness, she said,

"Please don't send for them or let them know of my arrival, my dear Monsieur Cocfigue. I've got so much to tell them, I'd like it to come as a complete surprise ... don't you think that would be nicer? Now, if you'll just be so good as to show me the way there ..."

They went through the verandah and out into the beaten earth road, as empty of people and vehicles as the desert.

"Go through the town, keeping your back to the port, till you come to the valley—we call it the settlers' valley—and then bear left. You will see a wood ... it's not difficult to find if you know the way—but are you quite sure you wouldn't like someone to ... ?"

Really, the man was absurdly persistent! He was beginning to annoy her, and patience had never been Stephanie's strong suit.

"No," she said, more curtly, though still smiling. "I'll find the place myself. Is it far?"

"Three ... four miles."

"Is that all? I thought you were going to say ten at least."

"You have to go through ..."

But she interrupted him, in her impatience to be off,

and this time her manner put an end to any further temporising.

"I'll get through, don't worry. I always do!"

Vincent Cocfigue bowed, almost humbly. This eccentric person was prepared to pay through the nose, it would be foolish to irritate her. But Aimé looked after her wistfully, wishing he were going with her. In her present frame of mind she was quite likely to go haring up the steep slopes of the hill at the back of the town. It was impossible not to admire her, though ... she had all the wiles of a woman, with the strength and courage of a man!

As she hurried through the town Stephanie made a mental inventory of what she saw, noting its features with the sharp eye of a successful property tycoon. All that waste land ripe for development! 'Two thousand Europeans,' the captain had said. That wasn't much. 'But it's growing all the time,' he had added proudly, almost as if it were all his own work. 'Four hundred or so emigrated here from Alsace after the war of 1870, but they don't live in Noumea. Nor do the four thousand deportees who were sent here after the Commune uprising.' The Communards! She had often thought about them on the journey out, though she had been careful not to bring the subject up. To her the Commune meant violence: firing squads, that terrible camp at Satory to which she and Aimé had gone ... suddenly Elizabeth Dimitrief flashed into her mind. There was a real woman! Strong, resourceful, indomitable—not unlike Stephanie herself. 'While I am here I shall go to see your Communard friends,' she promised. 'Yes, I shall,' she repeated fiercely. Just then she found she had reached the end of the road, before her lay a muddy, much-trodden track and a wide expanse of open country dotted with trees. The track bore the imprints of men's feet, animal hoofs, horseshoes ... it took her back to her tomboy childhood, it suddenly unrolled before her like the very symbol of freedom.

'I shall go if I want to! No one can stop me! No one

is going to scold me for getting wet feet and mud on my dress, there's no one to keep reminding me that I've the honour to be Madame de Guinchamp!'

She strode out along the slippery, muddy track feeling as elated as a prisoner newly released from his cell. This moment alone was worth the two long months on the *Araucaria* when she couldn't stop wondering what had possessed her to leave family, children, friends and her life in Paris to cross the world on a sudden impulse. It was true that she was fed up with René and longing to be free of him when the fateful letter from Yves Kerdelec arrived. That letter . . . it had filled her head with dreams of adventures in the Southern hemisphere. But there was a streak of wanderlust in her, too, she realised that. A craving for freedom which haunted her as it used to haunt her brother Charles. He had set out for a strange country once upon a time—Algeria. And now here she was, twenty years later, walking along a mud track halfway across the world, in New Caledonia.

She picked her way along, looking for the dryest patches in the track and glancing round from time to time. Her path wound across a green, grassy expanse, looping back on itself in the most surprising way so that she would suddenly get the impression that she was walking back towards Noumea. Then, at last, behind a small hillock which she had not even noticed, she came upon a dozen or so square whitewashed buildings with verandahs. 'Settlers' Valley' she told herself, and it crossed her mind that these white men and women might well be on the Dytteville Company's payroll. She greeted them simply and cheerfully, as one greets a fellow stroller on a country walk, or a child at a farmhouse door. They replied with a guttural Alsatian accent which took her back to the time when she went to the gates of Paris to watch the refugees streaming in ahead of the Prussian advance. She felt a wave of affection for these sturdy folk who had chosen exile rather than life under enemy occupation. For all her outward toughness, Stephanie had her full share of sensitive feminine intuition.

"Am I going the right way for the Kerdelecs?"

"Bear left at the crossroads and you'll come to their huts," a stout woman called back from her doorway.

'Huts'? Coming on top of Vincent's mention of 'the tribe', and his 'You must go through . . .' to which she had replied, 'I always get through,' the word was disturbing.

"You wouldn't like us to lend you a horse? You could leave it here on your way back," the woman continued in her strong, pleasant voice.

"No thank you," Stephanie answered without thinking.

Then the generosity of the offer struck her, and she was just about to change her mind and accept, when the woman said, "You'll know what to expect then. Anyway, you'll be sure to meet someone—the kanakas are always on the lookout. Enjoy your walk, Madame."

"Thank you," said Stephanie giving her a cheerful wave.

In fact she felt less and less confident. What did the woman mean—'always on the lookout'? No doubt about it, everything to do with the Kerdelecs was beginning to seem more and more peculiar. After another ten minutes walking Stephanie realised why Vincent Cocfigue had tried to dissuade her, and why the woman had offered to lend her a horse. A stretch of swampy country and a large expanse of water lay between her and the wood she was making for. Her track wound this way and that across the swamp, like a ribbon of soggy piecrust, occasionally slithering underwater to surface again a few feet further on. When it entered the forest, she beheld a fearful tangle of roots like monstrous writhing limbs plunging into the slimy, sandy pools at their feet. 'Those must be mangroves,' she told herself. 'I've got about three hundred yards to go before I get to them. Well, there's no help for it but to go on!'

She snatched up her skirts and stepped boldly out across the swamp. She soon discovered that a marsh fed by sea-water, like this one, was quite different from the treacherous

Dobruja swamp country, with its deceptive green quicksands which would swallow you whole in a few minutes. Here she was on firmer ground. She reached the most serious obstacle in her path, the wide stretch of tideless water, and began hunting for a ford. The woman had said there was one. It should have been easy enough to see, though the dancing reflections of sunlight made it difficult to judge how deep the creek was here. She couldn't see anything remotely like a ford. She took her bearings from the point where the path plunged into the forest on the opposite bank, then she bundled up her skirts and set one foot cautiously before her, only to sink in up to the knees at the next step. She stopped, in a high state of irritation. She had said she would get through, and get through she would! She wasn't going to expose herself to jokes and sarcasm from Aimé or Vincent Cocfigue! It was a question of honour. She wasn't going back till she had seen those wretched Kerdelecs! In a sudden burst of defiance aimed at herself, the Kerdelecs, the water and New Caledonia itself, she pulled her skirt and petticoat up round her waist and stood trying to make out the best way across, when a voice sang out and she froze like a statue.

"Stop, Madame!"

Glancing up, she found herself confronted by the 'look-out' the woman had talked of. He was a half-breed with a striped cloth wound about his loins, and he was coming towards her.

"White Madame not understand big water!"

Standing there with her great bundle of skirts round her waist and her legs in the water, like a half-submerged tree trunk, Stephanie felt more than a little ridiculous. She dared not stir for fear of falling into a hole. 'Fool that I am!' she told herself, observing that the man's feet scarcely sank in at all and that the spot where she stood was the softest ground she could have chosen. 'If I'd gone a few feet further up I'd have got across on my own! But here he is, and I'd better be nice to him.'

He was the first islander she had seen. He wasn't the least bit alarming, she decided. His childlike smile, displaying brilliant white teeth, was as engaging and friendly as his merry, shining black eyes. A fine looking man, broad shouldered, bare to the waist; a little heavy perhaps for his age, which could not have been more than twenty-five. His skin, she decided, was the colour of honey.

"Climb up," he commanded, when he was close enough to stoop and offer her his back.

She hadn't much choice. Besides, she had already resolved to fall in with all the island customs so as not to offend either the whites or the natives ... pushing her skirts out of the way she measured the distance and jumped. Two large muscular hands grasped her bare thighs to hoist her up higher on his back.

"Dat's good, now hold round my neck."

His good humour was so infectious she found herself answering in the same vein, as she gripped him by the shoulders.

"Off we go then, I'm all right!"

It wasn't till he set off that the full absurdity of her position dawned on her. What would her Paris friends, and the shareholders, think if they could see her sitting astride the back of a dusky islander on her way to visit the representatives of the Company which paid them out such comfortable dividends. It really was too funny! Here she was, the beautiful Mme de Guinchamp, whose hand they kissed respectfully, to whom they sent the choicest flowers and the most exquisite chocolates, riding on the back of a savage who held her firmly by both thighs while her skirts ballooned out behind them like a train.

"You stranger here, Madame?" he asked as he set her down on solid ground again.

"I've just arrived."

"On the *Araucaria,* we long time waiting for de fine ship."

"I would like to see Monsieur Kerdelec."

"He happy to see strangers. You eating here?"

"I don't know."

"You follow me."

Much amused, she entered the dark green vault shot through with golden shafts of sunlight. Lianas trailed from the branches like rigging, studded with strange flowers of such vivid hues they looked false. Suddenly a smooth beech tree appeared, and she couldn't resist caressing the familiar, satiny bark with all its associations for her—her own chateau, her woods and forests in France. Imagine finding one here, thousands of miles away! Her dripping skirt was sticking to her legs. She tried to wring it out but it still flapped wetly against her calves as she walked. Water splashed out of her boots at each step. But it didn't matter. In this heat it would all soon be dry.

"How you called, pretty Madame? Dis Napoleon at your service, to please an love you."

'A figure of speech,' she told herself, and was about to reply when she caught sight of the first hut. A straw cone perched atop a wooden palisade about a yard high, with a low opening screened by a curtain of leaves. She saw another, then another, then four or five more, then some young bare-breasted girls, an old woman squatting as she wove a basket, a few men ... they were all staring at her. A little further on she found herself in a big clearing round which stood more huts, presumably belonging to 'the tribe' and some square whitewashed buildings like the ones lived in by the Alsatians, one large and three small. So they really were living like the natives? This was life in the islands with a vengeance! Still, best take it all in her stride and try not to appear scandalised by these strange customs.

"Old Master in dere," said her escort, pointing to the largest of the white buildings, "an de young Master dere," he added, pointing to the smallest.

The islanders came shyly towards her out of their huts, emerging from behind trees and bushes, rather like an operatic chorus as the great aria is about to begin. They stared at her wide-eyed. They were smiling, but Stephanie could not help feeling like some totem who had suddenly appeared in their midst, arousing feelings of awe as well as pleasure. The odd thing was that this scene reminded her of another, distant now in time, a warm, friendly scene, in some respects quite different, in others strangely alike. She turned to Napoleon, who stood beaming at her like a fisherman who has landed a fine fish, and smiled at him.

"Tell Monsieur Kerdelec a lady wishes to see him."

"Yes, yes, yes," he babbled ecstatically, and raced across to 'de old Master's' house.

She followed. As she walked through the crowd of natives she suddenly recalled the moment that had been eluding her ... one of the most memorable of her life ... the Gare de Lyon, with all the Zouaves crowding round her, accepting her among their number after she had marched with them through the streets of Paris, and helped to seize the railway wagon. There wasn't the colourful impudent street-arab gaiety here, but something of the same feeling seemed to press between her and these 'savages'. They greeted her with a childlike, admiring delight, expressed in cries, laughter and exclamations which she knew even without understanding a word, must mean 'welcome, we wish you happiness and prosperity'.

"Lovely lady for you, old Master," said Napoleon, raising the cloth curtain which did duty for a door.

She felt awkward as she went in, though she did her best to appear natural. Two long windows lit the single room, which was almost bare but for an immensely long rustic table. It was piled high with papers and files, and through a gap between the heaps she saw an old man with the puffy features of an alcoholic.

"Monsieur Yves Kerdelec?"

"At your service, Madame. What do you want of me?"

The voice was toneless, slow, as weary as the face.

"I am Madame de Guinchamp," she said, almost apologetically, so exhausted did the man seem.

"Sit down, Madame," he replied, pointing to a chair.

His lack of response was breathtaking! Thinking that he might not have heard she repeated loudly and distinctly.

"I am Madame de Guinchamp, Monsieur Kerdelec."

He answered, voice toneless as before, "I heard you quite clearly, Madame. I always hoped that you would come and that I should have the pleasure of meeting you before I died. I have read about you, you are Armand's wife, Georges' beloved daughter-in-law, that is good, very good. Excuse me ... I cannot get up, my legs ... forgive me."

He pointed to a chair again with a shaking hand, trying to control his rising agitation.

"Thank you," she said, drawing it up to the table.

"You must be thirsty with this heat. Moses, bring us some milk."

A white man as old and skinny as himself, whom she had not noticed because he was crouching at Kerdelec's feet like a faithful dog, rose and silently left the room. The thought of milk was not very attractive, as she disliked the drink, but she dared not refuse in case this was another island custom.

"When you wrote to me, Monsieur Kerdelec ..."

He raised both hands heavenwards as if invoking a blessing, and Stephanie did not finish her sentence.

"I was a long time in replying to you. Time means very little here, as you will find, it's the climate ... I owe a great deal to Georges. Are things well with him?"

An almost youthful light came into his bleary eyes for a moment and Stephanie was moved by his resemblance to her Uncle Camille. Camille too used to wait impatiently, imprisoned in his invalid chair, for her to visit him and bring him news of a world he would never see again. Yves Kerdelec would never again see Georges, or France. Out of compassion, she began to lie, to embroider the truth.

"He hasn't changed, Monsieur Kerdelec, he was anxious

to be remembered to you and your son. He is so full of energy and spirits, just like you remember him, I daresay, always busy . . ."

Out of pity and affection she continued to weave the fantasy she felt her listener wished to hear, omitting to mention her father-in-law's obstinate resistance to any schemes for expansion or modernisation, presenting poor Hippolyte as a daring and enterprising captain of commerce. This monologue, to which the old man listened in something like ecstasy, was interrupted by Moses holding half a coconut in each hand filled with a refreshing white liquid which bore only the faintest resemblance to real milk. She tasted it. It was deliciously fresh and unusual.

"Do you like it, Madame Dytteville?"

Startled at hearing herself addressed by her first married name, she turned towards the door where the figure of a tall, powerful young man stood silhouetted against the light.

"My son Yann."

"Delighted to meet you, Monsieur," she murmured, holding out her hand for him to kiss.

Presumably ignorant of this society ritual, he seized it and shook it firmly, as if she were a man, enclosing it in both of his to convey his pleasure in seeing her and his gratitude to her for having come so far.

"Nothing could give my father greater pleasure, Madame Dytteville!"

He must have been about her height or a little more. She could see her own blue eyes reflected in his dark ones, which shone like ripe chestnuts, their black pupils in striking contrast to the glowing bronze irises. She marvelled at the classic regularity of the face framed by tumbled chestnut locks whose blacker streaks recalled the veining of iris petals. Womanlike, she guessed at the powerful muscles of torso and body. She did her best to appear natural and at ease, but it was difficult to quell the strange disturbing emotion his presence aroused in her.

"I'm sorry, I feel a little peculiar ... the heat ..."

"Will you take a meal with us?"

She realised that life was an informal business here among 'the tribe' and that the Kerdelecs kept open house.

"Thank you, no," she said with an embarrassed, charming smile.

Instantly his face hardened and he dropped her hand. Afraid that she had wounded his feelings, she went on hurriedly, "I really cannot stay, Yann. I invited the captain and lieutenants of the *Araucaria* to dine tonight at the hotel ... but why don't you come ... with your father?"

She turned towards the old man and immediately wished she could have bitten her tongue off. The poor old man obviously never left the village now.

"Would you like that, Father?" Yann asked, his good humour quite restored. "Oh yes, he often travels to Noumea in his special chair, between two horses. He spends a lot of time at the agency ... his work is his whole life, you know. But at the moment we are idle, though, as you see, the paperwork goes everywhere with him."

Yann obviously adored his father and was anxious to show him in his best light. Stephanie listened, thinking what a good son he was, when suddenly a thin, high-pitched babbling sound came from the old man.

"No ... not tonight ... poor Georges ... poor Armand ... poor woman ..."

He babbled on, uttering disconnected words, gasping and choking. Stephanie turned and found his eyes fixed on her as if there were no one else in the room. It was to her these incoherent words were addressed, to her his imploring, tear-wet eyes were clinging. Something she did not understand was taking place. She stood quite still, repressing a shudder, amazed at Yann's apparent indifference. Why didn't he go across to comfort and soothe his father? Only a few moments before he had been speaking of him with so much love and respect? Moses, no doubt used to these attacks, got to his feet, holding out both large hands as if to catch the old man if he fell. Stephanie was frightened. Her nerves were tense with strain but she didn't move a muscle, following Yann's example. In a harsh, low voice Yann called out,

"Helène!"

A brown-skinned island woman with full, bare breasts, entered as if she had been waiting for the summons. She went over to Yves Kerdelec, moving with supple grace, laid his head on her bosom as if he had been a baby and poured a thin trickle of colourless liquid from a gourd in her hand between his half-opened lips.

"Alcohol?" Stephanie whispered incredulously.

"Yes," Yann replied.

She was about to leap forward and snatch it away when Yann's fingers imprisoned her wrist.

"They know what they are doing ... they look after him better than we can."

"But they're mad, it's quite the worst thing for him! It's his heart, I can tell, I used to be ..."

"A cantinière. Yes, I know."

The low voice rooted her to the spot. How did he know? But all she could think of was the old man and his beseeching eyes. She burst out angrily, "A son who lets his father drink in his condition!"

"Yes, when he is like this, I let him drink. I'll explain, Madame Dytteville, if you will come outside."

"No," she protested, trying to free her arm. "No! He should be put to bed, and ..."

"He is the master here. No one would dream of disobeying his orders, least of all me. When he is ... unwell, I am forbidden to stay with him. The only people he will have with him are Moses and Helène. What a pity it is that your coming here should be responsible for all this ..."

"Responsible!" she cried, hurt and shocked. "What a dreadful thing to say!"

"Please, I'll explain, I'll explain everything ... but not here, not *here*!"

She would have to obey. He led her towards the door by the hand. As they were about to lift the cloth curtain hanging over the door, he whispered, "Now listen. I am going to introduce you to my people now. Don't worry—I shall be there with you. I want you to forget everything that happened in here ... for them you must be Madame Dytteville, a queen!"

"Queen?" she gasped.

It was hard to tell which was the crazier, father or son. On the one hand liquor was being poured into a helpless, raving old man, on the other there was the son, apparently quite untouched by his father's plight, babbling about her being a 'queen'. Yann gripped her hand fast. She submitted, quite bewildered and disorientated. She didn't understand the first thing about these people. The best course would be to submit gracefully, then she would be free to take her leave and go.

Yann slowly lifted the cloth hanging. Then he led her out. The dazzling light blinded her for a second ... the clearing was packed with people, sixty, seventy of them, perhaps more.

"Madame Dytteville ... (why did he insist on calling her that when it was no longer her married name?) ... our Great Mistress, has crossed the seas to visit you in your own country. She is happy to see you and she takes you under her protection from this time forth!"

The words rolled out in the impassioned style of old-fashioned oratory. The kanakas' reaction astonished Stephanie. The men-folk leapt shouting into the air, women shook and wriggled and screeched like peahens, and the children rolled on the ground shouting with delight.

"These are the islanders," Yann whispered through clenched teeth. "Go on, smile at them graciously, royally!"

Once more she did as she was bid, playing the role he assigned to her. Hands fluttered about her, coming close but never touching her, and she had the feeling again of being something of a totem. As Great Mistress she was sacred, taboo.

At a lordly gesture from Yann, a man went running off. He returned with a horse.

"I ride bareback, Mistress. Will you ride in front or behind me."

Bareback! She had ridden bareback in the Vendée, but how many years ago was that? How would she hold on; how would he behave? And he had just addressed her so familiarly! The whole situation was as crazy as it was unexpected ... she must keep her head. With a smile which would have graced a Parisian salon, she turned to him and said carefully: "In front, Yann Kerdelec."

She must have said the right thing because the joyful cries and shouts redoubled. Yann sprang with amazing lightness on to the animal's back, and now there was Napoleon standing in front of her, anxious for the honour of helping her up. Having carried her across the ford on his back, the honour was rightfully his. At one bound, using Napoleon's hands as a mounting block, she was up. She felt Yann's hands steadying her. Nervously Stephanie leant back against him a little. She raised both hands in a regal salutation to the islanders. Just then the horse took a few steps, and a tremor of fear ran through her. Would she be able to keep her seat? Dreadful to fall off and make a fool of herself ...! Yann sensed her distress, and she felt his arm circle her waist stoutly as he took the reins in his free hand.

A noisy escort accompanied them as far as the forest verge, where Yann raised his arm and said quietly but firmly, "Enough."

A devout silence fell and everyone knelt. Stephanie felt like someone in a dream. This was another world and she must get used to it. The horse stepped into the creek, muddy water swirling round its legs.

"Madame Dytteville ..."

"But I'm ..."

"No, believe me, for these people you will always be

Madame Dytteville ... that's the Company's name. Guinchamp, Bourdeilles, that means nothing to them."

"You know everything!" she murmured, remembering with a twinge of annoyance how he had said: 'Yes, a cantinière, I know.'

"Monsieur Georges Dytteville wrote long letters to my father by each ship that came here, and so we came to know and love you."

"Love me?"

"Monsieur Georges sees you as the 'man' who will succeed him in the firm and keep the name going."

She could hardly believe it: Georges, the man who was for ever opposing her, turning a deaf ear when she urged him to make changes or improvements, or to design new posters and advertisements, or re-model the Company offices! She had had to journey 20,000 miles to find what he really thought of her. Yves' words stole into her mind: 'Georges' beloved daughter-in-law ... that is good, Madame, very good ...' Later, when his health improved, she would have a long talk with Yves Kerdelec. The thought prompted her to ask Yann, reproachfully, "Why do you give your father drink when he is ill?"

He didn't answer. The silence grew heavy, almost threatening, till she wished she had not spoken, and then ...

"The ship that sank, drowning your husband, also took with it my mother, who was pregnant, my brother Jean and my sister Stephanie—yes, she was named after you."

She was too moved to speak. She leant closer to him as if to share his grief, and the arm round her waist tightened.

"My father was working in Australia when a letter from his friend Georges arrived, proposing that he should take charge of the New Caledonian branch which your husband was organising. He wanted my father to be there to meet your husband when he arrived. He took me with him, being the eldest. My mother was to stay behind to sell up our property there and then follow us. How many ships foundered and sank in that one cyclone I don't know ... it hardly matters ... but my father never recovered from the loss. My mother remains the one woman he has ever loved, although Helène sleeps naked with him at nights to warm him. Don't be shocked, Madame Dytteville, here my father is a chief, and this is the way chiefs live. You aren't angry?"

"No, no, I'm glad you told me all this. But there's one thing I can't accept and that's the alcohol ... it will kill him!"

"Alcohol sends him to sleep and makes him forget. He had a bad attack today. He wasn't expecting to see you, you came, and ghosts came with you."

This was disturbing enough. But she had further cause for agitation in the warmth of the powerful hand at her waist, and the hard strength of his body jolting against her back at every movement of their horse. 'No, I've finished with love, that's all over! I must be mad, what's happening to me? Why, he's only ten years older than the twins, ten years younger than me, I must ...' Struggling to regain her self-command, she said, "Now I see why you said it was my fault, though I couldn't have known ... I must have brought it all back, and it was too much for him ..."

"So I had to call Helène."

"And Moses."

"There's no need to call for him, he's always there. He's a poor halfwit my father brought back from Pine Island because he was the only white man among the kanakas there."

"Monsieur Kerdelec ..."

"Go on calling me Yann."

"Well, then, Yann, thank you for being so frank with me."

"Don't thank me, it was my duty. Shall I take you as far as the hotel?"

"No, thank you," she said, suddenly noticing that they had reached the outskirts of the town.

"As you wish, Madame Dytteville."

He helped her dismount. She gave him a friendly smile and said in a teasing voice: "I shall be at the office tomorrow at eight o'clock."

"We shall be there at seven. At your service, Madame."

She was taken aback. She hadn't meant him to take her light-hearted challenge so seriously. She was about to explain, and tell him to come along to the hotel, when he wheeled his horse round and set off at a gallop. She wached him go, half hoping that ... but he did not turn back.

'I shall have to get away from here, go back on board the *Araucar*ia, never see him again ...'

And her thoughts went back to Amelie's wedding, where she had first set eyes on René.

Chapter Four

Stephanie walked on, still shaken by the tumult of feelings Yann had aroused in her. The exercise steadied her. As she turned into the Rue de l'Alma she realised with a pang why the sight of him riding off into the distance had reminded her of Amelie's wedding. Amelie's wedding meant, 'May I introduce Monsieur de Guinchamp?' and the great love which had been born on the spot. First love, with all its joy and subsequent anguish when she found herself alone again. Yves Kerdelec's 'May I introduce my son Yann?' had set her heart beating faster in almost exactly the same way. Yann had clasped her hand in his, and the warmth had set her blood racing as she stood mesmerised, looking into his eyes. The emotion was exactly the same as on that occasion twenty years ago, but now the eyes she looked into were not black, but tawny, with darker streaks, like iris petals.

'I must be mad,' she scolded herself. 'Even if he is dark and handsome and strongly built, the sort of man who attracts me—still, I must be mad ...'

She sighed, glancing up almost fearfully at the houses on both sides of the street as if some prescience warned her of a fate against which there could be no appeal. Unfortunately the young Breton had that warm, ardent sensuality which women instinctively recognise and respond to. The memory of his hand on her waist, drawing her closer, was so disturbing that she began trying to harden herself against him.

'Naturally after such a long time without making love a woman like me is bound to be ... impressionable! I must keep my distance and keep telling myself, "You are Madame Dytteville".'

She laughed. Yann was right. The name did give her a certain dignity. Then the thought came to her that such a virile, attractive man was unlikely to lead a celibate existence. His father had Helène, and probably other women too, and Yann, as the Big Master's son, must have his harem too. An unpleasant thought, but it helped her get a grip on herself. A woman as much loved and desired as she had been was not going to stoop to become one among many. Not even the favourite! The idea was degrading, humiliating. Everything was falling back into place, it was all over ... a rush of blood to the head, a flutter in the pulse, everyone experiences that from time to time. Yann Kerdelec, that handsome man with the deep voice and splendid eyes, was nothing more to her than her Company's representative, her own employee. His private life didn't concern her in the least!

It was not far to the hotel now. She began to think that she had mishandled her arrival that morning. It had been a mistake to wear such a plain, everyday dress. She would cut an even sorrier figure now, splashed, torn and muddy, her boots past saving. The moment had come, she decided, to make an impact on the people of Noumea. 'I'll unpack the trunks!'

That 'creature' was still sitting on the terrace. She had three officers with her now, as well as Vincent Cocfigue. Good. She needed him to show her the way to her room. The proprietor rose to his feet when he saw Stephanie, and she hurried towards him with a breathless torrent of words.

"My dear Monsieur, you were quite right. The Kerdelecs are charming people, quite delightful—but the trouble I had getting there! I'm in the most frightful state. I really must change. Would you mind showing me to my rooms? Lead the way ... I'm just behind you ..."

A plan was forming in Stephanie's mind.

Somewhat dazed by her volubility, Vincent led the way

up the stairs and along a corridor till he stopped outside a door.

"So this is my suite. Thank you, thank you so much! You will see that the chef excels himself tonight—I do want to treat my guests to a splendid meal! Good, good, you are too kind ... thank you again for all your help ..."

She was gone, leaving Vincent Cocfigue staring at a closed door.

The room, as Aimé had predicted, was a large one. Trunks stood open all round the room. Aimé had already put a mass of things away, and hung up most of her clothes in the cupboards. She ran a thoughtful eye over her gowns, she knew precisely the effect she wanted to create that night ...

The first person to catch sight of Stephanie on her way down was one of the maids. The girl stood rooted to the spot, open-mouthed. Gowned and jewelled as for an Imperial ball, Stephanie was a vision of beauty and elegance such as Noumea had never seen. Her gown, of velvet and silk, was of a shimmering, misty blue; its draped apron front was swept up behind into a great bustle from which cascaded a train of enormous ruffles caught here and there with silk roses. A froth of lace and two rows of pearls called attention to the daringly low neckline. Her only other jewellery was her diamond engagement ring and the magnificent sapphire Armand had given her.

"Could you show me the way to the dining-room, please."

The round-eyed girl dropped a frightened curtsey and backed towards a set of double doors. Just then, Vincent Cocfigue, who must have heard her voice, stepped in from the terrace.

"Ma ... Madame," he stammered, unable to believe his eyes.

"Madame Dytteville, Monsieur, of the Dytteville Company."

He stood petrified and incredulous.

"Don't look so surprised," she cried gaily. "I've come here on important business. I thought I'd just check that the dining arrangements for the captain and lieutenants of the *Araucaria* are satisfactory. I have every confidence in you, Monsieur Cocfigue, but tonight for some reason I feel all the qualms of the anxious hostess."

Aimé had done her proud. Her table stood in a corner, screened by a bank of green plants from the other diners, and it was attractively set with flowers, brass candlesticks and an embroidered cloth. The dinner service was nothing extraordinary but it was sparkling clean. This was obviously the best that the Island Hotel could provide. Stephanie exclaimed delightedly over everything, and to further her secret project, drew Vincent Cocfigue into conversation. The Company, she explained, imported rare hardwoods from all over the world. She travelled about a good deal in order to see things for herself, on the spot, as well as to keep an eye on the Company's affairs abroad. She had been longing to visit New Caledonia for ages, and now she was here it enchanted her . . .

In reality she was playing for time till Aimé arrived and some of the naval officers came in from the terrace.

Aimé entered, immaculately dressed. The doorway behind him was crowded with uniforms. When a sizeable number had collected, Stephanie pretended to have only just noticed them and launched into the attack.

"My dear Monsieur Cocfigue, do introduce these gentlemen to me. The seafaring world is a small one . . . I'm sure they must all be friends of Captain Plantain."

A good dozen sailors had kissed her hand respectfully by the time the 'tart' arrived.

'No snubbing or cold-shouldering,' Stephanie warned herself, 'I must be very careful. For all I know she may be sleeping with the governor and the king of the kanakas too.'

"Mademoiselle Yolande de Ferrière."

"Charmed, Mademoiselle," murmured Stephanie, noting the embarrassment of the proprietor and other men present.

'With a dress and a name like that she must have escaped from some cheap brothel, or off the streets!' Stephanie thought, watching the poor woman go through a parody of a curtsey, head down, shoulders drooping.

"So pleased to meet you, Madame Dytteville! When you're a long way from Paris, Lord, it's nice to meet someone who's just come from there."

The 'Lord' struck a jarring note. Stephanie saw that Aimé had been observing the lovely Yolande with a sceptical, not to say disapproving, eye during her little speech. She chose this moment to play her trump card, the invitation which would put the finishing touch to a splendidly successful debut. In the canteen in the Crimea, or in Tuboisquoi's barn during the Italian campaign, she would have sealed her popularity with a round of drinks. Well, she was going to do the same thing here.

"Monsieur Cocfigue, would you do me a great favour?"

"Oh, Madame ... Madame ..."

Charmed out of his mind, the proprietor flushed, bowed, smiled and hopped from one foot to the other.

"Would you try to forget that you are in your own hotel, and imagine yourself in my drawing-room instead? You, these gentlemen, the young lady, are my guests ... we shall have a drink together, an aperitif ..."

She made a sign to Aimé. She knew she could rely on him. In ten minutes' time they would have a choice of sherry, madeira, port, champagne, wine and spirits, even if it meant turning the hotel inside out and raiding the local wine merchants. She turned back to her guests and was struck by the change in their demeanour. Her motley crew of roistering sailors of many nationalities, had mysteriously acquired the gravity and refinement of polished gentlemen, while Yolande de Ferrière was behaving like a young creature about to take her first Communion. Most of the men present must have been her lovers, if not her clients, and here was the poor dear modestly pursing her lips and lowering her lids, cooing like a young maiden bashfully unaware of the mysteries of sex.

A radiant Stephanie circulated among her guests, chatting to some in English, which she spoke quite creditably, and in a sort of pidgin French to the Dutch, Germans and the rest. The men fell like ninepins, dazzled by her beauty and charm, but even as she flirted with them, her eyes involuntarily conjured up a certain full-lipped face of classic regularity and tawny eyes ... then the image was gone as she laughed and talked, only to return a moment later as she wondered whether Yann was thinking of her in his village, while making love to his own 'Helène'.

Captain Plantain seemed astonished to find her metamorphosed again into the society beauty who had dazzled Marseilles. She greeted him like a long-lost friend and conquering hero.

Dinner was served in a gala atmosphere, and Stephanie was agreeably surprised by the standard of the food. Time passed so quickly she did not notice at first how crowded and noisy the hall and verandahs had become. She glanced out through the windows and saw that there were as many people on the terrace as one would find outside a Parisian cafe. The Rue de l'Alma was rapidly turning into a Boulevard des Italiens! This didn't surprise her. Noumea was like a small provincial town where every new event or arrival is common knowledge in a few hours. Word had gone round town and port that Madame Dytteville, arrived only that morning, was holding a reception at the Island Hotel, and everyone had come hurrying along to see for themselves. Her shining eyes met Aimé's. As usual he had read her thoughts. He was smiling too, but his eyes signalled a warning across the table.

"It's time to leave, Madame ..."

As usual, too, he was right. The fair Yolande had quaffed a good few glasses of champagne by now, and as the talk grew broader around her she dropped her missish airs and was soon laughing and exchanging ribald remarks with the ease and freedom of a trooper. To the one-time Phanie none of this was in the least shocking or embarrassing; men in their cups were nothing new to her. However, if she was going to live up to what was expected of Madame Dytteville, the moment had clearly come for her to discreetly retire from the gathering.

"Will you give me your arm, Captain?"

He rose, bowing, and she moved through the crowded dining-room at his side, motioning to the men to remain seated because she wanted to slip away unnoticed. A radiant smile and nod to each one as she passed, as if to say: 'No, please enjoy yourselves, don't take any notice of me, I'm a little tired ...'

"Madame's first party in Noumea has been an unqualified success," Aimé remarked as they reached her room.

"I'm sure it was the right thing to do," she said, "and I'm delighted that it went so well. Everyone knows who I am now ... not some flibbertigibbet who can safely be ignored! Wake me early tomorrow morning, and bring breakfast to my room. We have to be at the office by eight o'clock."

Drowsy with the heat, the wine she had drunk, and the warm glow of a triumphant evening, Stephanie fell into a deep and dreamless sleep. The tropical night was caressingly soft and she was happy and relaxed.

She was rudely woken by howls and moans like those of a wounded animal. She sat up in bed. Feet thudded along the passage outside her room. Then she heard a woman's voice raised entreatingly only to be drowned by a flood of incomprehensible male oaths. Stephanie was fully awake in a second, clearheaded as a soldier expecting a surprise attack. She snatched up her frilly peignoir and rushed to the door of her room without even bothering to put on her slippers. She paused in the doorway just long enough to take in the extraordinary scene being enacted in the dimly lit corridor. A tall, stout man, entirely naked save for his boots, was in hot pursuit of the unfortunate

Yolande, who was also naked, and zigzagging desperately from side to side of the corridor in her eagerness to escape. The man brandished a whip in one hand and Yolande's plump buttocks, back and shoulders were striped with red, bloody weals. In a moment she would have reached the end of the corridor, where her assailant would be able to corner her like a rat and thrash her unmercifully. He was mad, he would kill her ...

Without stopping to think Stephanie raced after them, snatched up one of a pair of boots standing outside a door and flung it with all her strength at the running man. He stopped with a bellow of pain. The metal spur had struck him first and scored a deep furrow down his back, now spurting with blood. He turned and confronted her, still brandishing the whip. She parried it with another boot, and then with her free hand reached out and seized the leather thongs and jerked them out of Ludwig's hand. She recognised the man now; he was the German commandant Ludwig von Reinbinggen.

By now doors all along the passage were opening and men came running up in their nightshirts, one or two of them still struggling into a pair of drawers. They seized the naked giant's arms in an attempt to pin him down, but with a roar and a sudden spring he shook himself free and made as if to hurl himself at Stephanie. Still holding the boot in front of her like a shield, she struck him across the chest with the whip. The men overpowered him at their second attempt. It was only then, when she saw the red stripes she had drawn across the man's skin, that she realised the weapon she was holding was a knout.

... Sebastopol! A dungeon chamber and the vicious crack above her each time her tormentor spelt out another letter of her name ... hissing thongs biting into her flesh ... the tiny metal balls breaking her skin so that drops of blood spurted as the man raised his arm to strike anew ...

Yolande's muffled groans broke into her thoughts. She turned and saw the poor wretch crouching in a corner, arms folded over her bowed head, awaiting further punishment, torture or aid. Stephanie took two steps towards Ludwig.

"Swine!" she hissed, and spat full in his face as if ridding herself by that action of the accumulated rage of twenty years. She flung the knout aside. Then she went up to Yolande and threw her peignoir over her.

"Put this on and come to my room!"

Without realising it, she spoke as she used to speak to her Zouaves, or Pompette. As she got to her feet, dragging Yolande up with her, she felt a cloak settle round her own shoulders. It was Aimé. She was suddenly aware, from the way the men were all looking at her, that every curve and line of her body was visible through the transparent folds and flounces of her nightdress. Ludwig had stopped struggling and stood staring at her as if transfixed. He uttered one word in his hoarse, thickly accented voice, "Sorry!"

Stephanie paused in amazement. He must be quite mad! What did he mean by apologising to her? Observing her astonishment, Ludwig began again:

"Forgive me."

She shrugged, swept him from head to foot with a stinging glance, and turned to the men who had hold of him.

"Bathe the brute's wounds with alcohol and send for a doctor. I'll look after her. Get me what I need," she went on, to Aimé.

Yolande lay stretched out on Stephanie's bed, whimpering, weeping and writhing with pain as Stephanie tended the bloody stripes left by the knout. Rubenesque was the only word to describe the girl's body, handsome enough with its generous pearly curves. Her heavy breasts were still firm, and Stephanie could not help wondering how she had retained such a shapely bosom when her waist had thickened noticeably. She suddenly felt a strange bond between herself and this whore who too had suffered the vicious bite of a knout. She questioned her gently.

"How did it happen?"

"Lord, it's all in a night's work, isn't it?" Yolande answered, with disarming candour. "Look at it this way, he's a generous bloke when he's sober, but he has his manias . . . he's not the only one, they've all got their little preferences. He doesn't usually hit so hard. This time he produced this whip I'd never seen before and said he was going to do a cossack on me! A cossack, I ask you. Then he put his boots on and . . ."

"I know."

The whispered words slipped out despite herself. Looking up she saw that Yolande, and Aimé who was sitting on the far side of the bed, were both staring questioningly at her.

"Well, I can imagine," she corrected herself with a smile. "The little metal balls must be terribly painful."

"Lord, yes, you can say that again! I knew it wasn't going to be fun from the first stroke . . . it was like a Chinese torture! As for these scars, I don't know . . ."

"In a week's time you won't see a thing. I'm going to put some sweet almond oil on them."

She thought of Sebastopol, the dungeon, and her own stripes that healed of their own accord. Gently, almost tenderly, she massaged the oil into Yolande's back. There was one question she was burning to ask.

"What brought you to Noumea?" she said at last.

"The war, of course," the woman answered bitterly. "If it hadn't been for the war I'd have got out of it all."

"Got out of it?"

"I'd a good bit of money saved, and a rich man who wanted to set me up in a place, and then, bang, the Prussians upped and entered Paris! Well, I lasted out the siege as best I could and then I went off to Versailles because that Commune lark, it wasn't for me! Catch me sticking around with that penniless lot of ruffians in power! So I got out."

"Out of what?" Stephanie asked, not clear what the woman was talking about. Besides, she wanted to know more about her. There was something oddly familiar about her accent and way of talking which she couldn't quite place.

"Out of where I was, stuck away in the countryside without two francs to rub together. War is a scourge, Madame, a shocking horrible thing, and it wrecked my career, that's certain. The way they treated me at Versailles! Any respect for women went out with the Empire. Ah me, if I told you my life story you'd think it was a novel you were reading, and you'd see what a dirty place this world is for the likes of me!"

"I'm sorry to hear it," Stephanie murmured, amused by Yolande's frankly amoral nature and curious philosophy of life.

"Now you've got a pretty name. Stephanie, that's nice, and uncommon too. Stephanie Dytteville sounds better still. I was born Eulalie Bouton. You can imagine what a help that was for getting on in the world! I had to change it."

"You chose your name yourself?"

"Not quite. Yolande was the name of the wife of the first man who took me out of the farm and set me up in my own place. He said by calling me after her he was less likely to say the wrong thing when he made love to her, and also it made him feel less unfaithful to her in some way. I thought it was a sweet thought on his part. Then when I moved to Paris I kept the Yolande and added Ferrière because it sounded pretty and because that's where I come from."

"Ferrière?" Aimé asked quietly.

"Yes, well to be precise La Ferrière, near Roche-sur-Yon, in the Vendée. I added the 'de' because it sounds classy."

Stephanie's eyes met Aimé's and then returned to settle on Eulalie Bouton, native of ... 'It's odd how I felt there was some connection ... I knew I recognised the accent,' she thought, more and more curious to know how this good-humoured peasant, so innocently naive at heart, had found her way to Noumea.

Aimé sensed her growing interest. He was not altogether in favour of 'drawing the girl out', as Madame seemed bent on doing. She obviously needed no prompting to tell her life story, and the trouble with women of that type was that if you gave them an inch they'd take a mile! She'd think she could get away with anything if Madame was too nice to her.

"Are you feeling better, Mademoiselle de Ferrière?" he enquired pleasantly.

"Thanks to you," Yolande exclaimed, taking one of Stephanie's hands between hers. "I'm yours to command, Madame, through thick and through thin. You've been good to me, and if ever I can do something for you just say the word!"

"Why, thank you," Stephanie replied. Just then she heard someone knocking at the door.

Aimé opened it, and found Vincent Cocfigue together with a stranger.

"Doctor Verdonnet wished to see Mademoiselle," Vincent mumbled nervously.

"Please come in, Doctor," said Stephanie.

"See!" Yolande cried triumphantly to Vincent, holding up Stephanie's hand which she still kept fast in her own. "You weren't even going to introduce me to Madame Dytteville!"

The hotel proprietor might shift and squirm uncomfortably but the doctor was professional discretion itself. He examined the damaged back, now thickly coated with ointment.

"Congratulations, Madame, I could not have done better myself. The commandant, I'm sorry to say, is in not quite such good shape. The spur left a deep wound and seems to have nicked a shoulderblade. He's in no danger of course, but it looks as if he will be scarred for life."

"How awful, Doctor!" Stephanie exclaimed. "I ... he

was very drunk and laying about him with the whip and . . ."

"Now, now, Madame, you mustn't imagine I am scolding you, I know how it all happened and you are in no way to blame. I merely wanted to congratulate you on your presence of mind and excellent reflexes!"

"Shall I see you back to your room, Mademoiselle?" Vincent suggested, fixing Yolande with a look which seemed to expect instant obedience.

Stephanie had a strong feeling that this was more than a polite suggestion on his part. From the way Yolande struggled upright with a groan it was clear that he was used to giving her orders, and that she submitted to them in the way of a woman under a man's thumb. She remembered how the presence of 'Mademoiselle de Ferrière' at her reception had not seemed to scandalise anyone despite the fact that she practised the oldest profession in the world. And she remembered too how Vincent had busied himself among the guests, putting in a good word for the lady here and there as if . . . well, as if he were a good salesman anxious to impress possible clients with the quality of the merchandise.

'Well, if the Island Hotel is a bit of a brothel on the side, it's nothing to do with me and certainly nothing to get excited about,' she told herself. However, something about the man's tone annoyed her and she put one hand on Yolande's shoulder.

"I'll see Mademoiselle de Ferrière to her room in a moment," she said. "I want to make sure she's quite herself again first. I am sorry about the commandant," she went on, speaking to the doctor. "He was behaving like a madman and I really had no choice."

"What's done is done, Madame," he replied fatalistically. "And I'm not sure you may not have done yourself a good turn without realising it— people will treat you with more circumspection in future. Noumea has always been a typical port, with all that implies, but now we have all the people deported by the Republic to cope with as well. They are Communards to a man, and we all know what *they* are capable of!"

He spoke in tones of such withering contempt that Stephanie could not help adding: "They were no worse than the men of Versailles, Doctor!"

She regretted the remark as soon as she had made it. She suddenly saw Aimé again, in flashback, herded on to the quayside where 'his own people', the class he had come from and grown up among, were butchering people at random, indiscriminately, just because their hands were 'black'; she saw the two of them marching the long road to Versailles, reviled and spat upon like lepers . . . still, in the doctor's own words, what's done is done. Besides, the doctor might be an important figure in Noumea, and she had no desire to offend him. Her remark had been hasty. Now she tried to soften its effect without, however, seeking to withdraw what she had said.

"I feel you should know that I was arrested by the Versailles party by mistake, together with Monsieur here," she told the doctor, with a glance at Aimé, "so we know a good deal about summary executions and judgment without trial and men who would stop at nothing . . . I trust that explains my reaction. Tomorrow I would like to visit the commandant with you, if you'll permit me, and see if there is anything I can do for him."

The doctor bowed his agreement. Then he looked at Stephanie and observed with old-world courtesy: "The commandant will be delighted to receive you, Madame. A man might almost wish to be wounded if you were to be his nurse."

"You see the place where that old man is squatting," Stephanie told Aimé as they rounded the corner. "That's where the Company offices are. The old man, Moses, is something like a faithful dog to Yves Kerdelec. If he's there, his master must be too. I must say I'd prefer some other form of advertisement, but I suppose we must make the best of it. It's all rather different from what you would imagine looking at our publicity material in France," she added laughing.

The Company's brochures and posters showed the New Caledonian branch as a smaller edition of the London one, with a flight of stone steps, massive doors with brass handles and offices furnished with sober luxury. The reality was rather different. Stephanie stepped through a simple rustic door into a tiled hall, with four whitewashed rooms opening off it, a view over the harbour and small garden where some goats were tethered.

"This is Eugenie, and Antoinette!" said Yann, who was doing the honours. "In Paris I suppose you would call them ... secretaries?" He smiled brilliantly and the two young girls fell on their knees. "Their job here is to put things away and help in general ways. They can't write and they can barely read, but they have excellent memories which come in useful when we're negotiating for the purchase of standing timber. I hope you will do me the honour of accompanying us when we go up into the mountains to choose the next shipment."

The 'us' slipped out quite naturally. Stephanie was shocked. They must sleep with the girls then! She supposed such goings-on must be normal practice in the islands. The girls were young and pretty. Stephanie wondered if she had seen them the day before, at the village. There all the women, young and old alike, went bare-breasted. The girls smiled timidly, turning their heads away with a frightened, shamefaced air which puzzled her.

"You must get used to seeing me," she said softly to them. "There's nothing to be frightened of. And if there is anything you need, come and tell me about it, and I'll see what I can do," she added, as if she were at the Rue Vivienne.

"My father is here," Yann whispered, almost as if he were warning her.

"I know," she replied, somewhat astonished. "I said good morning to him just now but ..."

Yann put a finger to his lips, hushing her, and she realised that she had put her foot in it quite innocently. She should not have told the girls to bring their problems to her. In Noumea there was only one boss, who saw to everything, and that was the old man whom alcohol had pickled as efficiently as if he were a foetus in a bottle. His authority was absolute. The solution, she decided, was to win him over by stealth, using all her tact and charm. She didn't want to offend him, partly because he was old and ill and partly because she could not forget the beseeching look he had given her the previous day when he was delirious. She went back into his office, followed by Aimé and Yann.

"My dear Monsieur Kerdelec, I expect my father-in-law has told you that I go to the office every day. It's one of the great pleasures of my life. But I should hate to disturb you in any way, just tell me where you would like me to put myself, any corner will do."

"Here, in my office, Madame Armand."

The name upset her; she went pale. Only yesterday he had said, 'You are Armand's wife,' as if he were still living. And then he had whispered: 'Poor Georges ... poor Armand ... poor wife,' as if they were all connected with the death of his wife and children. Yann had explained it all to her: those tragic deaths were still fresh and recent in his mind, and when the thought became unbearable only alcohol would serve to soften the pain and recall him to the present. But she was not going to help bring the past alive. It was one thing to let them call her Madame Dytteville; it helped establish her connection with the Company, it amused her and made her feel young again, and it was pleasant to be able to forget that she had 'the honour to be Madame de Guinchamp' so long as she was in Noumea. But not Madame Armand, that was too much! Her reaction was prompt and decisive.

"Monsieur Kerdelec—I would rather you did not call me that. Please call me Madame Stephanie as everyone does in the Rue Vivienne. Thank you for letting me share your office with you; it is a gesture of confidence which pleases me very much."

He did not answer. He made a sign and Yann and the two girls hurriedly drew up a table for her—a table she would not have given house-room to in her kitchen at home.

'The islands, the islands,' she kept repeating to herself, 'everything is charming and unexpected, it's another world!' Without being aware of it her eyes were following every move of Yann's as she might have watched a cat or a tiger. 'Will you do us the honour of accompanying us?'—the phrase went round and round in her head like a hurdy-gurdy tune. She thought back to their journey through the swamp, his thighs either side of hers, their bodies jolting and swaying together with the rhythm of the horse's steps. A trip to the mountains would last several days. Of course she would be riding her own horse, but he would ride beside her, with the kanakas, the girls, porters and baggage mules following behind. When the Masters went a-journeying here, she imagined, it would be like medieval nobles on a progress from castle to castle, accompanied by their own furniture, bedding, cooking and eating vessels, even papers and documents. She had just recognised the pile of papers on the old man's desk as the very one she had seen in his house the day before.

After she had installed herself at her table with a pile of big black ledgers like the ones they used in Paris—she supposed Georges must have them sent out here—she suddenly felt at a complete loose end. Really, there was nothing for her to do here. Aimé was with Yann in the garden, asking about crops, flowers, all the things which he liked to be informed about. Secretely, she guessed, he must feel as superfluous as she did.

'I'll stick it out, I'll get used to it. Anyway, there'll be trips into the mountains and forests, and there's Yann ...' It was annoying the way her thoughts kept circling back to him. She stared at the columns of names and figures without seeing them. With peculiarly feminine self-deception, she told herself that her interest in Yann sprang from the fact that he was young and active, and would be invaluable to her in the work she planned to do. With Yann as her right-hand man, she would be able to get things moving behind the old man's back, quite unnoticed by him—he was as wedded to his directorial throne as ever her father-in-law was. They would expand both the timber and nickel production. And there was always Aimé, the cool, clear-sighted Aimé, so good at making things go smoothly and handling tricky situations.

She heard a horse stop outside the office. A client? It must be someone who knew the place because he walked straight in without knocking. She looked up smiling, gratified by this diversion. Doctor Verdonnet came into the room. He greeted her and kissed her hand rather affectedly.

"You look surprised to see me, Madame Dytteville? But don't you remember suggesting that you should come with me when I went to see the commandant. I've come to fetch you, I'm on my way to the hotel now."

"How did you know I was here?" she asked in some puzzlement.

He paused for a second, then he said curtly: "Everyone knows, Madame."

"Really!" she exclaimed, her smile growing fixed as she took in the not altogether welcome fact that she was never going to be able to take a step in this town without everyone knowing it.

"The commandant was most touched by your concern," Yves remarked suddenly.

She spun round to look at him. How did *he* know? Just then Yann's appearance, with Aimé, confirmed that last night's event was already common knowledge.

"So the spur tore his back and nicked his shoulder-blade? Reinbinggen must have felt that all right!"

"Madame Dytteville," the doctor remarked, bowing in her direction, "prescribed the best possible treatment:

"Pour some alcholol over the swine and send for a doctor!"

"Let's go, shall we?" Stephanie said, getting abruptly to her feet.

This conversation was getting on her nerves. Talk about small-town gossips! What must she look like ... a tigress, some sort of Fury?

"And Yolande?" asked Yann.

So he knew all about that too. And there was no mistaking the familiar way he said 'Yolande'; he must have sampled the pale skin as a change from all those brown and bronze ones! Doctor Verdonnet—she was beginning to dislike the fellow—answered him, man-to-man. "She'll be on her back in three days, my dear chap, Vincent will see to that!"

He could hardly have put it more bluntly! It confirmed her own suspicions. There was a working partnership, if nothing else, between the girl and the hotel proprietor. The girl was being exploited; that was something she would have to see to later. She changed the subject abruptly, to let them realise the conversation displeased her:

"Monsieur Kerdelec, will I have the pleasure of seeing you tomorrow?" she asked the old man sweetly.

"Why, every day, Madame Stephanie, should you wish to. This afternoon, though, I shall be down at the port seeing to the loading of the *Araucaria*."

"How lovely! I'll come and see you there," she cried, with almost filial tenderness.

'Georges all over again,' she told herself angrily, sticking his nose in everywhere, trying to run everything. Still, he won't be coming into the mountains to choose the timber, and weigh up the nickel. In my case, forewarned is forearmed!'

Chapter Five

'Finished with the social round at *last*!' Stephanie sighed with relief as she stood watching the *Araucaria* swing slowly round and head out to the open sea. She had had her fill of dressing up and displaying herself every evening, either at the hotel or at the house of some local notable. In a week's time their caravan would be out in the wilds, heading up into the mountains. Anywhere, so far as she was concerned, would do as long as it wasn't here! She hadn't escaped from René only to be swept up in a social whirl which was a pale reflection of the one she had left behind in Paris except that its moral outlook was at once more strait-laced and more tolerant. Presumably this resulted from the mingling of races and nationalities living and working together in the same place.

Adaptable she might be, but she was also determined to be accepted for what she was, as herself. Noumea accepted her as an utterly independent woman, whose talk and behaviour might sometimes surprise, but never gave rise to malicious gossip. Thus, it was generally accepted that the beautiful Mme Stephanie Dytteville never went anywhere without her steward, and that if you invited her to your home you also invited M. Becave.

She had electrified the company at a reception held by the Governor, by remarking in the most casual way imaginable that she fully intended to pay a visit to the Isle of Nou and the Ducos peninsula to see the deported Communards. Their first reaction was one of horror, the Governor included, but then thanks to her social standing, beauty and character, this was succeeded by timid admiration of her courage, unselfishness and truly Christian charity in turning her thoughts towards these dregs of humanity. She had even gone so far as to ask for a meeting to be arranged with Louise Michel, the Red Virgin of the Commune. The whole town knew of the meeting, and described it as an encounter between 'That angel, Madame Dytteville, and the she-devil of a Communarde.' The angel had gone bearing gifts and money, which the she-devil had refused: 'I'm not taking anything from you, you're what I've spent my life fighting against.' To which the angel retorted: 'I understand if that is how you feel, but you are not alone here—take these things for your comrades, share them out, you can do that better than me.' The visit stuck in Stephanie's memory as something close to a descent into hell. It was the rout at Dobruja, the horror of Chersonese all over again. Heat, filth, decay, misery in its most abject form. She saw a bleeding, unconscious man who had been sentenced to flogging, carried off by fellow prisoners, themselves about to undergo the same punishment. A man who had tried to escape was brought in, hands and feet tied to a pole like an animal, by a party of kanakas eager for the reward attached to his recapture. Aimé, sensing her anger and disgust, had seized her wrist warningly: 'I think we should go now ... we can return another day.' He was right, it would be foolish to cross swords with the prison administration right from the start. She would have to do something for these people, but first she needed to get the influential ladies, the 'aristocracy' of Noumea, under her thumb. She foresaw the founding of a committee to deal with the penal settlement; it would be a slow, difficult task, but she might carry it through if she were able to calm the ladies' fear of 'those criminals' and infuse them with a desire for good works.

The fact that she had taken Yolande de Ferrière under her wing, insisting on her attendance at the dinner Commandant Reinbinggen held in her honour, had given Stephanie a sort of haloed superiority to common mortals in the eyes of Noumea, which made her immune to criticism or malicious gossip. Her decision to join a horseback expedition into the mountains set her still more apart from the local ladies, who greeted the news with envious admiration. Everyone accepted her 'just as she is'. Stephanie was delighted. It was true she had her name, social status and the Dytteville Company on her side, but her triumph here was largely her own work.

Her first conquests had been among the men. That had been easy—all she had to do was to make an appearance, smile, flatter their masculinity, say a few words, laugh at a silly joke or thank them for a banal compliment, and look amazed at some commonplace profundity. Then she had had the harder task of captivating their ladies. She had done this by reassuring them. Aimé's constant presence at her side, the way they talked to each other and the irreproachable friendship between them, had touched the ladies' hearts. Seeing Stephanie as a woman who could not refuse any human being in distress, while remaining free from all human weaknesses herself, they would even have packed their husbands off to her to receive a good scolding, or sound advice.

Her performance was masterly, but it was only a performance, had the ladies but known! Not that they had anything to fear from her. There was only one man in the islands whom she thought about, and she thought of him incessantly ... his eyes were her whole horizon, the brilliance of dawn, the radiance of day, the tender mystery of dusk. All her prejudices, all the defences she had set up against Yann, had melted away like snow in the sun: harem, bastard children all forgotten. He lived his own life in the islands just as she did. He was free, unmarried, but he could have taken his pick among the white women; that was obvious from the way they gazed at him and talked about him behind his back. Stephanie sensed, she *knew*, that he was not indifferent to her, but with her his behaviour was always perfectly correct and no more. Just occasionally, when he stood back to let her go first into a room: 'No, please ...' or when he asked her something: 'Would you like ... do you want ... do you think ...?' his voice would go warm, vibrant for a moment.

Stephanie had never again seen him casually dressed as he was the first time she saw him. He turned up each morning at nine in spotless clean whites, open at the throat, worn with black boots polished to a jetty brilliance. It had occurred to her that he might be giving the role of seducer a new twist, showing discreet signs of interest and then sitting back waiting for her to make the first move. There were other times when she wished she could leave the islands, but she knew that it was too late—even if she could have left on the *Araucaria,* she would have stayed. The trip into the mountains would bring them closer together, it would crack that puzzling reserve of his. He was waiting for something, she sensed it, waiting with an uneasiness she found incomprehensible. Meanwhile there was nothing for it but to carry on ... and yet she knew with all her mind and body that he was hers as surely as she was his, it was preordained, inevitable. And Aimé was as sure of this as she was: with his infallible instinct where people and events were concerned, he had quite adopted the younger Kerdelec and referred to him as Yann as naturally as he once spoke of Boris as the Prince.

Two slaps echoing through the room next door to the office, where Stephanie was adjusting her hat, brought matters to a head between herself and Yann.

"It's nothing, Madame Stephanie," old Yves whispered, seeing her start and look up. "Someone is being punished for doing their work badly, that's all. Obedience is vital. The kanakas are impressed by firmness. A white person must never lose face."

It was Yann in there, she was certain. She had often seen him treat his two women, Eugenie and Antoinette, like slaves, but this was the first time he had struck one of them while she was at the office. She listened but there were no cries or sobs to be heard, though she could hear the thud of repeated blows. Then she heard two ferocious slaps, followed by the sound of a body falling and dragging itself across the floor. Yann's boots rang on the tiled floor, then more dull blows and a smothered cry. Unable to contain herself a minute longer, she stood up so sharply she knocked her chair over.

"Madame Stephanie . . ."

She ignored the old man and rushed next door where she found Eugenie cowering in a corner, trying to escape from Yann just as Yolande had tried to escape from the commandant.

"Are you quite mad?" Stephanie cried, flinging herself on him and seizing his arm.

He sent her spinning.

"It's none of your business!"

"Aren't you ashamed of yourself?"

She was beside herself with fury. What a country! They beat women here? Well, not in front of her! She pushed Yann aside and ran across to the girl. He seized her, and this time with such brutal strength that she reeled across the room.

"Not in the least," he answered. "What the girl did is unforgivable."

"Whatever she did you still don't have the right to . . ."

"I have all the rights!"

"Nothing she could have done excuses your brutality—you are worse than the guards at the penal settlement. You make me sick."

She made a movement towards Eugenie, but he barred the way.

"Let me pass."

"No, Madame Dytteville, I forbid you to touch her."

Flabbergasted by his cool impertinence, Stephanie spoke in a voice hoarse with anger: "You forbid me, *you*!"

"You don't understand, you've come from a long way away, things are different here. This is my affair, Madame

Dytteville, I beg you to leave us alone."

That was the one thing she was determined not to do. His eyes sought hers as if he intended to stare her down and impose his will. Really, such arrogance! She hardened herself, fighting him, she wanted to win this battle of wills. But there was a look in those strange eyes of his, imperious and yet almost beseeching, which touched her despite herself.

"What did she do wrong?" she asked, forcing him to recount Eugenie's misdeed.

He bit his lips, reluctant to answer. She knew that he was clenching his fists. He was weakening a little, she could tell.

"I'm waiting for an explanation, Monsieur Kerdelec."

His nostrils flared and his lips quivered for an instant. He was breathing faster, exasperated by her. Then, no doubt hoping that the sooner he explained the sooner she would leave him to finish his business, he muttered reluctantly and with a bad grace: "She handled your hat."

Stephanie was so astounded that a nervous laugh bubbled out of her as her eyes strayed to the charming confection of roses and pansies heaped on a velvet crown.

"You mean she tried it on?" she corrected him, laughing eyes fixed on his sombre ones.

"Handled it, I said," he repeated in a slow, grave voice.

His bright, intense gaze hardened. She felt bewildered. After all, what had the wretched girl done—yielded to a passing feminine whim, a coquettish wish to see how she looked in a Paris hat. Everyone in Noumea coveted Stephanie's clothes, and the island's few dressmakers were kept busy copying her gowns and hats.

"If she likes it so much . . ." she exclaimed nonchalantly, approaching the girl.

Again she found Yann barring her way.

"Now what's the matter?"

"Please, just believe me, and leave her be."

His tone was imploring. Mystery upon mystery.

"I want to make her a present of it!"

"Let me present it to her, on your behalf, then. I'll explain everything to you later. Now don't move ... stay where you are."

He stopped and turned in time to catch Eugenie creeping towards the door. He leapt across, cutting off her retreat, eyes smouldering as he stared at the girl, who retreated submissively to her corner again.

"Now, you must watch what I am going to do ... trust me ... I'll explain everything. But you must see ... for the sake of ..."

He came over to her and stood with his eyes boring into hers. Then, rapidly and so softly she could not be sure she heard him right, he finished his sentence with the astonishing remark: "... for *our* sake!"

She stood petrified, unable to move, watching him as he snatched up the flowered hat by its ribbons, swinging it like a censer. He crossed over to Eugenie with a feline grace which sent a shiver of excitement through her. It could have been Sergei, her brutal gaoler at Sebastopol, the only one of the men whom she could not resist, whose love-making brought her skilfully, patiently, to a long, sobbing climax all the more frenzied because it was wrested from her reluctant body by a sensualist who needed her consummation to crown his own. Yann belonged to the same breed of men. She had suspected this before, now she was sure. How he must love when he loved! She almost hated him even as she loved and desired him ... she almost wished that he were standing over her now as he stood over the terrified girl, who flattened herself against the wall as if trying to make herself disappear, or as if she were gathering herself up for a desperate spring for the door. Why was there a look of such abject terror on her face as her eyes flickered from the hat to Yann and then back to the hat again?

He sprang upon Eugenie, forcing one leg between hers so as to trap her against the wall while his hand, buried in her frizzy hair, pinioned her head. A terrible, inhuman scream came from the girl as he savagely ground the hat in her face.

Stephanie was aghast. She flung herself upon him like a wildcat, tearing at his arms in an attempt to free the girl. Yann was taken so much by surprise that he let go of Eugenie for a moment, time for her to give him a desperate push which sent him and Stephanie reeling back while the girl vanished through the door. Stephanie was too late to save herself and she fell heavily with Yann on top of her. With one lithe twist he was spread-eagled on her ... she did not even protest, all she could think of was that the man she had hungered after for so long was lying above her ... he was handsome, his body warm and powerful ... she felt her breasts harden against him and closed her eyes, waiting with parted lips. His mouth fell upon hers savagely. A long shudder ran through her and she opened her legs so he could lie between them. Raising himself, he murmured huskily:

"I had to do it, Stephanie ... for ... for your love."

"You ... you ..."

He cut her short with another kiss. But now she tried to free herself. He wasn't going to make love to her here, on the office floor! She turned her head aside just long enough to regain a little composure, and when she turned back to meet his eyes a plaintive protest escaped her which sounded more like an avowal of love.

"You are a coward ... I hate you."

"A coward for punishing a native girl? Or because I want you, because I love you," his voice was hoarse, breathless "more than I've ever loved before? Oh, Stephanie, if you only knew ..."

He was gentle now, beseeching, and she took advantage of this momentary weakness to push him away and jump to her feet. But he was on her in a second, forcing her up against the wall, his legs straddling her, his hands forcing her arms apart.

"No ... please ..."

"You must believe me, Stephanie, there was no other way."

"If I hadn't come in then, you would have beaten her to death: it's horrible!"

"But don't you see, she was trying to kill *you*," he burst out in a half sob. "Now do you understand?"

She stared at him petrified. Why should Eugenie hate her that much? No, he must be imagining things.

"She wanted to put a spell on you, Stephanie! She hates you because I have thrown her out ... I need to be alone at nights, to dream of you. She is a jealous, proud girl, a chief's daughter. Sharing me with another woman is all right, because this is the island custom, and I am the master here, but for her own people to see her rejected, driven out like an old woman ... that she can't accept. She was trying to revenge herself."

He was so eager, so childlike in his credulity! Stephanie murmured kindly, "You are imagining things, Yann, these things don't happen. We are living in the nineteenth century, you know."

"Oh, but they do happen, Stephanie, I've seen them, I've had proof," he cried jerkily. "I've seen people fade away and die because no one intervened till it was too late. Didn't you hear the scream she gave when I rubbed your hat in her face? I turned her magic back on her, she breathed in the powder and got the flowers stuffed into her mouth—that was the scream of a mortally wounded animal, Stephanie. Do you know what she did? She pricked each flower petal with a special thorn, picked just as the moon touched it, and when I caught her she was just sprinkling the flowers with a magic powder!"

'I can't take these old tales seriously,' Stephanie thought, and yet his sincerity and the anguish and distress written all over his face were more disturbing than she cared to admit. She realised that he had been protecting her and would go on protecting her, without her even being aware of it. Despite herself a doubt crept into her mind, like the doubts that torment an atheist on his deathbed. 'Suppose God does exist?' the atheist asks himself. 'Suppose these spells and thorns and powders ...?'

Stephanie wondered. Then, hoping to learn more, she asked softly, "How did you know Eugenie was working these ... spells on me?"

As if it was too obvious to need saying, he replied, "Why, Moses told me."

"What, that poor simpleton who never utters ten words a day!" she cried incredulously. "Now you tell me Moses is mixed up in this! Oh, it's preposterous, a lot of silly superstition!"

"Don't joke about these things, Stephanie, please ... I tell you, they aren't funny."

He looked dejected now as he stood, still crushing her body with his, fingers entwined in hers. He moved her heart as well as her body ... she whispered tenderly, "I won't, I promise you."

His eyes lingered on her face, her eyes, lips ... her eyes again.

"They believe here, and I believe it too, that simple folk are closer to the mysteries of nature than the rest of us. Moses is never wrong when he predicts rain, hurricanes, sickness among the animals, a tree about to fall, spells and magic, danger ... My father set him to keep guard over you."

An involuntary shiver ran down her back. She checked the disbelieving smile she was about to give and asked, "Why?"

"Because my father has never forgotten the shipwreck, and because my sister was named after you. When you appeared it was like a ghost rising out of the sea, it shook him terribly ... you remember how he was? He loved you immediately with the love he still keeps for his dead daughter. The next day he tried to recall the past by calling you Madame Armand. Moses is a faithful dog. All my father had to do was point to you and say 'Her' for Moses to devote himself to you utterly, to belong to you as he belongs to my father and to me. If my father told Moses to kill he would kill blindly, merely to carry out his orders."

Stephanie reflected for a moment. Then she said, "That's the one thing you've said, Yann, which I find real and humanly believable. I do believe your father told Moses to keep guard over me, and I'm deeply touched. As for the rest . . . well, I just don't know. We'll see."

"You mustn't let it worry you . . . I'm here!"

"It's all right," she told him, tender and half smiling because there was real anxiety in his voice. "I'm not worried. If to believe is to be saved, as the Gospels say, then I must be safe. I believe in your father, and Moses and . . . in you, Yann."

The way her lips formed his name was like a caress. He swooped on her mouth again, kissing her wildly, deliriously, and his body moulded itself against hers so closely and sensually that she knew it in all its animal grace, power and desire even through all their clothes.

Eugenie was not at the office the next day, which was no great surprise, but Antoinette had vanished too, which was more puzzling. Yann told Stephanie carelessly, as if it were a thing of no importance, that the girls had left their village, and to her annoyance, the news alarmed her. Later, when they left the office to return to her hotel she had the curious, fleeting impression that a dark shadow fell upon them, as if the air were full of fluttering, soft-winged bats. Ridiculous, with the sun blazing down!

Chapter Six

The look and the timid smile Stephanie turned on Yann gave her away completely.

"You know so much more about it than I do . . ."

They had been talking for over five minutes without saying anything. He had asked her to see him to discuss what she called 'the trip into the mountains'. Stephanie agreed, knowing that it was merely a pretext to be alone with her—but then she so badly wanted to be alone with him! He arrived in the afternoon with a pile of papers under one arm; there they were now, the formal-looking papers, on the round table.

"Mostly, I do know what's the right course to take, but where you are concerned"—his hand dropped over hers—"I . . . I don't know at all."

Stephanie looked at his hand lying over hers, stroking it. Her heart thundered clamorously inside her. It was like first love, the passion she felt for this man, a love she could lose herself in for the rest of time. It was like that blood fever which had seized her at the first meeting with René, all over again. That love was dead, but a great tenderness still remained—'The one I loved so much . . .' Then there was Boris, whom she still loved in her dreams: would she ever see Boris again? It had been a blood fever which threw her into the arms of Victor Hugo, and into those of Michael Lambersart, a superb lover but a dull and doubtless conventional husband. But Boris was in Russia . . . Yann was here beside her with his burning eyes, handsome face, his lips which had already tasted hers. She wanted his lips as badly as she wanted his body

... she knew that body so well already: the set of his shoulders, the lithe powerful swing of his hips ... She remembered how he sprang upon Eugenie, the way he walked, his leap on to a horse, the strength of his thighs guiding the beast, the hard muscles in his arms ...

'I am mad, mad! I must ...' She tried to pull herself together, think clearly. What was it he had said? 'Where you are concerned ... I don't know at all.'

"What is good enough for you will do for me, too," she said. "We scarcely had the bare necessities during the Crimean War. Here there won't be the cold, or the snow and ice to contend with, just perfect, cloudless weather."

His hand slid over hers, across the table, and took hold of her other hand. He sat staring at them. He must be worrying about how she would cope with the fatigue and discomfort, and Heaven knows what more! She had mentioned her war experience, surely that ought to have reassured him.

"I don't want to be a nuisance to you. You have put two horses at my disposal, which is one more than I expected. Don't you remember how you said, that day in the office, 'I hope you will do us the honour of accompanying us'? It wouldn't be doing you an honour, Yann, I love the idea of going off to explore the island with you. That's what I came here for."

Slowly, his glance travelled back to her face, met her eyes and held them.

"I know that you are afraid of nothing, Madame Dytteville, I know you are ready for anything, but ..."

His hands snatched hers up, gripping them, holding them to his chest.

"What would you say if I were to ask you to abandon the trip into the mountains?"

"I won't!"

The words leapt out of her. No! Why was he trying to make her give up the trip? This journey of theirs was a journey to freedom, to love—was he afraid suddenly?

"What are you afraid of?"

"Things," he murmured evasively, refusing to meet her eyes.

"What things? Tell me, Yann. You must."

"I don't know what to say. I am afraid for you because I . . . I love you. You can't understand . . . You broke into my world like a new sun, and the old one means nothing, *nothing* now!"

He got to his feet and she was obliged to follow suit because he had hold of both of her hands.

"You must trust me."

"Explain yourself, then."

She felt calmer now because it had just become clear to her that it was Eugenie and her evil spells he was afraid of, and this struck her as absurd.

"What would you think of me if I were to give the idea up now, and what would I think of myself? Can't you be serious?"

"I'm more serious than you realise, Ste . . . Madame."

He had faltered over the name which haunted his nights. She wanted to hear him say it the way only he could . . . he alone. Their hands were still locked together.

"Yann, these fears of yours are absurd, they belong to another age. How can you believe in such phantoms in a world where people have gone over to gas lighting, where Remington has just patented the typewriter, where a world-wide postal service has just been inaugurated? Do you realise that trains travel at eighty-five miles an hour, that the transatlantic steamers are all being fitted out with propellers instead of paddles, and that the propellers which churn the water now will soon be churning their way through the air, according to Nadar? In twenty years time we shall have horseless carriages! In a century which has seen such startling progress, Yann, am I really supposed to be frightened by three pinpricks in the flowers on my hat?"

"I don't give a damn about propellers, or trains . . ."

His lips were close to hers now, his arm ringed her

waist. He gathered her against him in a single, sweeping gesture.

"I love you, Stephanie, I possess the world when you are in my arms. I dream about you, you haunt me night and day like a spell—I am bewitched. And you say you don't believe in magic! I love you too much, with a love beyond love itself. Before you came I loved with my blood: I love you with my whole being. I am you and you are me. And it is because I love you as no man has ever loved that I want you to stay here in Noumea with Aimé, another faithful dog who would give up his life for you, just as I would. I don't want you to go up into the mountains, where the devils are. They *are* there, you can laugh at them, but I know their power! Stephanie, please, I beg you ..."

His lips crushed down over hers in something like agony, savaging them like ripe fruit, and his tongue slid between her parted lips. She responded, yielded, gripped him with both arms, pulling him closer, crushing her breasts and belly against him. She wanted to feel his lips on her breasts, her body; she wanted to give her body to those lips that tasted and tore at her hungrily. He swept her off the ground and she was in his arms, swooning, rapturous, weak with desire. He flung her on the bed and fell across her.

"Yann ... no ..."

Why was she protesting when every inch of her clamoured impatiently for him? Because she was a woman, and the wild desire which impelled her towards him terrified her by its violence. Because, woman that she was, she wanted him to enter her and spend himself in her in one last possessive spasm which would leave her, finally, in possession. Because she wanted them to be one blood, one flesh, one heart and one life.

Accustomed to the scant garments of the native girls, he was fumbling helplessly in a sea of underclothes, lace and ribbons. Their hands kept meeting, clasping, but it was her fingers which loosened the hooks and buttons and his which peeled away her clothes to reveal her in all the splendour of her creamy flesh. They groaned with impatience at each new rapturous revelation. Her clothes might be elaborate, but then he had his boots! He left her for a second while he tore them off angrily, then fell upon her once again. How delicious it was to slide away from under him as if she were trying to escape, to make him wait, then to slip away again! Raging, his two hands gripped her round the waist and his belly slid down over hers. He arched his back, and she beneath him arched hers. Masterfully, he entered her, and she opened to receive him. She was filled with him, they were one, and the knowledge left them incoherent, delirious, transported. He bruised her lips, passionately kissed her eyes, forehead, hair, breasts. She snatched at his shoulders and waist to hold him down, keep him there, close, but he broke away to roam where he would, kissing and biting. Then he was back, a brute male who wound his arms round her like hawsers, holding her fast while his hands gripped her and his nails dug into her flesh. His nails were steely hard and he used them like a cat uses its claws in play, a sudden bristle of sharp points spiking a velvety caress which she found thrilling in its suggestion of sheathed power. She was his prey, then he became hers, spending himself in a long delirium which left him exhausted and panting, relaxed as a beast after a hard chase.

"I love you ... I love you," they kept murmuring in broken incoherent fashion, and their murmurs rose and fell in a tender, sensual chant. Stephanie took hold of Yann by the nape of his neck and drew his face down to hers to whisper close to his lips, "Do you still think you will be setting off into the mountains without me, my love?"

He shook his head, sinking his face into her loosened hair and biting her ear. Then, in a deep, solemn voice he replied, "I love you. Rest assured, in Noumea, with my father and Moses and Aimé, you have nothing to fear."

It annoyed her that this man who had just shown himself so masterful, male and virile a lover should cling to these absurd superstitions.

"Let them come too!"

He rolled over on top of her again, astonished.

"They can come too," she repeated, "since we shall be together!"

"The two of us," he whispered, eyes glowing, ready to take her again. "The two of us! You, me, the two of us ... is that what you want, Stephanie?"

"Yes, yes, can't you tell?"

And they gave themselves up to love.

Having covered the first thirty miles of their journey the caravan halted just beyond Paita, where Stephanie had refused to stop for the night.

"I came because I wanted to live out of doors, in the wilds, like an explorer. I haven't the slightest desire to meet a lot of white people and show myself off," she told Yann, on hearing that the eighteen founder families had grown to fifty, and that the mere appearance of a stranger among them would be enough to spark off a succession of parties, receptions and *conversaziones*, the legendary Island hospitality. Besides, the Dytteville caravan was no ordinary one. The whole island knew about it and longed to meet her now that the news of her arrival had spread. But Stephanie had had more than enough of Noumea society, with its sailors and exporters. All she wanted, her one thought, was to keep Yann to herself, and live with him far from everyone and everything.

Yves Kerdelec, the lordly patriarch, had chosen their camp site—a broad grassy plain scattered with old trees. By the time the kanakas had unpacked the baggage and supplies, tent poles and canvas, a cauldron and battery of cooking pots, the scene vividly reminded her of Pompette and the Dobruja. When Yann began hammering at tent pegs she couldn't resist giving him a hand. They put up her tent together.

"You seem to know what you are doing!" he exclaimed, astonished by her supple strength and deftness.

She burst out laughing.

"I've put up more tents than you have, I'll be bound, and it was a woman who taught me how to tighten ropes and tie knots and make it all fast. I can assure you it took a gale to uproot our handiwork!"

"You like remembering those days, don't you?"

She smiled, then laughed again.

"Like any other veteran," she said gaily. Then, in a softer voice, thinking of all the suffering she had seen: "Those were appalling, magnificent, unforgettable times ..." She bent towards him, and whispered, "You remind me of those memories, but you are giving me new ones, all the time."

"Stephanie!"

His hand gripped hers like a vice and she stared at him. His eyes blazed in a white face, and his voice was hoarse.

"Yann!" she cried out, uncomprehendingly.

"Forgive me—Madame de Guinchamp," he said dully, after a long pause.

He said her real name as if he were returning her to her husband, as if he were already thinking of the time when they must part.

"I didn't mean ..."

"You shouldn't have said what you did. I don't want to remind you of your other lovers."

"Yann!"

"I saw by your eyes that you were thinking of another man, more than one perhaps. I know, I tell you, I know that man marked you for life, and you will never forgive him! I hate him!"

Tormented by jealousy, his voice rose in violent desperation. "I never thought I could love like this! I'd be glad to die for you!"

She took his hand and looked gravely into his eyes, and said tenderly, "Yann, I am Madame Dytteville here, you chose to call me that yourself. Why suddenly bring up the name I am happy to forget as long as I am here?"

"One day you will have to go, I can't bear to think of it ... I'm a brute, forgive me ..."

"No, I won't forgive you ..."

"Stephanie!" he cried distractedly.

"... but I'll forget what you said, I'll forget your anger and your jealousy of the past and you must forget what I said, too. The two of us—that's all that matters. Come!"

They made a tour of the camp site, an idyllically beautiful spot which would have made the ideal poster for a back-to-nature campaign. The kanakas would be sleeping under the stars, while four tents for the white members of the party stood a little way off, the largest for Yves, then smaller ones for Yann, Aimé and herself—but Yann would be sharing hers. They might as well sleep together right from the start since everyone knew about their relationship already. It was useless to try and hide such things from the natives; skilled at interpreting the hidden meaning of looks and gestures, they could tell at a glance when people were in love, whether they were sleeping together or not. It was all perfectly normal to them, indeed they enjoyed the situation. The Great Mistress was so beautiful, and the young Master was so handsome, that it would have seemed wrong if they hadn't become lovers. Love, in these sun-dazzled isles, was ardent and uncomplicated. What could be more normal than for a man to lie with a woman he desired, and for the woman to laugh with pleasure as she gave herself to the man? The Gods must have intended love to be like this or they would not have given men and women such pleasure thereby.

'On our return perhaps I'd better be a little more circumspect, for the sake of appearances.' Stephanie thought fleetingly, but without enthusiasm. 'But really, what does it matter? I'm free, happy and in love, and Paris is thousands of miles away. I've got a right to live!'

She woke in the morning to find herself alone. She had a vague memory of Yann leaving—he had whispered something about going to see if all the kanakas were there

—then he came back and they made love again, and she remembered no more.

She stretched and yawned in the early morning sun, feeling happy and relaxed, thinking of the night they had just spent.

'We'll go right to the far side of the island ... we'll dawdle along the way, we'll climb mountains and descend into the valleys and lose ourselves in the forests ... Oh, Yann, Yann, beloved one!'

She stooped at the tent's low entrance and stepped out. Moses, she saw, was crouched with his back against a tree just opposite. He pretended not to see her, but got to his feet and went across to the horses to attend to the Old Master's horse-borne litter. Yann appeared and came towards her.

"He must have been keeping watch."

"Yes, Father's orders. You wanted to come, so we arranged a guard for you," he answered, as if it were the most natural, normal thing in the world.

"The same old story!"

"We won't mention it again, I know it annoys you."

Yann's voice was soft and amorous, but it was the voice of a man who knew his own mind and was not prepared to enter into any further discussions of what she scornfully called, 'that old story!'

Stephanie was touched by this anxiety for her welfare despite her annoyance that it should be thought necessary. Her lover's nearness troubled her, but there was another feeling she was not quite so ready to admit to and this was disappointment—she would have liked to know more about this island magic, and how the witches and medicine men prepared their love philtres and magic powders and spells. But Yann had so firmly closed the door on that subject to her, that she could scarcely hope to learn more about it from him. Perhaps he didn't know. She glanced at Moses, who turned his head at that precise instant, as if she had called him. His blank gaze flitted over her face and then passed on, a gaze which seemed to see beyond bodies and solid walls into some unknown world of the spirit which he alone inhabited. Moses wouldn't tell her how one saw into the future either, though everyone was convinced that he had the power of second sight.

'I'm a fool to bother with such nonsense!'

"Do we strike camp now?" she asked, with all Phanie's gay swagger in her voice.

"That's not your job. Look, the coffee is just about to boil. My tent is down and my father's will be down in a second."

She was sorry not to take any part in packing up but it wouldn't do to behave too much like Phanie or she would lose face with the kanakas. As it was, they were perplexed by the lack of resemblance between her and the lady wives of Noumea who beat and scolded their servants, who thought of nothing but new dresses and furbelows, and would not have dreamt of leaving home without a parasol to protect their complexions from the sun; indeed they often draped a veil over their bonnets as further protection. Stephanie liked to feel the sun warm on her skin, and when she asked the kanakas to do something for her it was with a smile, and a thank-you. They were growing used to the fact that she was a Mistress of a very different stamp. Nevertheless Aimé's ostentatiously ceremonious and respectful demeanor towards her—quite intentional on his part—had the effect of setting her somewhat apart, and reminding them that she was a great lady. When Aimé saw her approaching with Yann, he hurried up with a folding chair for her to sit on. She looked at him in astonishment. Aimé was wearing his sulky face. When he spoke his quietly respectful voice had an unmistakable ring of command about it.

"Yesterday Madame picnicked on the grass, a charming rustic habit. From today our nomadic existence begins in earnest, and I trust Madame will permit me to see that she is comfortable and properly looked after."

What he was really telling her, as Stephanie knew from

her long experience of him, was that he disapproved of this 'expedition', but that having decided to undertake it Stephanie should remember her position. She might be a one-time cantinière, she might be Yann's mistress—impossible to guess what he felt about this development—but Madame must not overstep what was proper and fitting in a lady of her rank and station. He would make sure she did not. He produced a tray, teapot, two fine china cups and set about preparing her breakfast as he habitually did on the *Araucaria* and at the hotel, spreading butter and jam on her bread rolls under the fascinated gaze of the kanakas. Stephanie glanced towards Yann, annoyed at finding herself the object of these unnecessary attentions.

"It's a shrewd move on his part," Yann assured her, nodding his approval, "and his dexterity amazes them, they can't imagine how he does it all with only one arm. This is the morning ritual which reinforces your importance with the kanakas; Aimé is making sure they don't forget that you are the Great White Mistress."

"Thank you, Aimè," she said when he handed her her breakfast tray. "Where would I be without your bright ideas? Remember what I said to you all that time ago?"

He pretended to search his memory, and then murmured, "No."

"Old goat!"

A faint smile lit his eyes reminiscently. "If Madame would be so kind as to remind me . . ."

"Don't you remember, when you arrived in Paris in answer to my letter, I said, 'I shall rely on you entirely, your job will be to remind me of all the things I am tempted to forget . . .' "

"I remember as if it were yesterday, Madame."

He brought up a chair, which he placed close to hers, ate his breakfast, washed the china himself before stowing it carefully away in a specially designed case, and finally, when everything was neatly in place, turned to Yves Kerdelec with a respectful bow, awaiting his orders. It was a masterly performance!

The caravan set off in the same order as the day before. A party of kanakas who knew the route went on ahead. Then came Yves Kerdelec in his horse litter with Moses guiding the horses, Stephanie and Yann, followed by the pack mules and horses, Aimé behind as if to keep guard over them, and lastly a straggle of womenfolk with their children.

Stephanie was in ecstasies over the brilliant tropical flowers glowing in the dim green forests or flashing from rock crevices, by the trailing lianas hung with orange and yellow fruit like lanterns, by the bright plumed birds, and the shy deer which sprang away at their approach. The quantity of deer astonished her.

"They are all descended from two pairs presented to the Governor's wife," said Yann, who took pride in pointing out the island's features to her. "They have bred and multiplied like rabbits. We have no carnivores here, so their only enemy is man."

Winding down into lush, blossoming valleys was as exhilarating as toiling up towards the mountain peaks. The sunsets were the most spectacular Stephanie had seen anywhere, a procession of gorgeous fiery colours streaming towards the horizon as if some giant conjuror were stowing his fluttering silk scarves away into a trick box for the night. All of a sudden the transparent watery blue of the sky deepened to a pure ultramarine and then to a deep indigo studded with blazing stars. And there beside her under this fantastic starry vault was—Yann, Yann with whom her imagination made love the whole day long. His eyes sought hers, feasted on her lips, stripped her naked, and she gloried in it. They lived for and through each other to the point where nothing else mattered, and it was an effort to come back to earth again in answer to some remark put by Yves, Aimé or one of the kanakas.

It was on the morning of the fourth day that it all began. As she left her tent, Stephanie spotted Moses twenty paces or so distant, crouching at the foot of a tree. He was watching for her to appear. This was a normal occurrence now. When he saw her he got up and hurried off to see to the Old Master's horses, as predictable a feature of the morning's ritual as Aimé's appearance with her breakfast tray. Looking about for Yann, she discovered him some way off thundering and gesticulating at the kanakas as if he were threatening them with the wrath of God. One had to speak sternly and harshly to the islanders to instil into them the proper respect for their chief, who in their eyes represented authority, justice and protection. The white man knew many and great things, and they were happy to be his children. The Kerdelecs were worshipped by their kanakas. All the same it struck Stephanie that there was something nervous and exaggerated about Yann's gestures in this dazzling dawn light. The kanakas' eyes stealing towards Stephanie warned him of her approach. He turned and strode towards her, everything about him, his walk, shoulders, the set of his head, conjuring up her memories of the night before. He took her by the arm and led her across to their fire.

"What have they done?"

"One of the horses wasn't saddled up properly. I just happened to notice as I was passing."

"The girth was loose, I suppose?"

"Yes, that's it."

He was lying though. She could tell by his extra wide smile, the way his arm firmly marched her away from the kanakas. She wanted to talk to them, to find out ... still, there was always Aimé. The moment Yann left her, to help carry his father to his litter, she turned to Aimé and asked him point blank: "What's happened?"

He smiled and answered carelessly, too carelessly: "Two kanakas have ... run away."

And that was all she would get out of him. She smiled pleasantly and asked if he had slept well, to which he answered, as pleasantly "Yes."

The day passed like the ones before except that Stephanie could not stop thinking about the two kanakas who had melted away in the night. She dared not raise the subject although she knew perfectly well that the very same question was preying on Yann's mind. He had not talked about them to her, well then, she wouldn't talk about them to him. Besides, the natives were a capricious, wayward lot, capable of drifting off for no better reason than that some other spot appealed to them more, a certain tree, or house, or stretch of coastline. It was silly to worry about it and yet ... there was something odd about the incident.

That night, as she went to her tent, a flight of bats fluttered round her head. The small ones were black, the large ones russet-coloured. The meat of these bats was esteemed a delicacy in the islands; it reminded her a little of pigeon or some small bird. At nightfall they came out in search of fruit and flowers. But why were they wheeling round her in this curious, startled fashion? Was it because the glade where their tents were pitched had attracted them from the dense forest roundabout?

Warm, blue night lay over the place when Yann slid into the tent beside her. Just as he was about to make love to her they heard the mournful cry of a *notou*, a sort of frightened whinnying noise repeated on several notes, like a screech owl's. The bird's call did not worry her but it startled Yann.

"Beloved ..." she murmured, stroking and stretching herself against him as he lay tensely, listening.

"It's all right, Stephanie, we shall be pitching camp near the Thio mines tomorrow. No bats there"—so he had seen them—"and no *notou* either?" So there was something unusual about the bird call too? "It's bush country there."

He stayed with her the whole night long, instead of making his usual twice-nightly patrols of the camp, and did not depart till daylight stole into the darkness of the tent. Stephanie dressed, brushed out her hair, and went out. There was no one crouching at the foot of the nearby tree. Moses had deserted his post. She looked about for him and saw Yann and some of the kanakas securing Yves' litter in place on the two horses. Had Moses disappeared too? She felt a pang of dismay, though she still stubbornly refused to concede that anything odd or sinister or out of the ordinary was happening to her or the caravan.

However, when they set off later that morning she suddenly saw Moses in his usual place, leading the horses. It was almost as if he had sprung from nowhere, out of the earth. Where could he have been during those missing hours? What summons had acted upon that strange, blank mind of his which responded much more sensitively than an ordinary 'thinking person's' to the mysterious vibrations that Stephanie, with her lucid Cartesian mentality, refused to acknowledge? It was useless to question Yann, or Aimé, who had adopted a calm reserve of manner intended to put her fears at rest.

At the midday halt Stephanie noticed that one of the native women, two young girls and a small boy were missing. No one seemed to have remarked their absence. In the hopes that old Yves would share her astonishment, and perhaps suggest some explanation, she turned to him with poorly feigned surprise.

"How odd, Denise doesn't seem to be here."

She had grown used to the incongruous French names, bestowed on them by some priest or missionary along with a little crucifix and chain, a few coins and a bible. The natives adored receiving gifts of any sort.

"She has gone to see some relatives of hers, in her own tribe. She will be back in a few days, like Claude and Alfred."

Claude and Alfred were the two men who had vanished earlier. It was all perfectly simple, how absurd to think she had begun to feel anxious. Nevertheless she could not shake off the dull fear that seemed to have fallen, like a clinging shadow, across her heart. Perhaps the forest was to blame, and the monotony of its gently undulating terrain—and Yann's uneasiness, which she sensed, however much he tried to hide it from her. Had Yves been lying to her just now? It was quite possible.

She felt happier when the trees thinned out and the hanging skeins of lianas grew scantier. A more open landscape came gradually into view. Bare rocky crags towered up above her here, falling into more gradual curves at their own level. The soil was red, carpeted with sunburnt heather and blue gentians and guaiacums, with an occasional twisted thorn bush or stunted tree. They had climbed higher than at any previous stage of the journey, the scene was full of light and sky, and a soft warm breeze was blowing, carrying the scent of the ocean which lay far, far below, its changeable blue expanse streaked by the creamy band of surf breaking on the encircling coral reefs. Yann's shoulder touched hers, and he groped for her hand.

"I love you, Stephanie . . ." he whispered.

She let her head rest on his shoulder as she gazed up at his mouth and eyes.

"Will we stay at Thio for long?"

"As long as you like. In the morning we shall go to a deer hunt—we need some venison, and the forest just below here is full of them. In the afternoon we shall visit the mines. I think you will find that you will soon have seen all you want."

The gag muzzled the lower half of her face before she had time to cry out. Neither Yann nor the four kanakas with him could have heard her in any case, they had gone down into the forest after the wounded deer. She had refused to go with them.

"The hunt does not appeal to you, Madame?" Empress Eugenie had asked her, at the weekend houseparty at Compiègne.

"No, Your Majesty, not at all."

Yann had cried "Winged it!" and seized her hand when

she protested, "No, no, I don't enjoy it, you go. I'll wait here."

He raced off. A moment later the gag was whipped over her face, her wrists and feet were bound and she felt herself hoisted into the air and borne away. The savages must have been waiting and watching since the first day for a moment when she was alone and unguarded. Stephanie had suddenly decided to go with Yann on the deer hunt at dawn that morning and had left without telling Aimé.

Her kidnappers sped along almost noiselessly under the thick trees. Hands, many hands, swung her up in the air as if she weighed no more than a feather, lowering her again on the further side of the rocks. She felt like an idol, being carried off to some sanctuary. There must be ten, fifteen of them, she couldn't tell, all strong, agile, nimble-footed and silent. They were carrying her into the unexplored hinterland in the centre of the island, towards one of the inaccessible, unknown valleys tucked away among the mountains. All the towns, villages and European settlements on the island were strung out along the coast. Of course they would come searching for her, but what if, before they found her ...

A comforting thought suddenly struck her. Kanakas often hunted down escaped prisoners from the penal settlement to collect the reward money. She was a very, very valuable prisoner to them, worth far too much money to torture or kill. She tried to keep her spirits up as she was borne helplessly along by her captors, and yet she could not help her blood running cold despite the heat. She gnawed at her gag, feeling the blood drain from her face and tears gather in her eyes. An involuntary shudder ran down her spine.

'Eugenie is proud, jealous, savage and cruel. Eugenie, the chief's daughter, is seeking her revenge!'

Chapter Seven

Fear, terror, horror ... the words scarcely do justice to Stephanie's state of mind after her abduction. Her seizure by the kanakas was much more terrifying than her capture by the Russians during the Crimean War. Nothing seemed impossible at the hands of these unknown savages: slow torture, death by bleeding, fire, even the cooking pot —the worst horror of all!

After a journey of several hours as far as she could judge, four of the men who had been carrying her passed her through the narrow entrance of a round hut with a huge grimacing totem figure planted either side. They had reached their destination.

Of the country through which they had travelled she had only a confused impression of tropical undergrowth lit by faint gleams of sunshine, of sudden ascents and descents, and the occasional swish and rustle of branches and leaves behind them as if someone were concealing their tracks. How often had this happened? She had lost count. At one point, borne along on the men's shoulders, she suddenly felt a dazzling wave of sunlight pour on to her face and had to close her eyes against the glare. Now she found herself being laid down on a bed of leaves, moss and rags. Someone untied her gag, and she took great greedy gulps of air. The air in the hut was thick, stagnant with trapped heat. And there was a stench which almost made her choke, a smell of sweet, confined space, mutton tallow, and the strange acrid smell of the kanakas themselves. She closed her eyes again, tensing all her muscles to stop herself trembling.

'They mustn't know that I'm sick with fear and my

heart's pounding fit to burst!'

The men were cautiously untying her bonds now, touching the chafed spots on her ankles and wrists, and her face where the tight gag had reddened the skin, with almost motherly solicitude. They talked meanwhile among themselves in low, gentle, placid voices. It was a sing-song language they spoke, rising on the 'a' sound in the middle of words which frequently ended in a sharp 'i' noise.

'Must look at their faces.'

She peered out at them through half-closed lids, and found them as she imagined them, a frightening sight to European eyes with their chocolate-brown skins, thick lips, broad noses, deep-set eyes and wildly frizzy hair. Their bodies were finely shaped, with clearly defined muscles. After a low-voiced but animated conversation, the men left the hut.

'I'm lost, lost ... No, I won't, I mustn't let myself believe that!' But she found it hard to believe anything just then. A rustle was followed by a heavy footfall as a massive woman took her stand by the bed and started feeling Stephanie's ankles and wrists and then struggling to unfasten her dress.

'Better help this woman, she seems well disposed towards me. Her hands are gentle.' Stephanie partly undressed and the woman began to massage her with soft, subtle, intuitive movements that relaxed her muscles. She was rubbing in a white cream which resembled thickened coconut milk, persisting in the massage till Stephanie's skin absorbed it all. So they intended to take good care of her? This discovery was both reassuring and alarming. If they planned to hold her for a high ranson, they would think it worth their while to keep her in good condition. On the other hand if she were destined for human sacrifice, they would be equally solicitous in order to be able to placate their gods with the offer of a beautiful, healthy body. It would be left to their priests to maul and slash their human offering, cutting out the heart at a single blow to present it still quivering to their chief or idol.

'No, no, that's too horrible!' She thought of Yann and Aimé. 'They will rescue me, they wouldn't let me die, I must, I must ...' For a moment everything went dark, as she fell into a near swoon. She took hold of herself. This wasn't the moment for weakness. She needed all her wits about her if she were to survive. 'The kanakas aren't blood-thirsty people,' she reminded herself. 'They have always treated sailors and explorers well. They are, no, they *were* cannibals, but that's all finished with—or so people say. Is it true? Help me, God, save me ... I solemnly swear that if I live to see France and my children again I will make the pilgrimage to Lourdes on foot!'

The woman helped her back into her dress, her task finished. Perhaps she understood French, she might even be a potential ally. Stephanie had nothing to lose. Forcing an uncertain smile she said haltingly:

"Thank you. What is your name?"

"Aravihi, White Lady."

The answer came promptly. She understood and spoke French, therefore she must have had dealings with the Europeans. Flatter her, the natives revelled in flattery and compliments.

"You have done me a lot of good, Aravihi, I feel much better now. Your hands are soft and gentle, and they know the art of healing."

"Your skin too is soft, White Lady. It is the colour of sea shells and when I feel it with my hand it is like the fluttering skin they make dresses of."

She meant silk, the light blowaway silk made up into scarves and shawls and flounced dresses.

"Will you come back, Aravihi?"

"If they tell me, and you want me."

"I want you. I have a great affection for the people of your island. I only came here to meet them and learn to know them."

Stephanie was quite sincere when she said this, but she

also said it to be pleasant and friendly and to encourage this woman to return and talk to her.

"Yes, I know that, White Lady."

Aravihi's answer astonished her. Stephanie eyed her curiously, anxiously.

"Napoleon say to me, you Great Mistress!"

Stephanie's heart gave a bound. Coming after so much fear and anguish the woman's statement was a gleam of hope. Aravihi knew Napoleon! Napoleon had told her about Stephanie. Napoleon was the kindly native who had carried her across the swamp on his back. She felt much less alone suddenly, this was a link with the world outside.

"He is a good man, Napoleon. I know him well."

"No, not good," said Aravihi slowly, shaking her head so that her great breasts swung. "He go long white man, he not faithful to ancestors, he traitor."

"Traitor!" Stephanie echoed, hoping she had misheard the word. "Traitor to whom?"

"To Atai, Lady, you see Atai soon."

She broke off as a kanaka slipped into the hut. Eyes rolling furiously, hands waving like windmill sails, he stood and scolded the huge woman and pointed angrily to the entrance. The pair left together. The incident was a warning to Stephanie to be on her guard; she must not ask questions, she must wait and watch. Napoleon might be a half-breed, and hence feel himself superior to the kanakas, but the fact remained that he had told them about the Great Mistress. He must see them fairly frequently then. He must know about this secret place of theirs. It might occur to him that they would have hidden her in this God-forsaken spot. If he were such a traitor, he would willingly help the search party track her down. Then there was Yann who knew the island backwards. He would send word to the governor, the military commander ... they would send the army out to find her and rescue her from these savages. Meanwhile she would do what she could to spy out the land as soon as they let her put her nose outside; she had an instinct for this sort of thing which had stood her in good stead on the battlefield. Wasn't she, a solitary woman, going into battle against a whole tribe? Well, and why not, it wouldn't be the first unequal battle she had fought.

She felt full of fierce energy suddenly, nothing seemed impossible. She would regain her freedom and Yann, her beloved Yann. She would ask for mercy on behalf of her kidnappers. Comforting fancies and hopes thronged her mind. Abduction by natives was just the sort of thing which was always happening to explorers. Hope was flooding into her when a woman slipped into the hut. Stephanie assumed a weary but welcoming smile for her benefit. The smile froze, and her hopes crumbled to dust when she saw who it was—Eugenie! She had forgotten about her ... Eugenie the jealous and passionate chief's daughter whom Yann had spurned, driven from his bed—the unforgivable humiliation! What would she be prepared to do to get Yann back? Here she was now, gloating over her victory.

"Greetings, Mistress."

Eugenie bowed and spoke respectfully, as if she were back in the office again. Stephanie found this puzzling. She looked searchingly into the girl's eyes, and could find no flicker of hatred there. She seemed passive, somewhat in awe of her. Stephanie wondered what she should say. The important thing was to gain time, to avoid offending her and to allay her jealousy. She must try to win her as an ally, above all discover just what the girl was plotting. It would not be a bad plan to frighten her a little, the natives were impressed by a show of force. Why not show the girl that she knew what she had been scheming? Keeping her eyes and voice carefully neutral she said quietly, "I am fond of you, Eugenie, you know that I have always treated you and your brothers with kindness. Why should you want to do me harm now?"

"I can't help it, Lady, it's not my fault."

"Do you want to ... kill me?"

"No. But if I have to, I will do it."

Why should she have to, Stephanie wondered, suddenly prey to all her old fears again.

"What do you want from me?" she asked, almost as if she were trying to bargain over a piece of merchandise. "If I can . . ."

"Oh, you can, you can!"

The girl gave a little leap into the air, clapping her hands as delightedly as a child who has been promised a new toy of a treat.

"I want to know your magic over men, like you did do in the hotel and the town. All the men wanting to sleep with you, to keep you for themselves . . . that's not right or normal. You must tell me your secret. If you won't tell me . . . I shall make you!"

The girl was quite ready to cut her to pieces and drink her blood! A cruel gleam flitted across her face and was gone again.

Half paralysed by fear as she was, Stephanie succeeded in taking hold of herself. 'I must disarm her, flatter her, lie to her.' She cast about for something to say, but Eugenie did not give her time.

"One man never satisfied with one woman, he always have many women. But men all wanting you by yourself . . . why, why?" Eugenie stormed, in a sudden burst of fury. "How you do it? You witch! If you give me your secret magic, then I witch too and we be friends together. I want you tell me!"

She was growing dangerous, hatred and envy oozing from every pore. Stephanie was dismayed. Her secret? She had no secret, she was just Stephanie, one woman among many. Maybe she was more beautiful, more attractive than some . . . a woman can sometimes attract men without even trying to, simply by virtue of her radiant femininity, by the fact that they find in her what they have been seeking: beauty, tenderness, sensuality. And of course she loved to make love. Men seemed to sense this about her. But how could one communicate one's own essential nature to another woman, especially something so largely unconscious? Every woman has her own secret, and they are all different.

In her present situation, however, there was no time to be lost in disarming and softening Eugenie and making an ally of her. In her present mood the girl was capable of murder!

'I'll do anything to escape from here,' Stephanie thought, 'anything at all! I'll concentrate on that alone, it will be my one thought. The first thing to make sure of is that none of these savages, beginning with this girl, suspect how horribly frightened I am.'

"I would gladly share my secret with you but, alas, it's locked up with my trunks in Noumea. Suppose we both go and fetch it," she suggested in the most helpful, friendly tones imaginable.

Eugenie appeared satisfied with her excuse, and Stephanie was just congratulating herself on the success of this childish fiction when the kanaka girl suddenly burst into loud, desperate sobs. Stephanie was mystified by this sudden display of grief which racked the girl's body and limbs.

"Why are you crying, Eugenie?" she asked. "I didn't mean to upset you. I'm quite prepared to give you . . ."

"Atai not let us go," Eugenie cried, raising a tear-wet face. "Atai keep you here, till . . . I don't know. I too frightened to disobey Atai . . ."

Stephanie realised that there must be some further motive for her abduction than the simple jealousy of a kanaka girl. But what was it? Eugenie meanwhile crouched on the ground beside her, groaning pitiably, flinging out her arms, and addressing Atai and her gods in the same breath, as if he were their equal. Aravihi spoke fearfully of the mysterious Atai, Eugenie addressed him as a chieftain's daughter, as a suppliant but not as a slave.

"What am I doing here?" she asked Eugenie. "You can speak frankly to me, I am your Great Mistress."

"Not tell you, not tell you," Eugenie whimpered. "You prisoner Atai. He Mahana."

So saying she touched one hand to her brow, nose and lips, a gesture which must have been some pagan equivalent to the sign of the cross.

'Mahana? I should have learnt a few words of kanaka, like Aimé,' Stephanie muttered to herself. 'If it's just ransom money they're after, I should be free in a few days. I pray that's all they want.'

"Can I go out?" she asked, sure that Eugenie would refuse. To her surprise the girl agreed.

"You are free with us, Great Mistress."

Free! That was surely a trick? She would be watched, guarded all the time. Or were they confident that she could never escape from this place? Her anxiety returned. One detail reassured her, she was still the Great Mistress!

Eugenie's mood passed in a moment from lamentations to childish gaiety.

"You be having to tell me your secret. Atai make you tell, he friend of the Great Ones."

'More threats,' Stephanie thought, detecting the menacing undercurrent in the girl's prattle. She decided to brave it out, and answered in her sternest voice, "I am powerful too, Eugenie."

"You strong in you place. Here you in we place, Atai place, my place."

So it seemed her freedom depended on Eugenie and this mysterious Atai. Stephanie's blood ran colder and a fine sweat broke out on her face, but she controlled herself to give the impression of the Great Mistress whom nothing troubles or frightens.

"You give me you secret, I give you mine," Eugenie said eagerly. "Atai, Mahana, he write to you God! There, I tell you truth!"

What rigmarole was this? Stephanie grew exasperated.

"My God? One can't write to my God!"

"Yes, yes! He send bad people here . . . bad people who wanted to kill him."

Stephanie listened attentively but in some bewilderment as the girl went on. "He Mighty One, but he not good to us. We kanakas not wanting all bad people in boats," said Eugenie. "Atai want bad people to leave island, give island to kanakas. See? Till bad people go, you staying here."

Suddenly Stephanie perceived the true meaning of Eugenie's incoherent talk, and her first impulse was to reject it as too preposterous and lunatic. But then she began to see the cracked logic in it. The bad men must be the white settlers, the Alsatians who were steadily taking over the land for crops and cattle, and the thousands who had been exiled here after the Commune, and who were occupying more and more of the Isle of Nou and the Ducos peninsula. By Stephanie's God Eugenie meant the Emperor. How was she going to convince this girl, as well as Atai, that France was now a Republic under MacMahon and that it was not the Emperor but the Thiers Republic which had sentenced and deported the men and women of the Commune? Stephanie felt dismayed, helpless, but to make sure of her reasoning she asked, "When you speak of my God, do you mean Napoleon III?"

"I not know, I think yes maybe. Atai say you Emperor, he you God like Atai we God. They two make speak together and fix everything."

It all seemed very simple to her and she was quite lighthearted as she described the expected treaty between an unknown savage chief, whose name Stephanie had never heard of before, and the unfortunate Emperor who had been driven into exile, and died at Chislehurst!

'I'll never talk my way out of this mess,' Stephanie thought, appalled by such blithe and total ignorance. 'I'm finished, it's impossible.' Her mouth and throat felt dry with panic but she determined to make one effort to explain to Eugenie what the true situation was. She must try!

"France has changed its government, Eugenie," she began. "Its God is no longer the same ..."

The kanaka girl interrupted her angrily.

"God always same God. Atai never mistaken. Atai waiting reply to letter, and you waiting too."

In other words, Napoleon III's reply would decide her fate. It was hard to imagine a more final sentence, a sentence without appeal, since Napoleon was dead. When she saw Atai she would try to explain, she must make him understand. Her thoughts turned to the crazy business of the letter. It could have been destroyed in Noumea, or perhaps it was on its way to France where someone would burst out laughing before tearing it up, or possibly forwarding it to England to the Empress, as a malicious joke. No doubt it would make her laugh too, and shrug her shoulders. What business was it of hers that this conceited savage demanded the evacuation of his kingdom before he would relinquish Mme Dytteville, or Mme de Guinchamp whom Eugenie must doubtless have forgotten completely by now?

'I must keep on fighting, though,' Stephanie told herself. 'It's my duty to fight, for the people I love if not for my own sake. I must be strong and self-reliant, behave like a Queen to make these people treat me as one, lie, cheat, make use of the dead Emperor's name since they still think he's alive.'

"My Emperor is my great friend," she said calmly. "He will answer your chief, be sure of that. And his anger will be great and terrible if so much as a hair of my head is harmed. You may tell Atai that too."

"You tell Atai, he see you soon, he coming here."

"When?" Stephanie asked curtly, as if it depended on her wishes.

"For the feast!" cried Eugenie, clapping her hands joyfully.

"What feast?" Stephanie asked. "When is it?"

"Etahitaaroa," Eugenie replied with a shiver of sensual pleasure that set her swaying, supple as a liana. Her face clouded over suddenly and she buried her face in both hands.

Stephanie felt that there was something vaguely familiar about the long word full of 'a' sounds. Hadn't

Aimé said something about all the phases of the moon having a different name here? There were some twenty-eight of them, as she recalled, and their titles were as highly coloured as they were incomprehensible. 'The seeds sprout'—that one she could understand, it was like spring in the French countryside where one sowed and then waited for the crops to appear. But what about 'The night rich in many things', or 'The night where the fish hides', or 'The night small where the ghosts walk'? She only remembered the kanaka word Maitu, which Aimé had pronounced pointing to the full moon. Eugenie's word was quite meaningless to her.

'I must try and learn a few words of their language before Atai comes,' she decided. 'He will be flattered if I greet him in his own tongue, and that will make our talk easier. And I must find out more about this feast which makes Eugenie look so excited and happy.'

"What does it mean, the word you said?"

"Etahitaaroa? The Sacred Night, Mistress, the one when Yann send me away, make me old woman, make me barren."

Yann had picked his night unwisely and she was paying the consequences. What idiots they were with their superstitions! The girl was young and beautiful, she already had a child in the village so she was not barren. The first man who lay with her would get her with child. Hoping to reason with her Stephanie confided in woman-to-woman fashion: "I promise you, Eugenie, you are . . ."

The kanaka cut her short with a glance of burning primitive fury. "The witch tell me so."

What was the use? She was powerless against the witch-doctor. He ruled by terror, commanding and ordering what he willed, with an answer and explanation for everything, and the poor kanakas saw everything through his eyes.

". . . But I still hope!" Eugenie cried in a sudden burst of optimism. "I still hope, and I love you good if you give me Yann to make a son. You poor thing, Madame

Stephanie, you punished. Witch say you eyes all turn to water. Great Master he know everything, he love you like he daughter."

She changed the subject abruptly. "Great Mistress want go out?"

"Yes," Stephanie said, dismayed by the girl's incoherent flow of talk and anxious to see the village.

She slowly adjusted her gown and her hair. Eugenie would not have understood too great a show of eagerness. The kanakas are accustomed to waiting, and take a childish pleasure in fine clothes and appearances. Alas, what Yann had failed to do with all his sense, Eugenie had succeeded in accomplishing with her babble—she was beginning to feel a grudging respect for their magic and witchcraft. Why would her eyes turn to water? What did Yves, the Great Master, know already? What did the silly creature mean? Stephanie was angry with herself for feeling afraid, but odd as it might seem, Eugenie had sown the seeds of terror in her with her chirping voice and childish babble.

'Why did I ever come here?' Stephanie wondered, suddenly remembering Yves Kerdelec's letter. Now that she thought about it, that letter had had almost the power of a spell—hadn't she felt herself mysteriously drawn to New Caledonia almost as soon as she cast eyes on it? Was everything predestined? Could free will coexist with predestination? It reminded her of a tale called *This night at Samarkand*. Who had talked to her about that? Was it Boris, or Françoise perhaps? Not René certainly? Georges maybe? No, it came back to her now. Armand had linked the tale to their forthcoming marriage on one occasion: 'You were destined for me at your birth, Stephanie, we knew nothing about it then but we were fated to come together for life, all because the geometry of human affairs parallels the geometry of the cosmos, of the stars!' She had laughed, they had both laughed and then they had made love, blissfully. It all struck her suddenly as stupid, alarming and ... false! False because, being pregnant with the twins, she had been unable to travel with him, because he had died alone on the coast of this island he had so longed to visit, and died without seeing. And now she was there, seeing it for herself! She often thought of him, and she kept the sapphire ring he gave her on one hand. Odd, that; ever since her arrival on the island that ring seemed to have grown on to her finger. She seemed to be unable to take it off! Superstition? Or nostalgia? She touched it caressingly for a moment . . .

Eugenie was waiting. Stephanie got up and slipped out of the low entrance. The long, narrow clearing before her was a blaze of sunshine, and for a moment she was blinded after the darkness of the hut. She blinked, and everything came to rights in a shower of gold: huts grouped among the trees, the forest sloping away down to a narrow valley where a stream gurgled and sparkled along its way. Pigs rootled in the clearing, hens clucked and scratched and there were even some peacocks strutting about.

"May I take your arm, Eugenie?"

"Mistress," she breathed, thrilled by this mark of esteem.

"You are a chief's daughter!"

Eugenie preened herself proudly, not suspecting that by taking her arm Stephanie was assigning her an inferior role in the villagers' eyes, the roll of slave that one leans upon.

"Your village is very beautiful," she exclaimed, sincerely impressed but also wishing to please.

The lost paradise of *Paul et Virginie*! What a marvellous place it would be for her and Yann to live in, lost to the world, to everything but their love. But this was madness! She was in a terrible situation, a prisoner, no one knew where she was. 'Brave it out! Never show weakness or fear, dominate these people,' she told herself. Tense, watchful, her heart beating, she gazed about her. The forest rose on either side like a luxuriant green wall, leaving this sunny cleft where the stream sparkled. Where did the stream come from? Where was it flowing? Water flows towards the sea ...

Kanakas were materialising from all sides, stealing out from among the trees. Some wore loin cloths, others went serenely naked, their sexual organs swaying as they walked. The women wore small apron-like garments over their bellies. The faces around her were impassive, hard-featured, typically Melanesian, but she intercepted some gentle, curious glances, which fixed on her with some astonishment but no malice. The people kept their distance respectfully, their numbers steadily increasing all the while almost as if the forest trees were giving birth to them.

'So many of them to keep watch over me!' Stephanie thought with a pang of dismay.

"Are these all your people?" she asked Eugenie. Again her chief thought was to flatter the girl, but it was also true that in speaking to her she forgot the fear that gnawed at her mind and body.

"They are Atai's people, Atai the Mahana!"

A reply as unanswerable as: 'I believe in God who created Heaven and Hell.'

"Mahana?" Stephanie echoed, thinking that she would greet Atai by this title.

"Mahana is light of the sun, beautiful and good, it shine in we eyes and warm we backs. You too, Madame Stephanie, you Mahana. Mahana light and love. You light with you hair and you love too with you secret."

'One point in common with Atai,' Stephanie told herself, snatching at anything faintly reassuring.

"I shall be friends with Atai," she said, trying to sound confident. Eugenie dashed her by piping up, birdlike, "Maybe yes, maybe no. The Great Ones, they say if you be Atai's friend when feast begin."

What did she mean rambling on like a half-witted child, yet so mysteriously sure of her ground? The feast? That would mean dances, sacrifices, blood ... *Not mine*! The nearness of danger stimulated Stephanie, as it had always done. 'I shall get out of it somehow!' she told herself. She always had done in the past; in Italy, the Crimea, she had survived worse situations. The first thing was to get to know this little sunny valley, greedily drawing in air, light and warmth in the midst of the impenetrable forest. Still leaning on Eugenie, she traced the stream back to its 'source'. A waterfall some sixty feet high plunged into a rocky bowl something like a giant holy water stoup, where men and women splashed and played like earth's first children. The sheer basalt cliffs frowned down on her, unclimbable.

Still clinging to Eugenie's arm, and disguising her growing terror, Stephanie guided her back in the opposite direction. They moved into the forest, the clammy tropical forest of palms, giant ferns and unknown trees. A party of kanakas followed, crashing through the undergrowth round about.

"You wanting to see this?"

The gurgling stream plunged out of sight into a dark hole in the earth under her very eyes.

"Does it finish here?" Stephanie asked.

"He go back to earth."

Her escape was cut off in both directions. She would have to think of something else; a flight through the forest itself, making for the mountain peaks, perhaps? She thought of the island's deer.

"I've not seen any deer round here, Eugenie," she said wonderingly.

"White men bring him here to eat we trees, rice, sugar, everything! He not come here, mountains too high!"

With a sinking heart Stephanie realised that this green valley was inaccessible even to the deer. It was Atai's mountain fastness, uncontaminated by anything European. From there the first party of native warriors had set forth to repel the white settlers, the Alsatians first, then the exiled Communards. Revolt simmered among the kanakas: it would explode sooner or later, she was sure of that now. Alas! She was in the power of these people who opposed the colonisation of their island. She felt a certain sympathy for them, but the fact remained, she was their prisoner. How was she ever to find a way out of this hidden kingdom which Nature herself seemed bent on defending against all intruders? The full meaning of Eugenie's calm 'You free with us, Great Mistress' struck her, in all its horror. But as always with Stephanie, her stubborn will to live rallied in the face of despair and hopelessness.

"I will speak to Atai, we are equals in birth. I will tell him that I respect his island, and that if he is King here I am Queen."

"You wanting to sleep with Atai?" Eugenie asked. "He big, he hurt woman!"

It seemed these savages had but one thought in mind! Still, was this so very different from Europe where 'sleeping together' could change the whole course of political life? Men! The same everywhere, vain and boastful, boobies who could be conquered by a wink, a glimpse of bosom, or a promise as vague as it was insincere. The Maintenon woman had persuaded Louis XIV to revoke the Edict of Nantes, Lola Montez cost Ludwig of Bavaria his throne: as for Atai—well, she would see! She was not going to remain a prisoner of the kanakas all her days. Her life was at stake, and she would defend it with every weapon she had, her will power, her mystery and authority as a white woman. She would be haughty or gentle as the need arose. If money was in question she would haggle over her price, she would escape somehow if he tried to rape her ... no, never! Her whole spirit rose up in protest against this vision of a brutal coupling with a savage!

"You don't know what you are saying!" she cried angrily. "Atai could never sleep with me, he must keep his race pure and his claim to rule intact!" She might have been a duchess protesting against a misalliance.

Empty words, as she well knew, still they conveyed a profound respect for the personage and power of the great chief. But if she hoped she was protecting herself, she was mistaken. Eugenie turned to her with wide astonished eyes.

"Atai he kind, you Great Mistress, he real man, never tired, you beautiful. One tribe marry into another, this good? You son by Atai he kanaka by father, white by mother, and all island go to him!"

'My God, My God, spare me that!' Stephanie whispered to herself in revulsion. She must, she *must* escape! But how? She had inspected the valley and her famous instinct had failed her. Still it was only her first glimpse of the place. She thought of Aravihi and her connection with Napoleon, and the thought was a faint ray of hope. She groaned suddenly.

"The men who took me away hurt me, Eugenie . . . they didn't mean to, but my ankles are swollen and inflamed. I've walked far enough now. Send the woman to me."

"Very well, Mistress, I send woman and calabash."

That must be the name of her strangely soothing ointment. Eugenie left her at the entrance to her hut. Stephanie went in and lay down on her crude bed. She did not have long to wait. Aravihi entered with her calabash full of a white cream and began to massage her again.

"So you know Noumea?" Stephanie began, confident that she would be able to coax the woman to speak.

The fat woman shook her head.

"But you know Monsieur Kerdelec?"

Again the shake of the head. Aravihi was clearly lying, but her lips were sealed.

After a few more attempts Stephanie gave up. The woman was frightened, they must have threatened her, she would not say a word. Still, there was time ahead—and she was not a stubborn Vendéen for nothing!

She woke next morning thinking she must have overslept. 'Sunrise!' Light shone in a golden pool inside the low entrance to her hut. She rose and went out, feeling hungry, and called for Eugenie. Aravihi came hurrying up, her great body shaking as she ran. Stephanie found the fat woman somehow endearing; perhaps she reminded her of Pompette. She felt she could trust her.

"I am hungry!"

Avarihi went off again, her huge haunches rolling. Stephanie glanced round at the hanging walls of greenery, examining it with a coldly practical eye. She was walled in, all right, but where trees and plants could grow there would be foot and handholds. The rocky heights of Alma had been bare; a single leaf could have given cover there! The totem figures sneered down at her from either side of her hut. They were powerful and menacing with their flat, flaring nostrils, narrow eyes and ambiguously smiling lips all carved from massive wood. Aravihi returned with a platter woven of leaves on which were laid slices of raw fish, strips of dried meat, boiled vegetables and fruit. She entered the hut without a word and Stephanie followed, determined to wring something out of her this time. She had learnt caution from the previous day's experiences. She must approach the subject in a roundabout way, taking care not to put the woman on her guard or frighten her. She sat down and began nibbling at her food daintily, like a great lady picking at her hors d'oeuvres. Then she suddenly leant forward and whispered, with a puzzled look: "Where is Eugenie?"

Aravihi rolled her immense shoulders, like two waves of fat which threatened to submerge her head, then she stretched out both arms and waggled her hands in a mysterious semaphore. If this were some secret message it was lost on Stephanie. Perhaps the big woman did not know Eugenie's whereabouts. If she did she did not choose to reveal them. She had been scolded the day before for talking too freely and she was on her guard now. Her mistrust infected Stephanie.

'Well, I won't suggest that she tells Napoleon to warn Yann today! Patience, Stephanie, relax, wait, be calm ...' Then a sudden thought struck her.

"Eugenie will be here for the great feast," she declared, confident that this time she was on to a sure thing.

"Pilou-pilou," Aravihi murmured softly, her eyes glowing.

'That could be my chance,' Stephanie thought. 'They will drink and dance and make love! A native orgy!'

"And Atai, will he be there?" she asked, hoping despite everything that his presence would be some protection.

Aravihi nodded solemnly. Was he not the high priest of the pilou-pilou, the ancient bacchanalia in which the natives danced till their passions exploded in a frenzy of coupling, followed by a long sleep of exhaustion?

'I wonder what happens before the dance begins?' Stephanie reflected. 'If only I knew the rules of the game I could be sure of playing the right card. What was it the Zouaves used to say: "Go it, Phanie!" They were afraid of nothing, and I was their cantinière. I shall see that Atai honours me as an equal as well as a valuable prisoner. I shall sit next to him, like a visiting queen who has been promise a feast to celebrate her arrival. My one hope of getting away unscathed is to make them fear and respect me, and dread my vengeance.'

"Soon, pilou-pilou?" she asked, eyes sparkling as if she too looked forward to the feast.

"Raauroto!"

That must be the name of a phase of the moon, for Aravihi glanced skywards. It meant nothing to Stephanie.

"Raauroto?" she repeated, holding up her fingers as if to count them. She numbered off her fingers, one hand, the thumb of the next.

"Etahitaaroa!" Aravihi cried eagerly, slapping her thighs, rolls of fat bouncing.

'Six days,' Stephanie told herself coldly, joining in Aravihi's laughter out of politeness.

That was something to build on. If Yann arrived first . . . if he didn't, she would have to defend herself alone!

Stephanie ticked off the days as they dragged by slowly and it seemed interminably. Her inactivity weighed on her. She would have preferred to collect firewood, fetch water, cook her own meals, but she was forced to remain totally idle, in keeping with her station as a 'queen who looks down on the world'. She walked about the place freely, seeking some path or track which might give her a thread to follow out of the labyrinth, but she found nothing. The absence of deer puzzled her. Was there no way into this hidden valley? Yet an animal's instinct is as sure as it is infallible. True, deer were not like chamois, leaping from crag to crag. On the other hand Eugenie managed to leave this apparently impenetrable fastness, Atai would soon be arriving and there must be at least three hundred people there now ... so? This speculation did her good, focusing all her energies on the prospcct of escape. She was not so sanguine as to expect people to find her here and rescue her, but she did think she might stumble on the way out. The hole into which the stream vanished continued to intrigue her and she visited the spot daily; it was somewhere to walk to!

The kanakas still kept at a respectful distance, but they smiled and spoke to her. They were simple, kindly people, she decided, as she had so often been told. But—imagine them drunk, crazed by dancing, drink and ritual, all their savagery re-awakened ... then they would be capable of anything ... rape, murder! She lived under the constant threat of death and she had to remain poised, smiling and calm, to give the impression that nothing could frighten her. She was beginning to make out a few words in their tongue: anavaiiti was the stream; fetia tataouro meant the Southern Cross, which they kept pointing out to her and a few others, notably nau, or breasts, for the natives kept urging her to show them hers, smiling at her with innocent curiosity and astonishment, but without a trace of lust. They wanted to see them because they were all pink and white and they had never seen breasts like that before ... why did the Great Mistress hide them?

Stephanie sat staring thoughtfully at the stream as it plunged into the earth. Her mood was anxious and melancholy. She thought about the river on its journey to the sea. That way lay safety. Only two more nights to go before 'etahitaaroa'.

"Mistress, Mistress, come quickly!"

Eugenie's shrill, piping voice, Stephanie turned round.

"You secret—I have it! It here!"

What could she mean by this? The girl was in ecstasies of delight, clapping her hands and laughing. What secret? Stephanie steeled herself.

"You come?" Eugenie asked, dropping an almost stately curtsey before proferring her arm.

They made their way back along the stream towards the village. Stephanie stopped dead, unable to believe her eyes. In the centre of the clearing stood Aimé, with two kanakas behind him laden with bundles.

"Great Mistress, you tell me you secret in Noumea in boxes and dresses. Simple! I find Monsieur Aimé, tell him you give me secret and he go fetch it, not telling anyone and now we back here!"

It was all clear now. Unable to take Stephanie with her to Noumea, Eugenie must have tracked Aimé down in the forest and Aimé, thinking only of her safety, ready to die with her if need be, had carried the girl's plans out blindly without telling a soul. He feared no doubt that telling Yann, and seizing the girl, would have led to reprisals against Stephanie herself. Poor Aimé! What a hornets' nest he had blundered into. It was a double disaster now, the ransom money would be doubled for a start. And she could not possibly leave without him. It was Versailles all over again, when she had declared stoutly: 'I won't go without Monsieur Becave.' But at Versailles she had names to conjure with: Ladmirault, MacMahon, Guinchamp—here she had nothing. Tears of despair were forcing themselves into her eyes when a sudden hopeful thought struck her.

The secret way out! Aimé must know where it was. He had come on foot, unlike her, he must know the way.

His eyes shone as she approached, and he smiled. He

was happy, nothing mattered to him now that he had found her alive and well.

'How you must love me!' she thought, swallowing down her tears.

Chapter Eight

"So you saw nothing!" Stephanie repeated for the tenth time, her voice flat with despair.

She had been questioning Aimé for over an hour, refusing to believe that a born countryman could have made the journey without noticing something, a tree trunk, a twisting root, a rock, which might have given some clue or landmark they could use when they tried to make their escape.

She buried her face in her hands, rubbing her eyes in an effort to concentrate her thoughts.

"Nothing! I can't believe it," she repeated over and over again.

"Everything about this island is quite new and strange to me, it's so unfamiliar that one area looks just like another. Put yourself in my place!"

"My own place is quite bad enough," she said curtly, in the blunt fashion she sometimes used with Aimé. It did her good to speak her mind occasionally. Aimé endured her changes of mood, her raptures and despairs, with his customary phlegm, and his very passivity gave Stephanie new strength and courage. She was like a wave retreating, curling, breaking and rushing forward again. He was infuriating, impossible, marvellous and quite irreplaceable. He made it possible for her to live, to feel afraid, to go on. Just now he was as stubborn as a rock.

"When they took me away I was blindfolded and gagged and tied up like a parcel, and they brought me all the way from Thio on their backs, like a mummy. At least you came on foot!"

"Like Madame, I shall repeat myself. Half the time I

was blindfolded, and the rest of the way all there was to see was leaves, greenery blocking out the sky, the uneven ground under my feet and a strong smell of damp vegetation, like mushrooms."

"But how did you get into the valley?" she cried. "Where is the secret entrance?"

"There must be several of them, but I've no idea where they are."

"Do you realise we've only one night to go before . . ."

She buried her face in her hands again, seized by paralysing fear. Who was Atai? What did he want from her? It was all very well telling herself that she would find a way out: so far it had not got her anywhere.

"We've got to escape!" she muttered, advancing on Aimé who stood leaning against the central pole which held up her thatched hut. He watched her, quite unmoved. He was right, of course, but Stephanie had to have her say before she would calm down. She stared at him coldly, willing him to produce a plan, or at least a suggestion.

"Well, what do you think, Aimé?"

"I've brought Madame's secret weapons with me."

Was there ever such a provoking man, with his absurd philosophical remarks at moments like these! She was touched, all the same.

"You think . . ."

"If Madame will allow me to give her a word of advice . . ."

Really, he was the limit! Atai was arriving the next day, for all she knew she might be handed over to the whole tribe to do as they liked with, and here was Aimé with his polite 'If Madame will allow me' just as if they were safely back in the elegant Guinchamp mansion in Paris.

Stephanie began to rub the small of her back with both hands. It ached with tension and anger.

"Well?" she said in honeyed, but menacing, tones.

"Madame has everything she needs."

"Everything?" she repeated in bewilderment.

How he loved playing on her nerves, making her wait!

"Aimé, please," she said, hands folded as if in prayer, "come out with it. I'm at the end of my tether."

"The situation appears to be this: Madame has been kidnapped by a native chief who is using her as a political hostage if I understand Eugenie's childish prattle correctly. This is an important point. It guarantees Madame a sort of diplomatic immunity which will be of the greatest value to us. Now, this girl wants to know Madame's secret, which is—that she is herself! Which can hardly be conveyed. What we have to do is play off one situation against the other."

"And what do you advise me to do?"

"Look."

He gestured towards the opened bundles on the floor. She saw two or three of her most elaborate gowns, flowers, trinkets, plus a mass of things she would never have dreamt of wearing, yards of cheap beads, bright imitation jewels, shiny ribbons, plaques and pendants of brass and copper, tassels . . . she rubbed her eyes.

"What is all this for, Aimé?"

She spoke as an obedient woman only asking to be told what to do.

"I picked up all this trash at the little boutique in Noumea. It was an idea I had. The more Madame sparkles and shines, the more like a Christmas tree—if she will forgive me the comparison—she looks, the safer she will be. Madame must remember that we are among savages here."

Stephanie thought it over, her chin resting on her hands. 'He thinks of everything!' It was like the scene when she wanted to abandon all ceremony and eat a simple breakfast on the grass, a picnic, and he had insisted that she maintain a certain dignity and reserve in the eyes of the kanakas. The difference between them was that Aimé always had a reason for everything he did, he was objective, calculating, whereas she rushed into situations on a sudden impulse, full steam ahead. She dealt with the situations as they arose, Aimé looked far ahead. In short, they complemented each other splendidly. In some vague way she had felt stronger and safer ever since his arrival, and this was because he had given her a solid base from which to strike out, to hope, despair, plot and plan. She had to keep active, that was her nature.

"Aimé, do you think ..."

She couldn't quite bring herself to say, 'Do you think we shall ever get away?' But he answered as if he read her mind.

"Madame's infallible memory will be of considerable assistance to us."

How he loved his weighty phrases, his long words! Even now he couldn't resist bringing them out lovingly, like a professor. 'That's *his* nature,' she reminded herself, trying to be patient. 'It's useless to interrupt and try to get him to the point. If he has his harangue all prepared he'll make use of it whatever I do.'

"Thanks to Madame we escaped from the Satory camp. Madame saved me from the firing squad by rushing down the stairs, pushing me over in the mud and shielding me with her body. I came here to be with Madame, and I shall leave here with her; how I don't yet know—but I know that I shall. It must be done. Madame's children need her, and trust her, and Madame is not one to disappoint them."

Extraordinary man! Only Aimé would have thought of conjuring up her family in this stinking hut, hidden away in some lost, inaccessible valley, in the hourly expectation of a savage chief with life and death powers over them, to restore her confidence and pugnacity.

"I was forgetting! It's also because Madame saved my life at Alma that I now have the inexpressible happiness of joining my fate to hers."

A flood of images passed before her—twilight, then darkness, torches like will-o'-the-wisps, the plain piled high with bodies, wounded and dead. She remembered the feeble clutching of his hand at her ankle, and her first sight of his face pressed into the bloody pulp of his shattered arm. Vividly, she remembered her stunned, horrified cry of recognition—'Aimé!'

She flung her arms round him, overwhelmed by memories. "Aimé! You dear fool! You paid off your debts of gratitude years ago!"

It was good to be able to call him 'dear fool' with so much sisterly affection, so good ...

Aimé's single arm went round her waist, drawing her close. She turned up her face towards him as a drowning man might look for a floating plank. She gazed into his eyes, then touched her lips to his cheek, then full on his mouth, kissing him softly, tenderly, out of gratitude and affection. Then she drew back, kissed his other cheek, his neck, and finally laid her head on his shoulder. A rain drop fell on her cheek, then a second and a third ...

Aimé was weeping for his hopeless love.

"What do you think will happen, Aimé?"

She was afraid again, afraid of everything, of Atai, the feast, its inevitable sensual, sexual climax. It had been a dreadful day for her, surrounded by a joyful atmosphere of eager, almost hysterical anticipation and preparation for the coming feast. The kanakas had built a sort of platform or dais, and now set feverishly rolling tapers of wax and resin. Flowers had been brought in by the hundredweight, the dais was decked and garlanded with them, and all the women were beflowered from head to feet, they even wore them tucked between their toes.

"We shall soon know, Madame," Aimé answered calmly.

He had decked her out lavishly, and her appearance was literally dazzling. Her exquisite Worth gown had been desecrated by the ribbons and beads and cheap trinkets with which Aimé had festooned her—'It has to be done, Madame!' He had put together this music-hall costume with great speed and assurance, standing outside under the trees because she could never have got through the small entrance to her hut after she had been attired.

"Where will Atai appear from?" she asked anxiously.

"I know as little as you, Mademoiselle de Boisnaudouin," he replied.

He called her that to make her laugh, and she did laugh. It was marvellous the way he kept restoring her confidence and calming her fears.

"Do you believe ..."

"I believe in you, and that's all I need."

He spoke matter-of-factly, almost curtly. She was so fortunate to have Aimé here, he wouldn't allow her to weaken or make mistakes, to satisfy him she must be every inch a queen!

"When will he come?"

She could think of nothing but Atai and his impending arrival.

"Aravihi will tell us," Aimé said, "she loves Madame, and wishes to serve her."

It had not taken Aimé long to discover that the fat kanaka woman was Stephanie's devoted slave, and as such might prove useful to them.

"And Eugenie?" she asked.

'She's quite a different story. She is obsessed by love, or rather the sexual act, it is her consuming, ruling passion. Women like this are always dangerous. They can't help it, it's the fault of the way they were brought up."

"I don't understand," she said, puzzled.

"The subject is a little indelicate, Madame, though perfectly natural. It is true the custom is more an African than a Melanesian one, but I know it is practised here too."

"Oh, Aimé, what are you talking about?" she cried, exasperated by his long-windedness.

"To quieten a crying child and put it to sleep, mothers and grandmothers are in the habit of rubbing a certain part of the little girl's anatomy with a finger—with natural, predictable consequences. I fancy Madame understands me now?"

"You put it very clearly," she told him. "So you mean to tell me they send children off to sleep by ... er, tickling them?"

"Tickling up their nervous system, you might call it. Unfortunately, this precocious training makes the girls insatiable and hard to satisfy. The force of habit, Madame. I read this in a book by an explorer, it's an observation of some ethnic interest."

Stephanie could not repress a smile. "One can never learn too much, Aimé. I only wish I did more reading myself."

"I always feel I am reading for *us*, Madame."

There was something strangely sweet and protective about that 'us'; it seemed to set them apart from the rest of the world. What a strange fellow he was! Always, at every stage of her life, he seemed to be there beside her like a shadow, an *alter ego*. 'We complement each other; what I lack he has.' Stephanie returned to the thought which haunted her.

"What about Atai, Aimé?"

"Madame must stop worrying, everything will be all right."

Aravihi appeared as he had predicted, her agate eyes rolling wildly. She was in a state of such excitement that her large pendulous breasts seemed to have become taut and pointed again.

"He will be here in a moment," she whispered. She vanished immediately, but she had forewarned them.

"It's up to us now! You will have to help me, I'm single-handed!"

Stephanie parted the branches for them, her other hand resting delicately on Aimé's. She was reminded of Louis XIV presenting Madame de Montespan to visiting kings and ambassadors. Such formality might seem a little absurd in the jungle, but it had style. And, as Aimé had foreseen, the kanakas were impressed, melting aside to let them pass, throwing up their arms in greeting, even falling to their knees in homage. The great crowd was all streaming in one direction. Led by Aimé, Stephanie found herself following the river upstream towards the waterfall, where they stopped and waited, with a semicircle of silent, expectant kanakas gathered round them. What were they all waiting for? A miracle?

Later she would ask herself how Atai had brought it off; at the time she was as thrilled by the spectacle as anyone present. He seemed to burst upon their vision, rising with straddled legs from the water, handsome as a god. He was clad in a suit of shells, arranged so as to emphasise the virile bulge of his sex, the length and elegance of his legs and thighs, his flat belly, narrow waist, powerful chest and shoulders, sturdy column of a throat—and ugly face, with its harsh, severe features and glittering eyes. His high, narrow forehead was surmounted by a headdress of brilliant kagu feathers which rose in a curving plume and then swept down again, sparkling with drops of water which the setting sun coloured in all the hues of the rainbow. A great breastplate of sharks-teeth necklaces, doubtless made from fish he had hunted and killed, shone like strings of pearls across his chest. As an apparition, the savage king was breathtaking, irresistible. He stood like a statue while a long ecstatic cry went up from all the assembled kanakas, then with an astounding dancer's leap he soared and landed, light as a gazelle, at Stephanie's feet. Rising to his feet slowly, like a figure in a dream, he presented himself.

"I salute you, Gr-r-r-eat Mistress Stephanie."

The use of her Christian name was like a title, an act of homage. Stephanie was speechless. Apart from the matchless beauty of his body, what fascinated her about Atai was his vigorous rolling of 'r's. Aimé's hand quivered under hers, warning her. She bowed.

"I salute you, Great Atai, Mahana," she answered, speaking in a medley of their two languages.

He did the same.

"You are more beautiful than Fetia [the star], you are Tiarama [the constellation]."

Without understanding clearly, she grasped enough to know that he was treating her with reassuring respect, as between equals.

Prompted by his innate sense of occasion Aimé took the opportunity to proffer Stephanie's hand to Atai. The chief stood perplexed for a moment, unsure of what was expected of him, then he made a fist as Aimé had done and Stephanie laid her hand upon it. Aimé, having shown her the direction to take, was handing her over to the care of this savage king. Obey him, he seemed to be telling her, but play your part well and you may lead him too. It was an effective piece of theatre. Atai might be King, but she had become the one he presented to his people, the one who conferred honour on them ...

'Honour?' thought Stephanie. 'We are playing for our freedom, our very lives!'

Aimé followed a few steps behind the 'royal' pair for all the world like a Lord Chamberlain intent on rectifying any errors in protocol.

Stephanie took her seat next to Atai on the dais whose thrones consisted of interwoven branches and lianas decked with leaves and flowers. Atai flung up one arm, fist clenched, as a signal for the feast to begin. Aimé sat at Stephanie's feet.

With ritual solemnity the kanakas assembled in two groups below the dais, the men near by, the women further off. They formed circles, weaving in and out in two different directions, in a moving chain. The tom-toms' hypnotic thudding began, like a quickened heartbeat, accompanied by piercing high notes plucked from some odd mandoline-like instruments, and a chorus of quavering obligatos from reed pipes. Tension mounted. The rhythm of the dance quickened, becoming passionate, incantatory, and its excitement seized the brown, whirling bodies. The dancers arched their backs and flung back their heads—'they'll shake them off,' Stephanie thought—thrusting their breasts and bellies upward in wild pulsing movements.

This continued for some time. Then, suddenly, the men swept down among the women and began to dance with them. As they danced face to face, man and woman, there was no mistaking the meaning of their movements and steps. The women writhed and flung themselves about in frenzied abandonment, arousing the males, who stood jerking their loins in a mime of the sexual act, and then thrust forward suddenly in mimic and brutal possession. The women fled in mock terror, uttering cries which were so many summons to return and begin again. This was the dance of love and of life, and its movements, though apparently obscene, had a strange, savage and disturbing beauty.

Suddenly, as the music reached a crescendo of thudding tom-toms, wailing flutes and hysterical strings, the men tore off their loin cloths with a great cry of triumph. The women had roused them to a pitch where they could satisfy them. Stephanie closed her eyes to shut out the sight of so much triumphant manhood. When she looked up again she saw Eugenie dancing a dance of hysterical, impatient desire at the foot of the dais. She snatched off the cloth round her waist and her blank, tranced eyes fastened upon Aimé as she waved and undulated before him in a dance directed at him alone.

Frightened and anxious all of a sudden, Stephanie threw a quick sidelong glance at Aimé. He was looking at the girl without seeing her, staring past her, unmoved. Swept by a sudden fury, Eugenie slapped both hands on the dais, either side of Atai's feet, and cried hoarsely, her voice unrecognisable in the grip of sexual frenzy, "You give him to me, Atai?"

"He is yours!"

Instinctively, Stephanie laid a protective hand on Aimé's shoulder, but now Eugenie seized him by the arm and began tugging at him. He threw a quick glance at Stephanie, which told her not to interfere, to let things be, and allowed the girl to pull him down from the dais. With a quick, explicit gesture, Eugenie reassured herself that her 'impassive white man' was becoming aroused and eager for love. She thrust herself against him, rubbing her belly and breasts against him, at the same time signalling with one hand. An old woman, one of those retired from the love feast, whose duty was to serve the menfolk with liquor, held out a half coconut shell in which a pale liquid shone in the torch-light. Eugenie handed it to Aimé, who drank, and gulped for air, darting a rapid glance at Stephanie. She was about to move when Atai's hand clamped down over hers, anchoring her to her flowery throne. Eugenie was leading Aimé, in a ring of howling, shrieking women, towards the larger of the two totems.

'The totem, dances, torture, sacrifice, blood ... no, no, not Aimé, no!'

Stephanie snatched her hand free, and leapt up, bent on running after them, imploring Eugenie, offering her anything, everything—but she found the tall savage barring her way, holding both hands out to her. He laid them on her shoulders and their touch was both and firm and surprisingly gentle.

"What do you fear, Tiarama?"

His calm voice, amused expression, and the glittering eyes just visible through half-closed lids, disconcerted her. Was Aimé in no danger at all, then? Why were they dragging him towards the totem? She tried to keep her voice steady as she replied, "He belongs to me."

She claimed him as her slave, which meant no one had the right to lay hands upon him.

"Lend him, don't be jealous. He can give Eugenie the child Yann will not give her because of you."

So that was what the little slut wanted? She had decided that Aimé must be Stephanie's lover, and now she was stealing him from under the eyes of everyone. Poor fool, with her dreams of vengeance, and poor Aimé!

'Well, perhaps not so much to be pitied,' Stephanie reminded herself. 'She's young, beautiful and ardent; I don't suppose he'll find it too disagreeable. And it may help me. Atai has been on his best behaviour till now, but . . . the night isn't over yet.'

She turned a regal look on him, as one monarch to another. "I will lend him to her; I hope she enjoys herself," she said, with the air of one conferring a signal favour.

Atai smiled and then sat down beside her.

Stephanie did her best to appear at ease, and unafraid, but she was secretly trembling for Aimé. The women were stripping him naked and thrusting drink upon him at the same time. The aphrodisiac was racing hotly through his body, intoxicating and arousing him. Great tremors surged through him which brought admiring sniggers and murmurs from the women. When he was quite naked they tied him up to the post. Stephanie would gladly have closed her eyes but Atai was watching her as if determined that she should enjoy the ceremony.

'I must look happy and pleased and grateful for all the pleasures I am being offered,' she told herself. It was a comfort to think that Aimé, now dead drunk, would not remember any of this. He already seemed oblivious of what was happening, his head lolling this way and that as he gasped for air like a fish out of water.

The throng round the post grew denser, and Eugenie moved back a few yards from Aimé.

"A fine man," said Atai, bending forward to compliment Stephanie on her slave.

She thanked him with a strained smile, heart beating fast. She hoped against hope that Aimé was not destined for anything more sinister than a bout of savage copulation, but she did not have too much confidence in the chief's promises, and she kept expecting to see the flash of a knife in Eugenie's hand before it was driven home into Aimé's heart.

However, the girl's hands were quite empty when she finally sprang upon Aimé like a rutting tigress, impaling herself upon him with a long howl of pleasure. Women rushed forward to support her as she thrashed and writhed upon her white man like one demented . . .

'Let's hope Aimé gets her with child,' thought Stephanie. 'He's one of the Great Ones in her eyes, worth as much as Yann Kerdelec. She will be saved from the fate of a spurned old hag— which was how she saw herself— and the curse upon her will be lifted once she has got herself pregnant by a white man!'

She sat trying to take a calm interest in the revolting spectacle being enacted before an enthralled audience, who clapped their hands and swayed in time to the rhythm of the sexual act. At last Eugenie collapsed on the ground, groaning and twisting like someone in their death agony. Some men picked her up and carried her off to a hut among the trees as a new group of furies flung themselves shrieking and arguing on the half senseless Aimé. They all wanted to be served by him.

"It's sickening!" Stephanie breathed.

"They'll get a better price," Atai murmured indulgently.

"Price?" she whispered uncomprehendingly.

"You prefer half-caste workers in your mines and forests, Gr-r-eat Mistr-r-ess."

That was it! She remembered now. Yann had explained it all to her. 'Half-castes get better money because they work harder. The native women all wants sons by white men because they earn more and this assures them of a comfortable, honourable old age. The father of a half-caste often refuses to acknowledge his son, but the half-caste son never rejects his mother!' Aimé was reduced to the role of a stallion. Poor Aimé, they kept pouring drink into him, while the woman swarmed over him clamouring for his seed. Semi-conscious he might be, but his virility seemed unimpaired. Stephanie remained quite impassive, not daring to move. This was a feast, a pagan feast; in a moment Atai would fling himself upon her, and then all the rest . . .

Aravihi had cleared a passage through the struggling women around the totem. So she wanted Aimé, too?

Stephanie saw her from behind as she stood on tiptoe, lifting up the apron which hung over her massive belly. The excited women helped her to mount her unfortunate victim, supporting her round the thighs and back. The kanakas looked on in delight, laughing and clapping. Stephanie was disgusted.

"Atai," she murmured, bending towards him.

"Great Mistress?"

"Give me back my slave."

His expression was stern and unyielding. "While a man has strength he must continue!"

Contempt cracked in his voice like a whip. For a woman to make a request like that was to insult his sex. Stephanie realised that she had made a mistake, and made a desperate attempt to remedy matters.

"You gave him to Eugenie, not to the others."

"And you, will you give yourself to me?"

He asked the question as if the freeing of Aimé depended upon her answer. She knew what Aimé would have said: 'No, Madame, I would rather die!' But to refuse would mean angering Atai, and turning him against her. She was in his power and he could do what he liked with her; rape her, kill her, let her bleed to death, hand her over to all the men of the tribe. She had never felt more helpless, never needed all her powers of fascination more. She gazed at him, projecting her will, her spirit on to him. He must be the one to refuse, not her. She thought of Yann, Boris, René, trying to draw strength from these masculine presences. Then suddenly Moses, the half-wit, the shipwrecked sailor who saw so much further than other men, came to her mind as she remembered him crouched on the threshold of the offices in Noumea, leading the horses, standing by Yves Kerdelec —as if by magic, a solution to her dilemma suggested itself.

"My apologies, Atai, Mahana. I am ashamed. You are a great chief, you are beautiful and your voice is gentle. May the gods forgive me, for they have afflicted me. Tonight is not good for me, Atai, I am . . ."

She bowed her head till it sank shamefacedly on her breast.

"Unclean?" he asked disappointedly.

She sighed and flung out her arms in a despairing gesture.

Stepping away from her Atai took up his position at the front of the dais, as impressive a figure as when he first materialised out of the water. From his lips, which remained half closed, an unearthly sound arose, a shrill animal cry which grew into a savage howl as he snatched off his shell apron and flung it into the crowd. This was the signal. The men of the tribe took up the love call and women began pressing forward, thrusting young virgins towards him, all drugged, half drunk and feverishly anticipating the imprint of a God. Atai flung back his head in a full-throated roar of lust, then flinging out his arms, sprang like a panther into the crowd. Stephanie felt that great cry of his reverberate through her entire body, such was its erotic power. This legendary male was a living challenge to heaven and earth and all the women upon it, and the line he engendered would wax great and flourish for century upon centuries. She had to make an effort to shake off his strange magnetism and return to herself.

'Well, I'm safe for tonight; so far, so good,' she thought. 'But what shall I do next time?' Suddenly Pompette's hearty voice rang in her ears: 'Cross your bridges when you come to them, my girl!' Her mind cleared, and she felt happier. Just then she caught sight of Aimé, abandoned now his duty was done, sprawled on the ground at the foot of the totem pole, the moonlight silvering his white skin.

Stephanie mopped Aimé's brow with a rag moistened in a gourd of water while Aravihi tenderly massaged his body. The feast had ended in a wild, nightmarish Dantesque scene where grotesque images thronged upon each other: the deflowering of the young girls, an initiation ceremony for the young men, then a general orgy—the men flung the women down and leapt upon them and the women were no sooner released than they offered themselves hungrily and drunkenly to anyone who would take them, only to shriek under a new and brutal onslaught . . .

At dawn she beheld Atai picking his way through the glade strewn with sprawled, drunk, sated bodies. He came towards her like a figure in a dream carrying the still unconscious Aimé over one shoulder, and flung him down at her feet. The night of frenzied coupling had left no traces on his face, and his powerful cat-like grace was unimpaired. Drowsy as she was, Stephanie had tried to speak to him, to leave a good impression with him. He smiled, raking her with the proud gaze of an eagle. His eyes lingered on her lips, then slid down to her neck, shoulders, the rounded curve of her breasts, her hips, then back to her eyes again. There was no mistaking the fact that he desired her, and was promising himself the enjoyment of her one of these days. His voice, when he spoke, was soft, as caressing as he could make it.

"We shall be meeting again soon, Great Mist-r-r-ess! May the valley protect you! I have returned your slave to you as you asked."

At the time she did not take it all in clearly, but later the words went round and round in her mind, and they seemed to take on a sinister meaning. 'May the valley protect you!' reminded her that she was a prisoner in this hidden cleft in the earth, while 'as you asked' meant I've kept my part of the bargain, now it's up to you to keep yours.

'But what could he mean? I haven't committed myself to anything.'

Meanwhile all she could do was sponge Aimé's brow. His breathing was becoming slower and more regular now. He was coming round gradually. It would be some time before the lingering effects of the powerful aphrodiciacs, which had rendered him unconscious and temporarily deranged, wore off. When he was back to normal they would be able to sit down and take stock of their situation again. By then perhaps Yann would have found them . . .

'I must hope against hope. It will be many days, weeks before the moon returns to the position it was in yesterday. We must think of something by then.'

In the first radiance of dawn she had seen Atai stride towards the foaming pool at the foot of the waterfall, dive into it, reappear for a fleeting second and then vanish!

'There,' she had decided, 'must be one of the secret entrances into this valley.'

Chapter Nine

"Quick, Mistress, quick!"

Stephanie woke with a start to find a shadowy form bending over her. The voice she recognised as Eugenie's. For a moment she was disorientated, then she sat up swiftly, put her feet to the floor and stared like a cat past Eugenie to where she could just make out a quaking, blubbery mass in the darkness: Aravihi! And beyond her the shapes of three men, recognisable by their long legs, powerful shoulders and narrow waists.

"What do you want?"

"We go, at once!"

Cold fear ran through Stephanie at the thought of leaving the hidden valley where, in spite of everything, she had felt safe.

"Why?"

"We must, Mistress, I ask you humbly."

Eugenie seemed quite terrified, but these kanakas always exaggerated everything so, they'd mistake a glow-worm for a lantern . . .

"What about Aimé?" Stephanie said harshly, her tone of voice implying that she would not leave without him.

"He dressing now, I come quick quick after hearing alarm."

"Alarm, what alarm?"

"Soldiers not far from here, all sleep now. If they find us Atai very angry, he kill everybody."

They had sent the troops out to search for her. In a short time she would be free! Naturally she would do what she could for Atai, who had been gracious to her. She would act as a mediator between the Whites and the natives, easy enough to understand in their childlike simplicity and ancestral code of behaviour.

"Light a torch!" she commanded.

"Ah, no, Mistress," Eugenie whispered, more terrified than ever, folding her brown body smaller as if hoping to melt into the night.

'No lights, no sounds; well, that's normal;' Stephanie thought. 'The troops must be about to besiege the valley. I daresay Napoleon gave them the precise location on the map. I shall delay Eugenie and her people and wait here till dawn. If they try to force me to leave, I'll scream—cries carry a long way at night.'

"What do you want, Eugenie?" she asked, lying back on her bed again.

It was heartening to defy them for once. But just then the hut doorway darkened as several men pushed their way in; there must be four of them. Suddenly, from the silhouette of his empty sleeve, she recognised one of them as Aimé.

"What should we do, Aimé?" she asked, quite sure that he would find a coded way of telling her that they must stay here till the troops arrived.

"Leave immediately, Madame, with all possible haste."

The opposite of what she expected him to say. She did not even protest, however, she had too much confidence in him. If he said this was what they must do, he must have good reasons. Ever since the love feast he had been sleeping with Eugenie every night, determined to make her pregnant so that she would become their ally and accomplice. He had not told Stephanie so, but he did not need to; a glance, even a silence, was communication enough.

"We shall take everything with us, Madame."

He made a sweeping gesture which took in the walls of the round hut, and the kanakas hastened to do his bidding, their bodies flickering to and fro in the half darkness like black flames. It was all like a strange ballet, danced in total silence. It took them three or four minutes to pack up all her possessions. Meanwhile she put on her dress and Eugenie helped to lace her boots up. The glade seemed quite luminous as she stepped out into the high, blue, whispering tropical night.

'I shall see the secret way at last!'

The knowledge would be useless now that they were on their way to an unknown destination. She saw that the whole village was hastily preparing to evacuate the valley. One group hurried down to the waterfall, and a moment later vanished from sight. Another went to the point where the river plunged into the earth. Her own party, with Eugenie guiding them, was heading west—in the direction of Bourail, Poya, Konë and the populated coastline.

The climb was precipitously steep, and they had to haul themselves up by hanging branches and roots, occasionally leaning against a tree trunk to take breath before scrambling up a rocky outcrop whose outline they could barely distinguish in the darkness. Aimé had cut a length of liana to fasten round their two waists as a lifeline if one of them should slip. She could not see Eugenie, Aravihi or the kanakas but she could feel their presence all around her. As they plunged deeper and deeper into the damp, steaming forest starlight reduced to a few paler chinks glimpsed between waving tree tops, Stephanie had the feeling of moving about at the bottom of a giant aquarium full of luxuriant, waving underwater plants.

'Mountains don't go on for ever,' she thought. 'We'll get to the top soon and I'll be able to take a breath of fresh air.' At almost precisely the same moment the slope became more sheer and dangerous, falling away suddenly to right and left in a dizzying drop. There was no time to be frightened—that would come later! Stephanie didn't want to break a leg now; she moved with infinite care and caution, never letting go of one handhold till she was certain that her foot had found a secure root or rock to wedge itself against while she groped about in the dark with her free hand. Aimé seemed to be making better progress with his one arm to her two. Anyway, even if she did slip, she wouldn't fall very far in this tangle of undergrowth. It wasn't as if she were alone, if anything happened she would be picked up and carried the rest of the way. But she was determined to keep up with her escort. Absurdly, a childhood memory flashed into her mind, comforting her.

'That time I climbed out of my bedroom window after knotting my sheets together . . .'

She could have been thirteen again.

'I know it's silly, but here I am escaping all over again and I'm beginning to enjoy it. My body is strong and agile, it hasn't changed. Well, escape isn't the right word, I'm moving from one prison to another, just as I move from one rock cleft to another, but I can make it on my own; I'm quite sure of that now.'

And she tackled the next slope with surefooted alacrity. Suddenly she felt the ground underfoot growing hard and rocky. They must have reached the summit. In the distance something glimmered white, like the exit from a tunnel. It was merely a shaft of moonlight, but the contrast with the enclosed forest made it seem as bright as sunshine. Suddenly she heard Aimé panting "Quick, Madame, hurry!"

He tugged on the liana between them like someone jerking on a dog leash. She almost dug her heels in, but then it struck her that if he was pulling like this it must mean . . .

"Hurry!" he repeated, as if it was the only word he knew.

"Why?" she asked, coming up beside him.

"Poisoned arrows . . ."

Eugenie sped ahead of the party over the damp lichens which covered the rocky ground underfoot. As they reached the edge of the jungle the kanakas materialised suddenly out of the shadows and fell in around them, both guard and escort. Aimé did not have time to finish what he was saying. Stephanie stood close beside him, clutching her skirts up in both hands, fighting to get her breath back.

"Yann is leading them," he breathed almost inaudibly into her ear.

How could he know that? Could Eugenie have signalled the information back? Her heart ached ... Yann, her beloved! It would have been so easy, so natural to fling back her head and call his name, summon him to her rescue. But Aimé read her thoughts almost before they had time to form.

"Are you crazy!" he hissed, with such contempt that it was like being struck across the face. He suddenly shortened the length of liana between them by binding it quickly round his wrist.

"Fall down!" he commanded her.

Almost simultaneously he lunged against her with all his strength so that she fell heavily to the ground in the moonlight. "We mustn't let them use the arrows," he muttered close to her ear. "*His* life and many others' depend on it. We must shake them off, get clear away, put a distance between us ..."

His cry of concern throbbed with simulated anxiety as he propped himself beside her on his one arm.

"You aren't hurt, Madame?"

Meanwhile his clear, cold gaze riveted itself to hers: she would have to read his thoughts, there was no time to explain. Staring at him, it suddenly became clear: the motive for this headlong evacuation in the night was to save Yann from a murderously unequal confrontation with the native forces. The kanakas were desperate, and the forest was their domain. They could melt into it like shadows, keep watch, prepare a deadly ambush. By now a dozen faces were bending over her, but it didn't matter now, she had received and understood Aimé's warning.

"Mistress!"

Eugenie sank down beside her, a quaver of fear trembling in her voice. Like Aimé, she feared that the approach of the Whites would unleash all the pent-up savagery of her tribesmen.

Poisoned arrows, sudden death ...

"I tripped, Eugenie, it's nothing, I'm all right now," she said, getting to her feet and looking round at them with a sudden assumption of authority.

She knew now what she must do ... she must follow these people freely, with all the speed and readiness she could muster. Anything was better than that Yann and his men should be destroyed stealthily in the forest. This way there would be no ambush, no fighting, no slaughter. She tilted up her chin commandingly and said crisply, as if she were the leader of the party, "Take me to Atai, at once!"

The men glanced at her like lost children in their sudden bewilderment. She had just countermanded their orders—they were not on their way to see Atai at all, but to another high, hidden valley to which the God-King would come in due course, stepping out of the water like a deity come to earth. It occurred to Stephanie that Eugenie might be more amenable. She had seemed much gentler, almost docile, since the feast night.

"It is Atai I must see, Eugenie," she explained, her voice gravely impressive. "We are both of royal blood, don't forget."

The kanaka girl hung her head almost apologetically. Stephanie's order had placed her in a sudden dilemma which she could not resolve. She was like a trapped animal in her perplexity.

"Atai and none other!" Stephanie repeated, still more firmly than before.

With these simple, fearful people the essential thing was to take command. Eugenie looked up slowly, her face aghast and her eyes glistening with tears.

"Not know where Atai, Great Mistress ..."

'She's telling me the truth. All the same ...' Staking everything on this throw, Stephanie put an arm round the girl's shoulders.

"He must have a hut, a wife, children, like other men."

"No! He free—like bird!"

There was admiration in her voice for the man who could still belong to all women.

'A man who flits from valley to valley and womb to womb isn't going to make my task easier,' thought Stephanie.

But she was not going to give up so easily. She squeezed Eugenie's shoulders encouragingly but urgently.

"I must see him and talk to him! Everything depends on him—and on you!"

"Me?" Eugenie was flattered, though her eyes were anxious.

"You are my messenger, my friend, I trust you."

The kanakas were looking about them impatiently and Stephanie made one last urgent attempt to convince the girl,

"Take me to a place where he often goes, that will be enough."

Eugenie fell to her knees, kissing Stephanie's hands. You could never tell what these confounded kanakas were going to do next.

"Take me to him, I will follow you. Don't deceive me," Stephanie said, lifting the girl to her feet. She transfixed her with a cold, severe stare. "I command you!"

Eugenie's glance wavered and her lids fluttered. Suddenly she stiffened as if she heard a distant summons. Gazing into the distance, she stood panting like an animal. Then she was gone, Aimé and Stephanie at her heels. The escort closed round them and once again they plunged into the black, hostile forest.

Imperceptibly, the sky lightened, and a milky pallor seeped into the forest darkness, revealing the snaky curve of a root, a slippery, matted patch of earth. With startling suddenness a dazzling shaft of bright warmth swept the vegetation like a lighthouse beam, varnishing the leaves with brilliance, hanging bright vaporous trails between the tree trunks: the sun was rising and the sight of the dawn and the sunshine gave Stephanie back her strength, courage and hope.

'Nothing is ever lost while the sun still shines and one's heart is still beating!'

Her own heart was beating more rapidly than usual and she felt a little breathless and weary after her long march, but it beat strongly and regularly, stout enough to meet any emergencies. Stephanie felt a sudden irrational happiness and elation wash over her.

'I'll find a way out of all these problems, I'll get through somehow, I always do!'

Could the White Man ever be trusted?

Atai's retort took the wind out of Stephanie's sails, and for a moment she could not think of anything to say. Because of course he was right. The kanakas had sold their islands and peninsulas to the Whites on condition that no one interfered with their traditional crops, or invaded their forests, but everywhere now White farmers and planters were laying waste to acres of jungle to plant crops, and fencing in the rich soil on the hillsides.

"Don't you trust me, Atai?"

"I trust you, Madame Stephanie, you are loyal to our cause, but the others are not like you."

What could she say? There was no gainsaying the truth of what he said. Then he said gently, "Your Emperor will reply to me. He is your great friend, so Eugenie tells me."

She had indeed said so. It would have been impossible to retract the lie now. In fact she felt obliged to reinforce it if only to gain face with Atai.

"He will reply, he is an honest and kindly man like you. But you ought to set me free before then!"

He laughed shortly. "You must wait as I do. We both trust him. It is many moons before a ship may sail to France and back. You are not unhappy?"

"You are gracious, Atai."

He would reappear every three or four days. Things had turned out rather differently from what she had excitedly pictured to herself. Atai kept her in this most secret and inaccessible valley where every cave in the basalt cliffs provided a hiding place. The sun shone down on them from a sky of the bluest blue imaginable. Stephanie was spinning out the luncheon, which she took with Aimé and Eugenie, for as long as she could. They were served by Aravihi, who bustled about as breathlessly as the old nurse in a classic play. The menu, which never varied, consisted of baked yams, which she adored, taro root, strips of raw fish, more fish baked between heated stones in lieu of an oven, game birds roasted on a spit, haunches of venison which she found dreadfully over-seasoned, fresh juicy fruit and coconut milk. Eugenie was chattering happily, toying with the yards of imitation pearls Stephanie had given her and which she wore as if they were worth a king's ransom, when a tall kanaka suddenly jumped to the ground a few feet from the rock where they were sitting. He leapt about screaming and shouting like a man possessed by the devil, spreading alarm throughout the entire camp. He knocked over the cooking pot with one sweep of his spear, scattered the glowing embers with a kick, destroyed the hot stone oven and then raced about in demented circles.

"Hurry, hurry, Mistress."

Eugenie was in a panic. Stephanie and Aimé had only understood one fact clearly from this scene—the 'enemy' had encircled their valley. But were they Whites or kanakas? She knew from Aimé and Eugenie that the natives waged war between one tribe and another and one valley and the next. A hard core of the old kanakas blamed Atai for his 'softness' towards the Whites, and his repeated attempts to come to terms with them.

The next moment saw the whole camp filled with frenzied activity. With Aimé half-dragging her after him, Stephanie scrambled up the rocky slopes to her cave, reached through an almost invisible crack in the hillside shrouded by a trembling curtain of greenery. Once safely inside she lay down on the rough earthen floor, with Aimé one side and Eugenie the other, her face pressed against the opening from which she could observe what went on down in the valley. At the sound of shuffling footsteps she turned her head and saw that they were surrounded by a guard of kanakas standing with drawn bows and arrows pointing.

The fires were still smouldering faintly though the valley was quite deserted when the first man came in sight, quite alone, wearing black boots, white breeches and shirt open at the breast. Yann! Her heart stopped beating for a moment. She closed her eyes, clenching her teeth to repress the cry of love, fear and terror which rose in her at the sight of him. She flung a despairing look at Aimé, beseeching him to do something. He quelled her with a glance, and mouthed the single word 'Silence'. Everything depended on her self-control now—and there were more than a hundred poisoned arrows aimed at Yann's heart!

Yann's men filed uneasily into the valley, guns at the ready. They walked slowly, glancing all around them anxiously. Yann examined the smoking remains of their fires, shaking his head doubtfully. Someone must have signalled their approach. Either the kanakas had fled, or they were lurking in ambush somewhere. He pointed out the jagged spurs of rock enclosing the valley and the troops began a cautious ascent.

With Aimé and Eugenie gripping her fast and the guard of archers following, Stephanie shrank further and further back into the dark recesses of the cave. At last she crouched in a narrow crevice, followed by Aimé, Eugenie and Aravihi, and the guard stood covering them.

A sound of boots and voices. "Anything there?"

"The swine have cleared off! I don't like the look of it."

Had they but known that at that moment seven deadly arrows were aimed straight at them!

"Shall we dig in here?"

"No point. The place is deserted."

The click of boot heels faded away and the pressure

of bodies weighting her down gradually eased. She was obsessed by her longing to see Yann again, she could think of nothing else.

She crept back to the mouth of the cave, still guarded by Eugenie and Aimé and the escort of kanakas. Yann was down there, giving orders to the men and watching them climb each rock face before returning to report: "Nothing, they've gone, sir."

'Oh, if only they'd give up and go and look somewhere else!' Stephanie thought in anguish. 'It only needs the smallest thing, for someone to stumble, or let off a gun by accident, and they'll be struck down by a hail of poisoned arrows as surely as Saint Sebastian—and *he*'s the most tempting, easy target imaginable!'

It looked as if he might be struck dead at any moment. For Stephanie, forced to look on in helpless silence, it was an appalling torment, and it lasted more than two hours!

At last his voice rang out strongly in the order to depart: "This way, men!"

Stephanie watched him disappear feeling quite weak with the strain of the past two hours. The soldiers vanished into the jungle like termites. The valley was once more deserted, and she was free to return. She turned suddenly and buried her face in Aimé's shoulder, she needed the consoling strength and warmth of a man just then. And no one knew better how she felt than Aimé, he who was always her port in a storm.

"Thanks to you, Madame, they are all alive and well."

It was just what she needed to hear. He held her close to him, as he had done once before in the Place de l'Etoile. She huddled against him: in spite of René, Boris, Yann, in spite of all the others, he was still the most important man in her life. For him she was the ever-present but inaccessible ideal, eternal woman, the universal Maya.

She looked into his face imploringly, still shaky from her recent experience.

"When are we going to be rescued? These natives aren't cruel people. They could easily have murdered them all but they didn't. I don't want them killed, I don't want any bloodshed. We ought to confer with them, they have their rights, this is their country. Aimé, when ... when can we get away?"

"Soon, Madame."

The reply was prompt and assured, and it took her breath away. He spoke as if it was settled that they should leave that night, or the next morning. What had he found out, what was he planning? Of course he still slept with Eugenie every night and pillow talk is pillow talk, whether the filling is grass or feathers. Usually men talk more freely, but with a man as reserved and calculating as Aimé, it would certainly be the women who unburdened themselves, fascinated and a little unnerved by his enigmatic manner, his long silences and the dark, brooding intensity of his eyes. He knew how to make his eyes eloquent, charging them with mystery and promise.

"You were saying?" she asked, all her fear and anguish forgotten.

"Nothing of importance ... Madame honours me with her trust, I would advise her to relax and be easy. It will all come right in due course."

He laid her down gently on her bed of ferns, stood contemplating her for a moment with a quiet, reassuring smile and then slipped out, leaving her in Aravihi's care.

The days followed upon each other with depressing monotony. The moon waxed and waned in the sky and Stephanie lost all track of time. The thought of another love feast approaching sapped her courage and confidence. The prospect terrified her. She was helpless, and helplessness was demoralising.

Atai always appeared in the evenings, almost as if he were born anew of the setting sun. He always appeared where one least expected him. On one occasion her heart would skip a beat to come across him leaning against a rock, motionless as a statue; another time she would suddenly come upon him perched in a tree as if it had given spontaneous birth to him. If she happened to be in the cave where she slept, the welcoming cries of the kanakas, a strange, vibrant sound which arose and subsided as swiftly as a snuffed candle, were the first warnings of his arrival. He would stride to meet her, a sure-footed, virile figure, as if the valley were quite deserted. It was not till he had paid her his respects that he condescended to notice the kanakas prostrated along his path.

'That's all very fine,' she would think, 'but it means nothing at all unless he views me as his equal, or a valuable hostage. I mustn't count on any of these people. I am fond of them, but they frighten me. They belong to him. Even Eugenie jumps to obey at a snap of his fingers. Still, it's a good thing that Aimé spends so much time chattering to them.'

Aimé, as usual, was full of surprises.

"Napoleon knows where we are," he announced one day.

Her hand flew to her throat. 'I mustn't let myself appear too excited,' she reminded herself. 'But really, Aimé shouldn't fling these thunderbolts straight in my face without warning.'

She moved nearer to him. "Who told you?"

"Aravihi."

"But how could she have seen him? She's never been out of our sight!"

"I don't know, but perhaps . . ."

"Perhaps what?" she cried, infuriated by his habit of leaving unfinished sentences hanging in mid-air.

"Perhaps because of what took place when I was . . . er . . . unconscious. It seems that during the feasting she . . ."

"She raped you, my dear man, you didn't know a thing about it!"

He answered with a touch of male pride, "I seem to have earned her gratitude, Madame."

A faint, almost imperceptible smile twitched the corners of his mouth and glimmered in his eyes. He was enjoying himself.

"Do you think it's kind to keep me on tenterhooks?"

"I think we can trust Eugenie too, she has come over to our side."

"You mean she was undecided before?" Stephanie exclaimed in some surprise.

"W-e-ell, let us say she was waiting to see before making up her mind. She is pregnant. I am going to be a father, Madame."

The news was scarcely astonishing in the circumstances, but Stephanie stared at him open-mouthed for a moment. Then she had to stifle an irresistible urge to laugh. There was something ludicrous about his approaching fatherhood. So the Becave children in the Vendée were to be blessed by a little half-caste brother or sister whose existence they would never know about!

"Madame's mirth is hardly tactful in view of the fact that the infant was fathered in her service. My one motive was to win her a useful ally. Now that she believes the curse upon her to have been lifted, Eugenie is definitely for us."

It was not like Aimé to repeat a statement without good reason. He must have a plan.

"You think Eugenie . . . ?"

"Thanks to her, Atai has consented to see Yves Kerdelec. That is more than I dared hope for. I had to put the idea into her head without asking her outright, and it has taken me some time. I did not tell Madame before because I was afraid of falsely raising her hopes."

Stephanie was stunned by the news. All this had been quietly arranged behind her back, without her suspecting a thing. But why the helpless old invalid rather than his son?

"But the poor old man will never be able to get through the forest in his condition. Yann should have come instead."

"Madame is being foolish if she supposes Eugenie would wish Atai to receive Yann after what happened between them," Aimé protested. "There are many things Madame does not know. The Great Master has always protected the natives, and they look to him as their sole arbiter. This is quite unofficial, and has nothing to do with the administration or the law, but it is a fact. As a rule any 'disputes' that arise are dealt with by him in the village. Madame seems to forget that our release from captivity has depended for the past weeks on the hypothetical reaction of a non-existent empire and a dead emperor!"

This was the literal, brutal, frightening truth.

"The whole situation is quite incredible!" she murmured.

"If Madame read more history she would know that what has befallen us here is by no means incredible or extraordinary even though it doesn't happen every day. Worse things have happened in the past."

"I believe you, Aimé. All the same I find what is happening to us now, hour by hour, quite dramatic enough. Do you think we shall be allowed to return with Yves?" she asked, trying to sound nonchalant.

Aimé's eyes held hers for a moment. "Let us hope so, Madame," he said at last.

"You mean you don't know for sure?" she cried.

"Now, listen—even if we aren't set free at once we shall automatically come under Yves' protection. Talks between Atai and himself will have begun, and Atai will have had to guarantee our safety. Our value, you might say, will have greatly increased. This way we are certain to be released sooner or later: previously the outlook was much less hopeful. With the army and police out searching for us, and planning bloody reprisals, our lives were in continual danger. I can tell you now that there was a time when I expected to be tortured and killed at any moment. But now everything is settled and it has all turned out for the best."

He sounded so confident and pleased with himself that Stephanie knew he wanted to be questioned further.

"How do you know all this?" she asked.

A faint smile flickered over his face and he coughed

discreetly. "They keep me informed."

"Who do?"

He paused, for dramatic emphasis. "My two ... women!"!"

"Two?" she exclaimed admiringly. "Congratulations."

"I can joke about it, Madame, but I assure you it is no joking matter. We have Eugenie to thank—a mother-to-be finds it hard to refuse the father of her baby anything—and Aravihi too. The poor creature has great hopes of me; there is a shameless explicitness about her caresses which would make a monkey blush!"

"You aren't blushing though!" Stephanie pointed out, amused by Aimé's bland way of recounting the most indelicate facts with an air of cherubic innocence.

"Didn't someone say that a man can become accustomed to anything?"

"Especially if he enjoys it," Stephanie retorted. "Well, I find it an encouraging proof ..."

"Encouraging?"

"Proof that man has come a long way since his monkey days. Take your own evolution: nothing shocks or offends you any more. You have learnt to accept Aravihi's caresses as a worthy tribute to your procreative powers!"

"Madame embarrasses me ..."

"Nonsense, you know quite well that you've been dying to get me to talk to you like this. I've yet to meet the man who could resist the cult ... the cult of himself."

She could not quite bring herself to say 'the ancient cult of the phallus' but Aimé guessed what she meant, and he glanced down as coyly as a convent school miss, secretly flattered by the references to his virility. Like all men he was delighted to picture himself in the role of stallion.

'Where would we be without men?' Stephanie was thinking. 'Without men to make us live and love and swoon under them, we would be empty, nothing! Oh, Yann, Yann, how long will it be before you make love to me again? I want to belong to you, to feel you on top of me, crushing me to you till I groan with joy, and melt and sink away into oblivion with you ...'

"She keeps trying to catch me unawares, or to drug me so that I can go through a repeat performance," Aimé went on, unable to drop this enthralling topic of conversation. "Anyway, thanks to Eugenie and Aravihi, I've managed to build up a sort of information service."

The last remark was uttered with such cool matter-of-factness that it brought Stephanie up short.

'Information service indeed! What a canny fellow he is! He couldn't resist telling me about his conquests—that was the old Adam preening in him—but now we are back to the sturdy peasant who knows exactly what he's playing at, and why.'

He was rubbing his hands now, as he flashed a searching, but ambiguous look at her.

"Monsieur Kerdelec's visit will be my first victory. Everything is going very well, very well indeed!"

"Aimé ..."

"Madame will forgive me if I ask her not to interrupt. I must ask her to trust me implicitly, and to accept whatever may happen without protest. Madame will obey ... not me, exactly, but whatever proposals I may put to her as a result of circumstances as yet unforeseen."

What lay behind this pompous rigmarole? What was Aimé hatching? Suspecting that she was going to be asked to do something unwelcome, she asked carefully, "What, without argument or discussion, Aimé?"

He brushed all future objections aside almost flippantly.

"Knowing my eternal devotion to her, Madame will realise that I am acting with her best interests at heart. According to my information Monsieur Kerdelec will be arriving in two or three days. His arrival will be celebrated by feasting. They will dance the pilou-pilou. Madame need not be anxious on my behalf: decency and respect for her presence will oblige me to remain out of sight, but I shall not be in any danger. Exhaustion, perhaps, but one recovers! I am not over-partial to their alcoholic beverage, I can't help worrying about its effect on my liver. However, at the time, it is quite astonishingly effective; one feels ready and able to satisfy all the ... er, suppliants!"

How characteristic of Aimé to mix anxiety over his health, satisfaction at his own superhuman prowess and the frankest and most scurrilous details with an elaborate courtly manner which would have done credit to an eighteenth-century Marquis!

The feast began on a somewhat subdued note.

Stephanie had been watching the sun's course in the sky, which gave her a rough idea of the time, when Aimé appeared to conduct her to her cave. "He has arrived, everything is in order for this evening," he told her.

"Where is he?"

"Patience, patience ... these people set great store by the proper ritual, and we mustn't do anything to upset them."

She went with him docilely. She spent some time on her face, creaming and powdering it and applying discreet, flattering touches of colour on her lips and eyelids. Eugenie arranged her hair. Aravihi laced her into her corset and tight boots, rubbing the latter with a dab of spit to make them shine. And, as before, Aimé set about decorating her like a Christmas tree: bunches of artificial flowers so bright they made the real ones look insignificant, shiny ribbon bows, sparkling pendants and drops, hideous festoons of imitation pearls threaded in and out of the folds of her skirt and neckline. She wore one jewel on her fingers—Armand's sapphire ring, hoping and praying that it would bring her luck.

"Madame will stay here until he arrives."

Unexpectedly, however, Atai paid her the courtesy of coming to fetch her from her cave. The valley below was lit by dancing, flickering torch flames. Yves was already in place on the dais. She recognised his chair and the rug over his knees, and, to her surprise the figures of Claude and Alfred, the two runaway kanakas, standing on each side of him.

'Either they returned of their own accord, or—which seems unlikely—Yves had them recaptured, or they are also part of Aimé's information service.'

Cross-legged at Yves' feet, like Buddha himself, was the inevitable Moses. He sat watching her approach like an inscrutable idol, but for the very first time, she saw something like life flicker in the depths of those dim, blank eyes.

Remembering the elegant way Aimé had walked with Stephanie's hand resting lightly on his, Atai escorted her to the dais with old-world ceremony. His legs and torso were bare, apart from a loin cloth interwoven with pink and pearly shells. She counted more strands of sharks teeth necklaces than the time before, and on this occasion sprays of feathers adorned his arms, shoulders and hair.

She reached the dais and took her seat. With a sudden, impulsive moment which made her shrink back a little, Moses seized her hand and kissed the blue stone in her ring. The thought of those lips touching Armand's stone seemed almost sacrilegious. Stephanie shivered. She had to snatch her hand away because his fingers had tightened on hers like a child who doesn't want to give up a toy.

"My daughter!"

Yves held out his arms to her and his dry lips brushed her cheek. Though somewhat surprised to be addressed as 'daughter' she returned his kisses with filial affection, pressing her lips to his parchment cheeks, murmuring her gratitude for his arrival.

"Thank you, Father!"

"Take your seat, child."

First daughter, now child! This must all be part of some mysterious plan too obscure for her to follow. As she took her seat between Yves and Atai she remembered that they had spent several hours in conversation together that afternoon, according to Aimé.

'Don't try to rush things.' She remembered his warning. 'Bear in mind that here on the islands men make the laws and the women hold their tongues! Yves will speak to you in good time, let him speak first.'

She managed to assume a serene, queenly smile as she watched the dancers circling to the dull beat of the tom-toms, but inwardly she seethed with impatience.

Slowly the rhythm of the drums quickened, and flutes and strings joined in; the circle of dancers split in two as the men surged forward to the dais, feet drumming. They flung up their arms in salutation, and voiced their greetings in staccato shouts to which the shrill cries of the women arose in response. The women were gathered into a half circle now, swaying and clapping excitedly. As the men began falling back to join them, Yves bent closer to Atai.

"Your warriors are valiant men, Mahana, Child of the Sun."

"To behold you and dance for you is an unforgettable honour for them, Great Master," Atai replied.

'The exchange of civilities is beginning,' Stephanie told herself. 'Protocol must have its way. Now they'll be raining bigger and better compliments on each other till ...'

"Your courage, Atai ... and yours, Great Master ... the valour of the one, then the other, the greatness, goodness, wisdom in judgment, purity of soul ..." the compliments fell as thick and fast as hailstones.

'This inventory could go on for ever,' Stephanie thought, seething with exasperation beneath her smiling mask. 'He came here on my behalf, I'm the prize at stake and I might just as well not be here. I shall insist on seeing him tomorrow, or even tonight ... I have to speak to him!'

She was quietly working herself up into a fury.

"Doctor Verdonnet asked me to pay his respects to you."

Stephanie gave a startled jump. Through at last with the polite speeches due to his host, Yves was leaning towards her, assuring her of the continued respect of Doctor Verdonnet. Stephanie was surprised that he should choose such a banal opening gambit but she snatched at it nevertheless.

"Thank you very much, how nice of him. Could you tell me . . ."

He laid one hand warningly over hers and she stopped.

She let him speak. He chatted to her about the folk at the Island Hotel, about sailors who were complete strangers to her, and a whole lot of other people she scarcely knew, but he avoided any reference to the judge, military commander or governor, any of the people searching for her now. He was showing her that she must avoid the smallest allusion to her kidnapping or subsequent captivity. All she could think of was Yann. Yves must have known, but for all the mention he made of his son he might never have existed.

"I am here for several days, Stephanie."

The first encouraging thing he had said! She fixed imploring eyes upon him but he chose that moment to turn back to Atai, leaving her alone with her thoughts.

'Several days,' she thought miserably. 'But will I get a chance to see him alone or to talk to him without witnesses? I must tell him about the poisoned arrows, tell him to warn Yann. Yann must stay and wait for me in Noumea, I'll get back there one of these days . . . Yves must tell him that I love him, that I think only of him . . .'

"Atai . . ."

Stephanie did not hear what Yves asked him, but a moment later the Mahana sprang to his feet, an imposing figure towering over the valley and his people. A great yell went up from the kanakas, and with that he launched himself into the air like an arrow and landed on the grass below with the slow panther-like grace which fascinated Stephanie. The men fell back a little way and some women entered the ring of dancers and the dance of provocation and desire had begun.

"Don't move, Stephanie, don't take your eyes off him. He is dancing for us . . . smile at him and listen to me.

"Two nights hence a young boy will take your hand

and guide you away from this place. He will take you to the sea where a boat is waiting and Yann ..."

Till then she had heard him out without so much as a flicker, but at the mention of Yann one hand flew up to screen her trembling lips, while the other gripped the arm of her chair to steady herself.

"And you?" she finally asked.

"I shall stay here to take your place."

Her smile froze, and her eyes remained fixed on Atai as he mimed the overtures to sexual passion before the twenty or so women who offered themselves to him, opening and closing their thighs in a hypnotic rhythm counterpointed by the harsh cries of the men whose bodies mimed the thrust and withdrawal of physical possession. Stephanie closed her eyes, love was too much on her mind already.

She could not think of accepting the frail old man's sacrifice. She could never abandon Aimé. Besides, Atai trusted her, she mustn't deceive him and betray him as all the other white men did. In Atai's eyes she and Yves were people apart, vastly superior to the rest of their countrymen.

She sighed, composed her features and then murmured in a faint but firm voice "No!"

Yves' eyes, with their other-worldly gaze which seemed so much more penetrating than most, fixed upon hers for a moment during which he seemed to be peering into her soul and reading her innermost thoughts.

"I understand your feelings, and I admire them, but ..."

His strange eyes flickered away and they seemed to draw her soul after them.

"I know what you are thinking, daughter, but you are still young and you must obey. Atai will hear how you refused to escape; he will see that you acted honourably. I shall protect Aimé, he is in no danger. One day you will be returning to France. Many things have happened, much will have changed. Life is all and it is nothing, a mere dream. Two nights hence! Don't protest ... don't say a word . . . Yann is waiting for you!"

She was too overwhelmed to speak. Brushing aside her strongly held objections as if they were of negligible importance, Yves had come straight out and ordered her to go and find Yann. It appeared that she had very little choice.

"I will follow the boy," she whispered.

Chapter Ten

A SOFT but sturdy hand grasped Stephanie's.

She had lain down that night fully dressed, wearing her laced boots and the simple unconstricting dress she had been wearing on the day of her abduction.

She followed the young boy whose adolescent figure was silhouetted for a moment against the mouth of the cave.

Not a word, silence.

Outside the entrance stood the two impassive totem sculptures, and a pair of kanaka guards sprawled on the ground in sleep.

Stephanie and the boy stole along the flank of the narrow valley, keeping to the shelter of the shrubs and trees, and using any available cover to cross any exposed places there might be. Suddenly the boy stopped and gazed up at the thick, tumbling mass of tropical vegetation.

'Behind this wall which seems to reach up to heaven we shall find the sea, the west, Yann!'

The lad was still holding her hand. Now he clapped both of his round it and shook it vigorously three times as if sealing a pact between them. As abruptly, he relinquished it and slipped into the torrent of greenery. Stephanie seized the first branch that came to hand and begun pulling herself up. The young kanaka hovered close beside her, a watchful, sturdy guide, showing her where to put her hands and feet, steadying her, giving her a helpful push from below. She knew instinctively that she could trust him.

The climb seemed endless, an exhausting battle with Nature in her most unhelpful mood, matted bushes and trees, great trailing lianas which threatened to trip one up. In her eagerness to get to the coast Stephanie took risks which would have made her shudder in normal circumstances, scrambling up hand-over-hand blind to the dangers of falling, broken limbs, and all that might bring in the way of pursuit and revenge on the part of Atai and his men.

A pale, slender moon hung in the sky but only the faintest glimmer of light filtered through the overhanging branches and leaves. She soon grew accustomed to the darkness, seeing her way like a cat. As they climbed the soil grew rockier and the vegetation thinned out.

'We'll soon be at the top, then down the other side and then ... Yann!' she told herself encouragingly as she swarmed up a smooth rock which seemed to offer nothing in the way of a hand-hold.

They reached a sloping plateau thickly covered with matted, prickly scrub, too dense to cross. They were forced to push their way along one side, scratching and tearing themselves on the thorny branches as they plunged through the elastic tangle, their feet slipping and sliding on the uneven, treacherous ground beneath.

A light breeze heralding the approach of dawn carried the scent of mimosas with it, and this told her that they would soon be descending below the thick belt of scrub they were painfully crossing.

The boy went ahead, reconnoitring the way. The night sky paled and grew milky. The sun was rising. There was nothing to be seen on the horizon but trees, and more trees. The blue below was the blue of the sky only. She had been so desperately eager for a glimpse of the sea that her eyes filled with tears. She fought against the pang of disappointment. This wasn't the moment to turn soft. She stood looking about her.

'It's a blow, but it would take more than that to slow me up now. Anyway there's water all around me, since I'm on an island.'

The boy glanced at her, then came striding back towards her. She could see his face now, and the colour of his skin. He was a half-caste, combining the strong, supple build of the kanakas with a face which, apart from a slightly thickened nose and lips, could have been pure European in its chiselled clarity of feature.

"You want rest, Madame?"

He thought she was tired. Well, she wasn't a bit!

"I was looking for the sea."

"Beyond the banyans, Madame."

At first glance it looked like green, and more green, but when she stared harder she could make out a great swathe of paler green—the scanty foliage of the niaoulis.

"You rest, Madame," the boy repeated with touching gentleness. "Plenty time. Boat for tomorrow ... tonight we sleep in forest."

"No!" she cut in." We'll sleep on the coast!"

He smiled widely, then flung up his arms and said in the same quiet gentle, friendly voice: "Forbidden! Tomorrow I take you like they told me."

She realised that nothing would induce him to go against his instructions. She wondered who had given them to him, not that it mattered.

"What's your name?"

"Maurice."

The name was like a blow to the heart and she reeled for a moment, overwhelmed by the weight of memories it conjured up. Maurice de Bourdeilles! André's son, little Maurice, and Valentine ... then she thought of her oldest children, the twins, for whom she always had a soft spot: her four children who were living with Françoise. All at once she ached to hold them and kiss them. As she thought about them, and the happy home they lived in, it never even entered her mind that she had another child, Diane, her daughter and René's. Everything to do with the Hotel de Guinchamp was sponged clean from her mind.

She composed herself, swallowed back the tears and then murmured with a special tenderness for this boy who would have been about the same age as her own Maurice, "That's a nice name."

"Pure chance, Madame Stephanie."

"Chance?"

"Missionary gentlemen got a list, and Maurice came up for me—his feast day 22 September, when I was born. Saint Maurice loved horses, like me—I adore horses."

Yielding to a sudden impulse and hoping to persuade him to change his mind, she cried: "I tell you what—I'll give you a horse of your own if you will get me to the sea tonight!"

He flinched, staring at her angrily. In the space of a second his charming, open expression had changed to one of hatred. What had she said? She had promised him a horse? He should be jumping for joy! The truth hit her like a thunderbolt. She had wounded him to the core of his native ideal of honour by trying to bribe him like a worthless person. These poor natives were really quite morbidly touchy, the most innocent suggestions were received as unforgivable insults. The boy was trembling with anger, and when he replied the words burst out disconnectedly.

"If you give me a horse I kill it! I take you to sea tomorrow, Madame Stephanie, because my grandfather, Yves, tell me so!"

She went rigid with shock. If Yves was—what he said, then his father ... and just then, as the sun shone into them, she saw that his eyes held the tawny glints of Yann's.

"Maurice," she pleaded, taking a step towards him in the hopes of placating him and excusing herself.

He sprang away like a fish. "Don't touch me. Follow."

His voice was the harsh, toneless one she had heard before. He would carry out his orders—she had nothing to fear on that score—but she was miserable to think she had unintentionally wounded his pride. She would explain to Yann what had happened, he would know how to put matters right and convince the boy that she had not intended to bribe him or humiliate him. She walked behind in silence. She was worrying about the forthcoming night to be spent under the banyans and niaoulis, and she couldn't help wondering why Yann had forbidden them to wait for the boat on the coast. Maurice had clearly received precise instructions, and he had an instinct in these matters.

The day was a long and harassing one. She repressed the slightest signs of weariness. They picked fruit along the way to quench their thirst, and prepare themselves for the trek across the arid plain where the niaoulis grew. At the first belt of banyans she told herself that surely they could rest here. Maurice was examining the soil, sniffing at it like a hunting dog.

"Here!"

The first word he had spoken the whole day long. She sank down against a tree trunk. He stood looking down at her, weighing up her physical condition with an unfriendly eye. Stung by the contempt in his eyes, she said calmly,

"I stopped because you told me to. If Monsieur Kerdelec entrusted me to you, it must mean you are worthy of his confidence. But I'd like to point out that I am not tired, and I could go further!"

He nodded. Yes, it was true, she was strong. However, he was pleased by the compliment she had paid him, and when he spoke his manner was friendlier.

"Forbidden, Madame Stephanie."

"Why?"

The bluntness of the question disconcerted him. He gazed round suspiciously, then prowled in a circle scanning the ground and occasionally glancing up into the trees.

"Not safe," he said, returning towards her.

There was something like fear in his voice. He was very much on his guard, on the lookout for danger. Had he seen something? What was he afraid of? She knew it would be useless to ask, he simply wouldn't answer her. She took a long look at this half-caste son of Yann's. For Yann's sake she wanted to make friends with him, and still more to make him forget the tactless remark she had made in a thoughtless moment.

"Maurice, come and sit down beside me. You have rescued me, guided me here, you are as strong and brave as a man."

His eyes shone and he thrust out his chest proudly.

"I was chosen."

In those three words there was all the vaingloriousness of a man combined with the excitement of a child believing itself invincible. She knew that by speaking to him and complimenting him as a man, she would be increasing his prestige in his own eyes and in those of his tribe.

"Maurice," she half-murmured, half-chanted the name in gentle, maternal tones which touched the boy's heart.

"Madame Stephanie ..."

His voice was stern, but it was softening just perceptibly. She must go carefully, on tiptoe. She wondered how best to win him over. A look of Yann about him, and her knowledge of the kanakas' sexual precocity, led her to compliment him quite sincerely on his looks.

"You are very handsome, Maurice, and the women you love must be very happy."

"Maybe! More women always coming to me ... so I think they happy, and I pleased to make them happy with me."

Nothing could have been more simple, frank or natural. He seemed to be placing himself at her disposal, she felt, though without insisting upon it. He sank down cross-legged a few feet away, looking at her with candid pleasure as well as respect.

She suddenly couldn't think what to say to him. There were so many questions she burned to ask, but she knew he would resent them. It was a pity, as she had been longing to spend the night on a beach under the palms instead of on the hard earth under the sombre canopy of banyans.

"I don't seem to remember seeing you in the village the first night I went there."

"Napoleon carried you across ... I could have done ..."

He seemed genuinely distressed that he had not had the opportunity, and Stephanie was touched. His tone was frankly sensual but that was the way of the islands and Stephanie found it natural and appealing.

"I still remember the wonderful welcome I received."

"You most beautiful woman we ever see in our life! You one big world of love!"

Stephanie was a little taken aback by the violence of this declaration. She laughed lightly.

"You exaggerate, Maurice, I'm a woman, nothing more."

Manlike, he burst out, "You bewitched Yann!"

He was frankly envious of his father, and Stephanie was troubled for a moment. She thought of Yann, dizzy with longing for his kisses, his arms, his loving—she would be seeing him tomorrow! Maurice, she noted, had said 'Yann', not 'my father', almost as if he was forbidden to use the word. If it had not been for his outburst that morning she would not have discovered that Yves was his grandfather. Just then he asked, diffidently,

"Please not repeat what I tell you this morning when you say bad things to me like man trying to buy wife."

She recalled that a girl's dowry in the islands consisted of lengths of cloth, weapons, chickens, pigs, and where possible, a horse. The latter was obligatory in cases where a girl came to her wedding with one or two bastard children.

"It is a secret between us, Maurice. Tonight you will watch over me."

His face grew serious, and preoccupied again.

"Tonight and tomorrow, on the coast."

Why was he afraid of approaching the coast? Was there some threat hanging over them? She was afraid to cross-question him for fear of offending him again. He was on the alert for their safety and she trusted him. Nevertheless, a dull apprehension slowly took hold of her.

They were through the forest of banyans at last. Stephanie was rejoicing at the sight of waves creaming over the coral reef when an arrow whistled past and stuck quivering in the ground at her feet. She froze, paralysed with terror, gazing round for Maurice who had disappeared from sight, when another arrow struck the ground just behind her and a third fell a short way ahead. They all just missed her! Frightened as she was, she drew comfort from this—it must mean they wanted her alive! But who? Was it Atai's men?

"Don't move!"

Maurice's voice floated down to her from a great height. She suddenly saw him perched up in a tree. He must be trying to get an idea of the numbers against them. Just then he saw them—three of them, kanakas, who had come up silently as cats and now stood grinning and staring at her with cruel, gleaming eyes. Maurice broke the silence. He was speaking to them in their own tongue. Stephanie could not understand a word. As soon as they heard him the kanakas drew their bows, ready to defend themselves, and loosed off some warning arrows. Convinced that these must be Atai's men, although she did not recognise them, and hoping against hope that if Maurice escaped he might be able to return with help in time to rescue her, she cried out wildly,

"Don't shoot! I give myself up!"

"You escaped prison camp!"

So these were hunters of men engaged in running to earth the unfortunates who had escaped from their living hell? No doubt with her torn dress, scratched face, tousled hair and look of terror, she must have resembled some cornered animal.

"But I'm not..."

"You be punished, you kill your husband or your brothers, you bad woman," one of the kanakas suddenly roared out.

These were the lies the guards fed them when they talked them into hunting down convicts. And of course there was a reward to be collected too. What a bunch of swine they were! All the men and women who had been exiled for their part in the Commune were treated as murderers and criminals, quite indiscriminately and irrespective of their sentences. Stephanie realised that she must expect no pity from these men; they would carry her back to the settlement suspended by bound hands and feet from a pole, like an animal. Horrible! She had seen a man brought in like that, and then dumped, half dead, on the ground. His comrades had carried the poor wretch away while the chief warder paid out the money offered for his recapture.

But the worst of it was that if they took her to one of the small forced labour camps on the coast or in the interior, no one would know her or vouch for her being Madame Dytteville. These penal colonies were remote, isolated places to which the hard core of prisoners were sent as a punishment. It might be days, weeks, before she was found and rescued. She had obsolutely no idea where she was now. But Maurice knew ... Maurice would race off to the shore and look out for a fishing boat ... he might belong to Atai's tribe but he was first and foremost a Kerdelec. The Kerdelecs were known throughout the length and breadth of the island, she knew that for a fact. Maurice was Yann's son, and she placed all her hopes in him! It might be a vague hope but it comforted her.

The kanakas were calmly gathering up their arrows, making sure that the points had not been blunted. This did not surprise her. They had to bring back their quarry alive to claim the full reward. She shivered as she took in their strapping, brutal appearance. She hoped they would reach their destination before nightfall ... she was afraid of what they might do to her. The prison administration would be some sort of protection to her, but she knew her real help would come from the Communards themselves because the terrible experiences they shared had given these men and women a greathearted tenderness towards each other.

"Get along, go, you!"

They fell into step around her, pushing and prodding her forward. As fas as she could judge from the position of the sun, they were moving north—Noumea was to the south!

Stephanie had the impression that the path they were taking ran parallel to the coast.

'What will Yann do? Maurice must be attempting the impossible on my behalf.' She never doubted his good faith for a second. He had been entrusted with a misson, the mission had failed through no fault of his own, and he would feel bound to do all he could to rescue her even at the risk of his own life. His grandfather had commanded him to deliver her safely to his father. A sacred trust! Until he had carried out his part successfully, Maurice would know no rest.

There was a short halt for food. The kanakas took some strips of dried meat and fish out of a bag, and unwrapped a bundle of leaves to reveal a ball of some whitish substance. They offered her some.

"You want?"

She took it and tasted it; mushy, overcooked rice mixed with corn and bits of chicken. 'Well, it'll keep me going,' she thought, choking down the pasty, over-seasoned food.

"More?"

Not the moment to be dainty. She held out her hand and a dark palm passed her another sticky mouthful.

All that afternoon they pressed on, Stephanie and her three captors. She did what she could to delay them, pretending to be exhausted, dragging her feet, all in the hopes of giving Maurice time to catch up with them. But the men did not seem to object, they walked at the pace she set quite cheerfully, as if they knew they had time to spare. As they went Stephanie took mental notes of anything which could serve her as a future landmark. You never knew what might happen! She was more and more convinced that she was being taken to some inaccessible forced labour camp, miles from anywhere. She had no illusions as to the sort of treatment she might expect there. Still, anything was better than the company of these three savages whom she believed capable of anything.

'I'm not afraid for my life,' she told herself sturdily. 'The forced labour, well, I've known worse things. I'll get out sooner or later, I always do ... it'll be a matter of a few hours, or days perhaps. Maurice knows who these men are, he won't find it difficult to pick up the trail. And these savages have their tom-toms and drums for sending messages ... maybe they're beating out the news of my capture right now across the mountains and valleys of the island!'

She went on to herself in this vein, to keep up her spirits and pass the time. A few hours later the men halted a second time. She devoured the food they gave her hungrily, anxious to keep her strength up and to show no signs of defeat or discouragement.

'Keep going, that's the thing, while there's life there's hope.'

The sky flamed. Sunset! Night was approaching, and the thought oppressed her anxious heart. Night was a time of insidious terrors, of stealthy menace and fear. Stephanie belonged to the day, to the sun and wind, and she felt helpless against the subtle and sinister influences that gathered around her after dark. She suddenly told herself that never again, in future, would she suffer the gradual decline of daylight—the minute it began to get dark she would have everything lit around her—paraffin lamps, gas lamps, candles. This little sortie into the future cheered her, and gave her new courage.

"Here!" said one of the kanakas.

The exclamation brought her back to reality with a bump. Night was coming on, and now they proposed to camp here in the shade of the banyans for the night—three young, lusty males and herself! She lay down. The three men stretched out around her and she curled up nervously like a beast trying to keep warm. After such a long, exhausting day, she knew she would have no difficulty in getting to sleep—alarming though the circumstances were.

A tapping on her feet made her rear up like a startled snake. Then she saw that she had nothing to fear. Day was dawning and the three kanakas squatted round on their haunches, waiting for her to awake.

"You walk?"

"I walk!" she exclaimed, leaping to her feet. She was surprised that they had not tried to take advantage of her that night. If they had, what could she have done? Nothing. She would have suffered them. It showed that they were not such bad men after all.

"Is it far?" she asked.

"Over there!"

This was an exaggeration as she had to walk for several hours before the banyans thinned out and the soil grew stonier and more arid. Stephanie longed so passionately to hear the sound of waves breaking on coral reefs, imagining Yann's boat waiting at anchor in the lagoon to rescue her, that she seemed to hear a faint roaring in her ears and could not decide whether it was real or imaginary. Abruptly the path turned a corner and she found herself confronting a grey, stony desert of a place, a rocky canyon cleft by a fast moving river. On the banks she counted one, two . . . five stark buildings and some sheds. A prison camp; it could be nothing else. Stephanie felt grateful to the men for not having trussed her to a pole by her hands and feet like a dead deer. It was because she had shown herself docile and obedient. She gazed around her. There were human shapes standing in the rushing torrent, wraithlike under the glaring sun, and here and there she saw uniformed figures carrying guns.

She scrambled down the rocky path ahead of the kanakas, and when they reached the flat, pebbled ground below they nudged her towards the nearest hut. A flag hung from the pole beside it. She realised that this must be the office where new arrivals were checked in. Most of them would be forwarded here from the other convict camps at Nou and Ducos as a punishment for rebellious behaviour, or for trying to escape. As far as the authorities here were concerned she would be just another escaped convict recaptured by the kanakas.

She went into the building. A man stood up behind the thick wooden barrier which cut the room in two. A small man with a puffy face, swollen and flushed with alcohol.

"Where does she come from?" he asked.

"Not know," replied one of the kanakas.

"Better find out, she's not one of ours."

Terrified by the thought that he might reject her and send her back into the jungle with the kanakas, Stephanie cried challengingly, "I am Madame Dytteville!"

"Like hell you are!"

She wasn't going to start bandying insults.

'Just wait till the kanakas have gone, then we'll see,' she thought.

Hope thrilled in her briefly when the man suddenly disappeared behind the wooden partition and she heard rattling drawers and the chink of coins. He came back, unlocked a little gate in the partition and approached her captors. The coins clinked monotonously into the outstretched hands, five coins to each man. She seemed to remember that the minimum reward was thirty pieces, which meant that he was keeping half back for himself.

'That's handy,' she thought, 'he takes bribes.'

"Off you go then, boys. Bring me more of these scarecrows and I'll pay you for them at the same rate!"

"Thank you, Great Chief."

The kanakas, unaware that they had been cheated, went off happily with their money and Stephanie turned to face the prison guard. She was quite confident that the misunderstanding could be cleared up in a minute.

"Monsieur, I really am Madame Dytteville," she repeated, keeping her voice steady.

"Balls to that one!"

"That's all very well, but it isn't an answer," she said, adopting a haughty manner which she thought might impress him. "Even if you don't recognise my name you must have heard of the Kerdelecs."

"I've heard of them, they hang out in Noumea. Every single time they bring me in an escaped convict I have to listen to this rigmarole about rich protectors, and references. You make me puke!"

"I swear . . ."

"Save your breath, I don't give a shit for your promises!"

"I know, but . . ."

She was ready to promise anything in return for her release, but he didn't give her time to begin.

"But what?"

A stunning slap across the face sent her reeling back against the partition.

"You'll pay me back for that slap, capital and interest, just you wait and see!"

"Oh, cheeky are we? Haven't you had enough, you dirty slut?"

He looked like a madman, advancing upon her with bloodshot eyes, lips trembling, and fat, stubby fingers outstretched like claws. She flung up her arms defensively, unprepared for the kick and the brutal knee jab which doubled her up moaning with pain.

"You dirty, stinking slut, where d'you come from?"

"I . . ."

"You're shit, nothing but shit, d'you hear? You tried to get fresh with Pepere did you? Nobody gets away with that, let me tell you, nobody gets fresh with Pepere round here! It isn't healthy! They don't last very long!"

"That's too bad," she replied, her voice flat with weariness. She wasn't going to knuckle under to this brute, no matter how useless defiance might be. It was no use expecting anything of this gross little man with the piggy eyes and purple flush of a habitual wine drunkard.

A blow struck her head that would have felled an ox and she dropped to the floor, huddling against the wooden partition in the faint hope of averting some of the kicks and blows that rained on her. She began to miss the kanakas. At least they had left her alone, while this little brute . . .

She lay still, groaning feebly, too weak to fend off the blows. Abruptly, they ceased. She heard a door open. The man called out hoarsely in his thick, alcoholic's voice: "Fernand!"

Through a mist of pain, she was conscious of approaching footsteps.

"Take this dirty cow out of here for me. She's to do two yards a day! Show her the ropes."

'Two yards of rock breaking a day!' That was what the convicts had to do at Noumea, she had seen them!

"She couldn't do that in the state she's in, boss. Anyway it isn't woman's work."

That must be Fernand. She saw him bending over her.

"Come along."

"Do what you like with her," said Pepere.

She felt sympathy in the man's touch for his fingers were gentle enough although he made as if to seize her roughly to please Pepere.

"You need gloves to handle creatures like her!" Pepere bellowed.

"I'll manage," the other man muttered disgustedly, "though . . ."

He slipped both arms round her to lift her. She struggled up to receive another kick from Pepere across the shins. A parting gift. She gave a faint, smothered cry. Fernand half dragged her out of the hut.

"Pull yourself together."

She uttered a faint sound by way of an answer.

"What's your name?"

"Stephanie," she gasped.

"No, your surname."

"Dytteville."

"What, same as the company?" he whispered, so startled that he almost let her go, and her knees buckled dangerously. He tightened his hold and she leant against him, trying not to make herself too heavy while he pulled her along. She murmured "It's true, I am ..."

"I can't do anything, Pepere's watching me, the swine. Look, I'll have to drop you now, the others will come and get you ..."

He let her fall and the stony ground bit painfully into her aches and bruises. He shouted to the prisoners.

"Three of you, that's all I need. Keller, Greboura, Lafaye—that'll be enough!"

Three faces swam into focus above her; two were men's, one a woman's. They all had the same tanned, leathery skin stretched tightly across their bones. Their eyes seemed unnaturally large due to their emaciation, but there was a flicker of kindly concern in them, as well as something feverish and strange. Their bloodless lips were strips of cracked, crumpled skin.

Arms went round her, picked her up, carried her off ... she closed her eyes, dead to everything.

"After what she's been through the best thing would be to stick her in the water."

The voice was precise and authoritative, like a nurse's voice prescribing anaesthetics.

Stephanie felt herself being lowered into the river, with someone supporting her head. The water, which must have been about two foot deep, foamed and bubbled round her as if she were a new rock in its bed, washing and soothing and easing the pain of her bruises.

"Courage, child."

A man's voice. Her eyelids struggled open, and found herself looking into the kindliest eyes she had ever seen, the eyes of a father bent over a sick and suffering child. The face that went with the eyes seemed ageless. The voice was gentle ...

"Courage, child, stick it out, you aren't alone here, there's all of us."

"He'll get himself killed one of these days," said the woman, whose eyes had the hard brilliance of agates.

"Maybe I won't kill him, but I'll give him back the

kicks and blows, I'll see him spit his teeth out!" Was it really her, Stephanie, thinking things like that?

"Who are you?" the man asked.

"Madame Dytteville."

The face lengthened, and the skin seemed to stretch even tighter over his face and skull as the man reflected. Then he whispered slowly "Dytteville ... I seem to have heard the name before, a long time ago."

"In Paris?" Stephanie breathed.

"Paris!" The same smothered exclamation burst from all three of them simultaneously, and their sunken eyes lit up. Paris! The city where they had spent their youth, city of memories both joyful and sad. Perhaps they had been born there, still had families living there. Unforgettable, faraway Paris, heart and centre of the civilised world.

"Maitre Keller, barrister," said the first man, introducing himself almost as if they had met in some fashionable drawing-room.

"Greboura," said the other in a light, attractive voice. "Georges Greboura, G.G. to my friends and the ladies, a journalist."

"There's no time for that nonsense," the woman broke in hurriedly. "Juju's taking aim."

A bullet struck the ground two yards off and Stephanie started.

"A warning," the woman remarked indifferently. "We're doing too much talking, he doesn't like that. He's enjoying himself. Here, we'll get you back on your feet now."

They set her upright, supporting her as if she were a sapling whose roots needed planting. She concentrated on keeping her balance.

"Stick it out, you've got to, understand?" the woman told her, turning her bright, intent gaze upon Stephanie as if trying to hypnotise her. "You've got no choice. I'll be back soon."

She let go of her and made her way over to the cobbled

pathway where she slipped her feet into a pair of wooden clogs. Then she went across to a sort of log cabin where the tools and implements were kept. An armed man stood guard at the door. It was only then that Stephanie noticed the state she was in, her torn, muddy dress, the bodice in rags and tatters. If she had been a beggarwoman standing at the doors to a church her plight would have touched the stoniest heart.

She looked the lawyer and journalist over slowly. On the former the ragged remains of a once sturdy canvas jacket hung upon a skeletal frame. The journalist's shoulders and body were still sturdy and massive, though there was little flesh on the bones. Then, moving her head with difficulty, she scanned the river banks and the rushing torrent between. Human beings, live human beings, all clad in the same coarse spun uniform, faded to colourlessness in some cases, almost new in others, were engaged in dipping large round wooden platters into the water, shaking and apparently washing them ...

"What are they doing?" Stephanie asked, dismayed.

"Looking, we'll show you," said Keller.

"How many of us are there here?"

She asked the question softly. It wasn't till she had spoken that she was dismayed to realise that she had included herself, quite unthinkingly, in the 'us'!

"Twenty-one men, five women," Greboura replied, as matter-of-factly as if he was reading off the contents of a cattle truck.

She was the sixth woman to be flung into this Gehenna!

"Watch out ... Pepere!"

The warning came from a man who passed them in the water a few feet away. He spoke without moving his lips or glancing at them. She looked after him, as he made for the shore.

"Don't look!" Greboura commanded. "You take things in here as though you weren't listening. This is a prison camp! Now, you're on your own, my beauty."

He released her abruptly at the precise moment when

Keller relaxed his hold.

By some miracle, through sheer strength of will, she managed to stay upright.

The woman returned with a large sieve like the ones everyone else carried. She left her clogs on the dry paved area and joined them.

"I'll show you," she murmured, quickly scooping up a sieveful of water, gravel and pebbles. "Quick, the bastard's looking this way!"

Stephanie realised that the bastard must be Pepere, and that she was going to have to learn how to wash pebbles and gravel.

"This soil is gold-bearing, but not to any marked extent," said Maitre Keller, bending towards her. "So you see ..."

His practised eye detected some pale, yellowish granules in the gravelly sand at the bottom of the sieve, and these he deftly extracted and stowed in the pocket hanging from his belt.

"When your pocket is full you empty it over there."

She saw a large barrel, into which two men were engaged in emptying their bags.

"Allow me, lovely lady."

Greboura fastened a cord with a bag round her waist. The woman must have given it to him.

"Now you're ready to start," he said, showing her how to hold the sieve and the proper movements for bringing up gold-bearing river gravel.

"Do it like ... no ... yes, that's better ... keep it easy and rhythmical ... bend towards the water like this, but don't overdo it or you will tire yourself unnecessarily ..."

A bullet ricocheted a few feet away.

The woman straightened up angrily, set her hands on her hips and shouted: "If you want me to show her, give me time! Do you want to show her yourself?"

Stephanie followed the direction of her stare. A guard sat watching them from a rock fifty feet or so higher up the ravine. He let off a bullet from time to time, it seemed, as a warning to the convicts not to spend too much time talking, and to get on with their pan-handling.

"Hop to it! Juju's worse than Pepere and there's nothing he enjoys more than practising his marksmanship. He can riddle a tin thrown into the air or cut a hair clean in two. I'd better leave you now or I'll be due for a bit of 'treatment'!"

'Treatment must mean punishment, in this case the whip.'

Stephanie began working on her own, sifting the cloudy water in search of the dull glint of gold. If she concentrated on the job with all her strength she might be able to forget the plight she was in, or so she hoped, but she reckoned without her poor, bruised and battered body which kept seizing up on her like a rusty machine part. She had been so proud of its supple strength during her escape through the jungle; now, it was letting her down. What was it Saint-Arnaud used to say? 'If the will holds, the body will fall into line!' Something like that.

'Well, I'm not going to let my nerve crack, no matter what happens. They must be out searching for me now, and it won't be long before ... *how* long, I wonder?'

How long? It might be weeks, months even, before Maurice and Yann picked up the trail leading to this camp.

A wave of despairing terror swept over her and she stumbled.

"Stick it out, child," came Keller's encouraging whisper.

"Stick it out, Dytteville," Greboura called a little more loudly.

"Come on now, you don't want to give Pepere a treat!" the woman said sharply.

"Don't give up," said an unknown voice.

"We're here," said another.

A choir! Like the different parts in an oratorio the voices seemed to reach out and comfort her. She knew nothing about any of these people and they knew as little about her, but they were all thinking about her, responsive to her suffering. 'I'm working in a convict settlement!' It was hard to believe, and she still couldn't take it in. But how marvellous that such compassion and brotherly love should be born of misfortune, injustice and hatred. She was no longer alone! One and twenty men and five women, as Greboura said, were her comrades and friends. She dug her boots—stretched and badly worn after her long trek through the forest—more securely into the river bed, gripped her sieve tightly and swung her arms as she had been shown ... as the minutes passed she found her stiffness and soreness lessening almost miraculously. At each step Armand's ring, which she had hidden in her waistband, chafed against her skin.

'What luck!' Pepere had been so busy beating her up that he'd neglected to search her. 'What luck, what luck!' The ring was worth a fortune. But more than that, it was her most precious souvenir, of Armand her husband, of the arranged marriage which had changed to a marriage of true love. At each step she took, at every breath she drew, she seemed to hear his voice whispering: 'I'm here, my one and only love, I'm with you, watching over you, keeping you safe!' And then there was the compassionate tenderness of the convicts supporting her like an outstretched hand. At Dobruja the men had come to her for love and comfort, and her help in their dying, but here it was the other way round—they came to help her! Perhaps destiny was rewarding her. Faith in humanity, faith in mankind ... Armand had had that. Her eyes blurred over with foolish, loving tears. Almost without noticing it she had found the right rhythm for the job, as at each swing her sieve took up gravel, sand and river water. She shook it carefully, looking for grains or tiny nuggets of gold, setting aside any pebbles which seemed hopeful ... her bag gradually filled up.

The barrel, now. It was time to have a look at the thing. She redoubled her efforts, and soon managed to fill the cloth bag flapping at her side. Trying to look confident, though far from feeling it, she went across to the barrel and tipped the contents of her bag into it.

"From Paris, aren't you?"

The man knew without being told. He was unhealthy looking, flabby with fat.

'It must be the food they get,' she thought. 'In some cases, like Keller's, they burn it up but with a man like this it accumulates. I suppose they stuff themselves on potatoes, lentils, dried beans and peas.'

"Keep moving!" an unknown voice warned. "Don't ever look," Greboura had counselled.

Her face was quite impassive as she emptied her bag.

"Yes, I'm from Paris," she answered the man.

"Which district?"

"Better not mention the Hotel Guinchamp, that's much too grand." She thought of the Dytteville mansion, where her children lived and replied without moving her lips: "Observatoire."

"I'm from Port-Royal."

She was speaking without moving her lips as if she had been born to ventriloquism.

"We're neighbours," she said, almost gaily.

"What are you in for?"

"A mistake. And you?"

"I strangled my wife and brother. He was her lover but I got even with them ..."

She didn't hear the rest. Her blood ran cold: what was a common-law criminal doing mixed in with the Communards? She stepped back into the water which rushed past, buffeting her noisily. She trembled a little as she took up her former position.

"Keep working, for God's sake!"

That was the woman.

Stephanie swung her sieve again, but she was shuddering. "A murderer!"

"They mix us all up together ... that's the system!"

Keller's voice now, resigned, soft. "In defiance of the law ..."

"And of our rights ..."

"We're political prisoners ..."

"It's iniquitous ..."

"We'll get our own back one day ..."

Words and phrases were lost in the raging of the torrent, but there was no mistaking the anger.

"How many from the Commune?" she asked as she swung forward with her sieve.

"Fifteen ... two women ..."

"You'll be seeing them ... one of them's confined to barracks."

The words came bouncing towards her. It reminded her of something ... yes, that was it! As a child she used to make flat pebbles skip along the smooth waters of the Vendée, fascinated by the way they hopped again and again before finally disappearing into the river's depths.

"Which are they? Where?" she asked. She had learnt how to make her voice carry further now.

She wanted to get to know all the prisoners, and find out why they were there and who had sentenced them. The common convicts terrified her, but she must make an effort to get to know them too, there was good and bad in most people.

Someone had heard her because the reply came promptly, "We'll all be getting together tonight."

"In the barracks, child." That was Keller, he always called her 'child'.

"How long have you got?" A Parisian voice that, a voice that smacked of cobbled streets and crowded alleyways, a voice that went straight to the point. But she hadn't got any 'time' at all. The blunt question was disconcerting because it suddenly made her feel inferior to these people, many of whom were serving long sentences simply because they were prepared to fight for an ideal. Whereas she was nothing but a drawing-room idealist, an emancipated woman. She lived in an elegant district, owned property, goods, shares—why, she even owned nickel mines on this very island! Why lower herself in their eyes by admitting that she was there by mistake, a bird of passage who would soon be released? She would have a chance to explain all that tonight in the barracks.

The appearance of a guard patrolling the paved path along the river bank saved her the trouble of replying. The moment he was out of earshot the talk started up again, broken, staccato words and phrases. She learnt that one of the men had gone through the ordeal of Satory like herself and Aimé. She could have talked to him for hours, sharing recollections of that appalling prison camp and the long march out to Versailles through the rain with women prodding at them with umbrellas, men spitting on them, crusts of bread thrown into the muddy gutters for them to pick up. A woman—there was no mistaking the voice—revealed that she had fought at Montmartre and seen the Federal troops skewered by bayonets when the Versaillais moved in. One of the men had defended the wall of Père-Lachaise cemetery ... he escaped the firing squad only to be captured later.

A bugle call, clear and shrill, gave her a fleeting sense that she was back in the Crimea. Everyone was moving towards the river bank. She followed, tipping out her cloth bag into the barrel and then laying her sieve on top of the pile in the tool shed.

"She hasn't any clogs, she hasn't got the right clothes or kit," said her protectress, emphasising the word 'kit'. "Pepere chucked her out like this after he'd finished with her."

"Yes, I saw. If she comes along tomorrow I'll make sure she has the right kit," said the guard. "She's been re-captured, has she?"

"Obviously," said the woman.

"Your name's Dilille, isn't it?" the man asked, turning to Stephanie.

"Dy-tte-ville," Stephanie spelt it out, syllable by syllable, hoping he would react with some interest. "That mean anything to you?"

"Nothing!"

That 'nothing', uttered in a rasping but not unfriendly

voice, was like a steel door slamming shut behind her. Her only hope of release would have to come from outside. As far as the guards were concerned she was merely an escaped convict, a Communard who had been recaptured, a filthy slut!

"Get a move on there, you women!"

Seizing her by the wrists in a grip like handcuffs the woman pulled her along and Stephanie found herself standing in a long line of convicts formed up in pairs.

"One, two, one, two, one . . ."

Stephanie was swept into marking time and swinging her arms along with the rest. The column marched off towards the longest of the various huts. On the way in everyone took an earthenware bowl into which their meal was piled—a ladleful of soup, lumps of sticky pork fat, a dollop of noodles like maggots clustered together, and to crown it all a black, rotting banana. It was disgusting, but she would eat it because her stomach was cramped with hunger.

Watched by four guards stationed in the corners of the hut the convicts devoured their meal as noisily as pigs at the trough. Stephanie was anxious not to appear lady-like or finicky, she wanted to win their trust and confidence, so she set herself to eat the same way, sucking the food down noisily, chewing with her mouth open. Tonight they would have their 'get together' in the barrack hut. She kept hearing the word, and it had come to sound like a promise, a ray of hope. She would be able to talk and listen to them there, and she hoped to convince them that her sincerity was beyond doubt. Names whirled through her mind: she could already see the doors she would be knocking on, the offices she would storm into, the 'powers-that-be' whom she would upbraid and pester and browbeat till some notice was taken of her complaints. She wasn't going to let them get away with it, it was illegal to mix common-law criminals with political prisoners, and that was only the beginning. This place needed reorganising, humanising; Pepere and Juju should be sacked, others too, very likely, the food should at least be as edible as it would have been in the army or a conventional prison . . .

Before the 'get together' everyone washed up for themselves, a simple operation which consisted of passing spoon and bowl under running water. As the spoon clattered into the bucket and she added the bowl to the pile, the canteens of the Military Academy, Gallipoli, the Crimea, rose to her memory. She shivered inwardly. Why should these memories return unbidden, reviving the past so painfully? That afternoon she had relived a period of her childhood as words bounced over the water to her like pebbles. Now, the sound of spoon and bowl, and she was back again in a military canteen. And strangest of all, these memories of the past strengthened her faith in herself and her future, as if an experience of prison camp had an essential part to play in her life. Stephanie stumbled out of the building. The convicts were forming up into a line again. Then they marched off to the dormitory hut.

Four double barred windows showed the dusky night sky. There was no lamp. A key squeaked in the immense lock, and someone slid back the bolts on the outside of the door.

"Give Antoine a shove; this one'll sleep beside me," said the woman.

The aforementioned Antoine shambled off to the back of the hut muttering a few coarse words which Stephanie did not catch. All she registered was that when this woman commanded, everyone obeyed.

"Your coverlet," she said, spreading a cotton square over the thin mattress which was now Stephanie's.

"Thank you," Stephanie whispered, beginning to unlace her boots.

"Wait."

The woman unlaced them for her, and then massaged her feet for a few minutes. Stephanie lay down, gritting her teeth as she tried to find a position which did not hurt her aching body. She pulled the coverlet over her and loosened her waistband. She suddenly remembered Armand's ring. Where was she going to hide it tomorrow if they confiscated her clothes when she got her convict's issue?

"Could you tell me . . ."

"Go to sleep," came the cold, crisp reply. "You can talk tomorrow."

"Thank you. What's your name?" Stephanie whispered.

"Lafaye. Have you forgotten?"

"I did hear it but it slipped my mind, I'm sorry."

"No harm done. They used to call me Annette once—but not here!"

"You'll always be Annette to me and . . . I'll always . . . be . . . Steph . . ."

"Go to sleep, you poor dear, you haven't the strength to talk. The first day in this place is gruelling, besides, you had a beating-up from Pepere to start with. He's got a heavy hand, as I have good reason to know! Now go to sleep!"

Stephanie shut her eyes and tumbled into sleep like a stone falling down a well. Now and then, through her slumbers, she was dimly aware of moving shapes and murmurs and she even distinguished a few disconnected words: "leave her be . . . Dytteville . . . leave her alone, will you . . . Paris . . . she's promised . . ."

Yes, she had promised to tell them . . . to speak to people . . . she must . . . At last, so as not to disappoint them all, she struggled out of the black sleep which had engulfed her, and at the first flutter of her eyelids the convicts pressed round her, whispering urgently, breathlessly:

"Tell us about France . . . Paris . . . what are they doing for us . . . has anyone registered an appeal on our behalf? And what about the rest of Europe? What hope is there for us?"

Her mattress was underneath one of the windows, and

the faint light from the night sky showed her an eager circle of anxious, haggard faces. What could she say? There was no hope for them. No one ever talked of the Commune in Paris these days, it was a painful, forbidden topic. She hadn't the courage to try and deceive them.

"Since Henri Brisson's and Louis Blanc's proposals for an amnesty, both of which were quashed, there's been nothing at all," she faltered. "Thiers is pitiless, and MacMahon won't do anything on his own initiative. You can only wait, hope ..."

"For how long?" Lafaye demanded angrily.

"I can't lie to you," Stephanie answered simply. Then her voice strengthened as she went on, "but I swear, I swear by everything sacred to me, that as soon as I get back to France I shall move heaven and earth to do something for you. I am Madame Dytteville, which may not mean anything to you, but it carries some weight in Paris. I know a lot of influential people ..."

From a heart overflowing with pity and affection, Stephanie threw them some crumbs of hope and comfort. She would intercede on their behalf, that she was determined upon. Just how it should be done she didn't yet know but she had given her solemn word and she meant to keep it.

"Maitre Keller," she said, recognising the emaciated countenance in the dim light, "why are you here?"

She sounded as if she were taking notes for a dossier.

"I hid Elisabeth Dimitrief in my house, that was enough."

"Elisabeth!" Stephanie exclaimed. "What became of her?"

Elisabeth ... the first aid post ... the Women's Union for the Defence of Paris. Elisabeth had said to her once, 'We could do with more women like you!' She had been a true friend. Another time, when things had begun to go against them, and the Versaillais forces were beginning to encircle the city, Stephanie told her, 'Whatever happens you can always hide out at my place!' Elisabeth had chosen Maitre Keller, the lawyer with the wise eyes, instead.

"Why did she go to you, I wonder?" she murmured, with jealous affection. "I offered to hide her."

"You did?" The lawyer was amazed.

"Yes," she persisted. "I am all the things I said I was, just now, but to Elisabeth I was just a woman she liked and respected. Where is she now?"

"Almost certainly in London, with Karl Marx. She was his secretary. He sent her to Paris."

The mere mention of Elisabeth's name seemed to have put new life into her. She studied the other faces, and one by one they named themselves. The names poured out, more than she could remember at one session. Later she would question them, find out why they had been sentenced, begin filling out her dossier. She seemed to remember seeing the journalist's name at the foot of an article somewhere. She turned to him.

"Why are you here, Greboura? I seem to have seen your name ..."

"It means something to you?" he asked, his voice eager and his eyes sparkling at the thought that he was not forgotten.

"I can't quite recall but ..."

"G.G., for your information, lovely lady, was arrested in a printing-press, type-setting. I used to write against Versailles, against Thiers, against everything! I was a journalist!"

There was such a desperate gaiety in the way he emphasised the word 'was' that Stephanie riposted, "And so you are still!"

She so wanted to rekindle his faith in himself and his past achievements. She saw tears of gratitude and joy sparkling in his eyes, blinked away hurriedly a second later, because a man does not weep. She felt like weeping herself, then, it was so extraordinary that a few words from her should be enough to restore life and hope in a man who was almost a perfect stranger.

They asked her about Paris, France, the Republic ... What would a stonemason earn there now? What had changed, what was new? The man from Port-Royal wanted to know if any of the streets in his district had been demolished or rebuilt. He spoke of the place as if it were his own native village, he had been born there, his mother still lived there. He touched her heart, he was so simple, so eager. She gave him her hand and he bent over it, and she felt it wet with tears—and he had killed his wife and brother! Others in the crowd wanted to know about new laws, votes, interest rates. She answered them all, inventing a little where she didn't know the answer; anything was better than leaving them famished for news, and all the while her head dropped lower and lower and she felt herself plummeting into semi-consciousness. Lafaye finally intervened in her crisp, commanding way.

"Leave her alone now, d'you hear, she's worn out, finished, at the end of her tether. She needs sleep, rest, she'll be stronger tomorrow ... give her time to get used to this life! Run along now, run along!"

"Tomorrow ... you must all talk to me ... I'm sorry ... so tired ..." Stephanie mumbled almost inaudibly." You must tell me ... names ... and where you come from ... I've got a good memory ... I'm your friend ..."

Her head sank back. The others went off, elated by her news and her assurances. For one night they would be able to forget their convict existence ...

No one even noticed that Stephanie, face whiter than death, had fainted clean away.

Chapter Eleven

Snatched from sleep by the frenzied clamour of the bell, Stephanie started up on the mattress and then fell back with a cry of pain.

"Pompette . . . I-I-can't make it!"

"Pompette? I'm Annette, old girl!"

Where was she? 'Old girl'—that was what the convent pupils used to call you when you were slow getting out of bed in the morning, but that wasn't a schoolgirl's voice, it was harsh, adult. It wasn't Pompette's cheery bellow either, it was . . . it came back to her in a rush: the penal colony, Pepere, the river, Annette!

"I can't, really I can't . . . my body aches everywhere . . . it's dreadful, I can't move!"

"Yes, you can!"

That was crisp and clear enough. But Stephanie had woken to limbs so stiff and battered she could not even sit up.

"I . . . no . . . I-I-can't!"

"Stick it out, ducks. Let's have a look at you."

'Ducks!'—that was a new one to her . . . Pompette used to call her 'my pet', or 'child'.

Annette pulled up her skirt to examine Stephanie's legs and thighs, and then ran her hands gently and probingly over her body.

"Your breasts, are they sore?" she asked.

"No, they didn't get hit . . . he kicked me in the belly. It's my back most, all round here, and down there. I rolled myself up into a ball, you see!"

"You've got as many bruises as raisins in a cake, my poor dear! Pepere must have been enjoying himself, the dirty swine. It'll take a week to heal. Those bruises are going to be a fine sight, you'll be rainbow-coloured! Now look, you don't need Pepere's help to get you on your feet again, do you? No, well you'll have to get back to the river and the sieve. Think of all the people who are waiting for you, who believe in you, who are out looking for you now!"

That was the best thing Annette could have said. Maurice and Yann *would* be looking for her. They would be certain to think of the convict camps because it was well known that the native search parties delivered their captives there. There was a boat waiting out in the lagoon for her, somewhere ...

"You were wonderful last night, you can't think how much good you did us," said Annette, helping Stephanie to her feet, and keeping up a deafening flow of chatter. "Cry out if you want to, it'll make you feel better—it's getting moving again which hurts, you've stiffened up. I must say you've got the gift of the gab all right, the way you made Paris come alive for all of us again! It's your education of course, I spotted that straight away. Dimitrief thought well of you, you said, that's good too. We'll give you a helping hand if you weaken, ducks, but you'll have to keep in the middle of us. See, you aren't doing badly at all! Now keep your legs moving, scream, cry all you want, I'm going to rub your back for you!"

Stephanie groaned through clenched teeth, as the fingers probed her bruised flesh, rubbing and kneading.

"No, please ..."

"Go on, yell, I don't mind," said Annette. "I've got to rub your back, though, it'll do you good."

"It'll help, child," said Keller. "We've all been through it one time or another so we know what we're saying."

"Courage, lovely lady." Greboura stopped in front of her and swept an imaginary hat off his brow. "When I get back I shall write a splendid front page article called 'Stephanie the convict'!"

Despite her pain she managed a shaky laugh.

"Thanks to you," the journalist continued, "I'm convinced I shall get away from here. You've brought me back to life! In the racy language of the convict colony, Stephanie, you're a pal!"

Beneath the youthful gaiety, Stephanie sensed the strong emotions of a man who has regained his faith in himself after sinking to the depths of despair.

"Thanks to me? Thank you, G.G., that alone makes my coming here worthwhile!"

G.G. conjured up Paris, her old life and loves, so vividly that she felt stronger already. The convicts came and went, with an encouraging word to her in passing, but it was George Greboura's gratitude that meant the most to her. No doubt about it—G.G. was a new man.

Falteringly, she forced herself to take one slow step, then another. It felt as if her legs were being driven into her body, grating against her hip bones.

"I'm still in one piece," she cried, to reassure the others.

"It would be a pity if you ..." Greboura used the formal 'vous' and she checked him.

"You were saying?" she interrupted, pointedly making use of the familiar 'tu'.

"I was saying it would be a pity if you were not!" and he dropped back into the 'tu' form of address, underlining a comradeship that cut across differences of class and fortune, "because, from what I can see of you, your hair, face, lips—and from what I imagine of the rest—you are a woman to inspire painters and sculptors!"

A brilliant smile flashed across his face as he spoke and he fixed his steely blue eyes on her with an appreciative connoisseur's stare.

"Idiot," she murmured affectionately.

She might have renewed his faith in himself, but he had now returned the favour by reminding her that she was beautiful, a woman to make men dream, and that he was even now dreaming, desiring, imagining ...

Stephanie knew she was surrounded by arms ready to

reach out and support her if she faltered or weakened, they were all keeping an eye on her. She took her place in the column. Keller was in front of her, Lafaye at her side, Greboura just behind, and she realised that they were falling into step with her, to help her. Her steps might be slow, uncertain, but she was moving! They were carrying her along with them. A new day had begun!

She was familiar with the day's routine now, apart from breakfast itself, which consisted of a dishwatery liquid called coffee and two slices of damp black bread on the verge of going mouldy. She ate it all! 'It fills you up, and you can't do without food,' as Annette would say and Stephanie agreed. Annette had taken charge of Armand's ring because Stephanie was to receive her prison issue that morning. This passed off without incident. Nenesse took an inventory of her few possessions and assured her that they would be returned to her if she behaved herself and got transferred to another camp.

"I am Madame Dytteville," she said almost apologetically.

"So you say, so Fernand tells me. But it's got to be proved. We get a new load of provisions once a month; you never know, there might be good news for you then."

"He's a decent bloke," said Annette when Stephanie returned wearing the coarse canvas uniform and wooden clogs. "I'm sure he'll do what he can. You're luckier than we are, ducks, they're out searching for you and they'll soon get you out of here."

'They're searching for me, they'll find me soon,' Stephanie thought. 'Maurice's mission was to take me to Yann. Yann's boat will be waiting out in the lagoon at the rendezvous.'

"Right now your job is to pan for gold," said Lafaye crisply, breaking into her thoughts. "A time for everything and everything in its time."

Stephanie dipped her sieve into the water, washed the contents, shook it and slowly began filling up her cloth bag. As she worked she kept up a staccato flow of talk with her fellow workers, catching the words and phrases which flitted across the water to her and replying without moving her lips. It was amusing to fool the guards. Juju fired only two bullets in her general direction. The 'game' helped her forget her battered, aching body. It was only when she attempted a movement outside her working rhythm that new pain stabbed through her. Fortunately the other prisoners kept her fully occupied—she was a new listener, a newcomer who didn't know the first thing about them all and they were delighted to fill her in with the details. And Stephanie wanted to know about all of them.

'They' still meant the Versaillais troops, and their harsh reprisals—firing squads, tribunals, sentences. Stephanie re-lived the recapture of Paris in this remote corner of the world as she had never lived it before. She remembered how she and Aimé had marched with their hands above their heads from Paris to the Satory camp at Versailles. Aimé! He was sleeping with Eugenie, spied on and coveted by all the other native women who wanted to bring a half-caste son into the world. How absurd to think of Aimé, the human stud, being pampered and petted in a remote, hidden valley on a Pacific island! Reality was stranger than fiction. In brief, bloody, unsparing language the convicts re-created those tumultuous days when the barricades were raised across the streets, only to be destroyed, then rebuilt, then finally recaptured again, street by street. Stephanie endured with them the gradual attrition, bullet by bullet, of the main Paris stations which the Federal troops had made their strongholds. 'My mate was killed under my nose ... head smashed open, arm blown off ... there wasn't anything I could do.' They conjured up for her the last bastion of the Rue de Rivoli, and the great conflagrations started by the Federals in the hopes of checking the advance of the official army. As they talked of the desperate, foredoomed struggle which had marked them for life, the men seemed to kindle into new hope that one day they would be able to begin again where they had left off . . . and this time they would win! Stephanie was deeply touched when, in the midst of some gory account of blood and death at the barricades, an occasional encouraging phrase reached her: "Keep it up, ducky . . . thanks for last night . . . I'll tell you more tonight, Dytteville . . . courage, lovely lady!"

"Just a minute," said Lafaye, raising a hand to check the other inmates of the dormitory barrack as they all made a move to gather round Stephanie.

"They've given her an ancient suit of clothes. I'll have to see what can be done about the trousers—they look as though they'll fall off. Look, yes, it's all coming apart down here," she went on, while Stephanie gazed curiously at her. "You don't want to go giving them ideas, they're quite bad enough as it is!"

Reading between the lines Stephanie understood this to mean: 'I'll sew your husband's ring into your waistband, nobody'll suspect a thing.'

Sewing without a needle and cotton was a laborious business. It involved unravelling a thread, poking a hole through the fabric with a stick, pushing the thread through, knotting it, and then beginning all over again.

Stephanie wrapped herself in her coverlet, and a moment later they had all thronged about her. Eagerly, anxiously, they questioned her about Paris. As she answered them the city seemed to rise up before her eyes like a mirage: Paris in the spring sun, Paris on a grey day, Paris at the hour when the lamplighter passed. These men dreamed of Paris, of their own 'quartiers', where they lived and loved, where they had their families, wives, neighbourhood bistros. A hoarse voice, choked with nostalgia, suddenly demanded: "Rue du Theatre, in the Fifteenth been down that way at all?"

The man so desperately longed for her to have been there, and his eyes shone so imploringly in the half light that she lied comfortingly. "I'll say I have! I went the whole length of it just six months ago, from one end to the other."

In his excitement the man retraced his beloved street, house by house, dwelling fondly on a shop sign here, a window there, a crooked doorway. Stephanie interrupted softly, "Ah, yes . . . a laundry, I remember it now . . ."

"La Gervaise?"

"I didn't take in the name."

"That's understandable if you were passing through. It's not as if it were your own quartier."

"I haven't got a quartier of my own, Norbert, I think of them all as my own," she said. She called him Norbert because using his Christian name gave him confidence.

"You make me feel as if I were back there myself! What luck you went that way, wasn't it? It's a fine street, don't you think?"

"Very fine, full of life, a place you don't forget."

"One window's got flowers in it . . ."

"That's right . . . some . . . some . . ."

"Geraniums!"

"I was just going to say geraniums, and . . ."

"Lines of washing?"

"Hung out to dry!"

"Yes, yes . . . and the little shopfront was painted yellow."

"A faded yellow," she cried, clapping her hands excitedly.

"Of course, old Mother Gervaise gave it a lick of paint when she could. I feel as if I'm standing there now! I tell you what, Stephanie, when I really do get back I'll think of you!"

"When you return, Norbert, you shall have me in for a meal with your family and we'll talk about the past, would you like that?"

In his excitement and agitation, overwhelmed by the rush of memories, Norbert burst into tears. She laid her soft woman's hand on the nape of his neck, and pulled his head down on to her lap where he wept like a child. It was then the unexpected occurred—life is full of surprises.

"You know Paris, that's obvious," said a man's voice. "But whereabouts in France do you come from originally?"

"From the Vendée."

'The Vendée': all at once they began telling her of their native regions, Auvergne, Gascony, Beauce, Limousin ... but the one name she was waiting for, she never heard! New Caledonia had a bit of everything, even the Breton Kerdelecs, but apart from Aimé, herself and a whore, Yolande de Ferrière there was no one who hailed from the Vendée. One of life's dirty tricks!

"What a chauvinist bunch," cried Lafaye as if she had decided to stem the flood of reminiscence. "All they can think about is their corner of a province somewhere. I bet it's the same everywhere, ducks, if you were in America they'd be telling you about Nevada and Missouri, in Italy about Piedmont and Calabria, in Norway it'd be some fjord; and in Africa and China it'd be the same story! No matter what happens you never lose touch with your roots."

"Where are you from, then?" Stephanie asked, nettled, because she fully entered with the passion for boasting about one's birthplace.

"Paris!"

"And your parents?"

"From the North. My dad came from Lyons. Now are you satisfied?"

"Yes, now I know why you're the way you are. You northerners, you're a tough bunch; when all's said and done, you are yourself, and I like you that way!"

Lafaye burst out laughing, secretly pleased. When she replied it was in language worthy of Pompette.

"Well, I'll tell you one thing, you came to this place like a blessing from heaven! They've all grown so much younger, it has to be seen to be believed! As Greboura says, you're a real oil painting yourself!"

Stephanie turned towards him. Darkness was gathering rapidly but she could just make out his shoulders and the shape and set of his head. He looked every inch a man again, and she thought tenderly, 'It's good to see them as they should be, strong and confident. Where would we be without them?' and Yann rose before her imagination; handsome, tender, masterful Yann.

"Shut-eye now," Lafaye commanded.

Regretfully they all shuffled back to their pallets, thanking Stephanie, wishing her a good night, a sound sleep.

"It's done now," said Annette, handing back her canvas smock. Then she added, "We've all got our stories, I suppose."

A catch in her voice alerted Stephanie, who said gently, "You've got your keepsake too, then? Why don't you tell me about it?"

There was a long silence. Lafaye finally confessed:

"A lock of dark hair softer than down—my son's."

She fell silent.

"Go on, tell me, there's no one else listening. Talk about it, it'll do you good."

"My son—I called him Louis-Nathaniel after Rossel who got shot— I wanted him to be like him, an idealist, pure as daylight. He'll be just on three now, I hardly knew him. My mother's raising him, I haven't heard a word from her. She can't write anyway, she probably doesn't even know where I am—and I don't like to write to her because a letter coming from here might put her in bad with the landlord, or the boss. I know she's waiting for me. When I go back all she'll say to me, as if I'd just gone out that morning, will be 'Sit down, child, you must be hungry' and she'll put the food in front of me crying very quietly because she doesn't like to show her feelings."

"Just like you, eh?" Stephanie whispered, impressed by the efforts Lafaye was making to keep her eyes dry and her voice steady and impersonal. "I've got kids too, you know, twins, Charles and Armand, then Maurice and Valentine and a girl a bit younger. If I get back to France before you—I don't want to upset you but it looks as if I will—I'll go to see Louis-Nathaniel, and I'll look after him and make sure he has everything he needs; he'll be like another child to me till you get back. I'll send you news of him and I'll tell him about you. What's your mother's address?"

"Rue Mouffetard ... number eleven," Annette muttered, her throat tightening. "I-I ... you're too much for me, you are—you witch!"

"Come here!"

Stephanie couldn't believe her ears. It was three o'clock, almost time for their midday meal.

"Come!" repeated Pepere with obsequious politeness. He took her sieve from her and handed it to Lafaye who always arranged things so that they worked side by side. There could be only one explanation for this uncharacteristic deference on Pepere's part: her heart filled with joy: 'Yann is here! Maurice tracked me down ... this nightmare is over!' She straightened up, looking round her and then suddenly, in a voice which reverberated round the camp, she cried: "I'll be back!"

Pepere took this without batting an eyelid. She glanced up at Juju on his rock, sorely tempted to shake her fist at him. Fernand and Nenesse, the only guards to show any human feelings towards the convicts, were rewarded with smiles.

She followed Pepere into the guard post. Yann, Maurice and two guards stood behind the massive wooden barrier. Al she had to do was walk through the low wicket in the partition to be free! Her eyes were swimming with tears as she gazed at Yann. Her lips trembled so that she could scarcely pronounce his name. She leant against the wooden gate.

"You must be tired, Madame," said Pepere with oily solicitude. He made a move as if to support her.

The swine seemed to imagine he was going to get away with it! What a bastard! Her eyes flashed, and she spat furiously at him, "Don't touch me, d'you hear, I forbid you! Don't you lay a finger on me!"

The bugle call for the midday meal sounded.

"We'll cut along now, boss," said the two guards casually.

"Off you go," said Pepere stoutly, but he looked uneasy.

The moment they left Yann tried to push the gate open. It was locked and bolted. Impatiently, he kicked it in.

'This is just the beginning,' Stephanie thought exultantly. 'He's going to pay dearly for beating me up!'

"Madame Dytteville will tell you that she has been treated well here," said Pepere, repulsively humble all of a sudden. He must be hoping that in her delight at being freed she would keep her mouth shut.

"Treated well?" Stephanie flamed at him. "What's this then?" and she pulled back her dress to reveal a badly swollen shoulder, "and what about my back, and my stomach, and the kick which winded me! What about my legs, and shins—you really worked me over, didn't you, and then when I passed out you threw me out for the others to take in and look after ..."

"You did that! You ... you ..."

Yann was choked by fury. His fist shot out and caught Pepere on the chin, sending him thudding against the partition. His fat, flabby body slumped to the ground. Blood spurted from his nose and dribbled from his mouth, and he whimpered, gasping and spluttering "You can't do this to me ... you can't ..."

"Can't? Who says I can't, swine, bastard, scab!"

Yann grabbed him by the waistcoat and shook him like a rat.

"You haven't the right ..." the words squeezed out of him.

"The *right*! I'll take it, d'you hear, and a whole lot of others too while I'm about it. I'm going to beat you to a jelly!"

A second stunning blow sent Pepere crashing to the floor.

"Help ... help ..."

The terrified whimper was almost inaudible through bloody froth. Yann snatched him up and dealt him two thunderous slaps across the face. The man flopped into the corner, half-conscious.

"That's enough, you'll kill him," Stephanie whispered.

Yann was too blinded by fury to hear her. He kept picking Pepere up only to pulverise him again. The man's groans grew weaker, ceased altogether, but Yann still went on pounding his insensible victim, shouting abuse at him, threatening to have him arrested, locked up, put away. Stephanie felt sickened by the slaughter he was working on the unconscious guard. Blood kept spattering from the blows. She went over, hoping to stop him. Maurice slipped an arm round her shoulders and she turned and buried her head in his neck, trying to shut out the dull, soggy, murderous tattoo of Yann's revenge.

"And now outside with you, you foul creature, and give your victims a bit of fun!"

Yann hoisted Pepere as if he were a sack of barley and dragged him through the bloody chaos of papers, broken chairs and inkwells on the floor. He opened the door, and kicked the limp body into the yard. Then he stood for a moment wiping his hands and staring at the inert shape lying in the dust. When ...

"Now it's your turn!"

It was Juju, with a loaded gun pointed straight at Yann. He must have suspected that something odd was going on, and come creeping up noiselessly.

Yann stood looking at him, arms akimbo, helpless.

"That's better," the guard sneered. "Not so chirpy now, are we? You're going to be a nice quiet boy now, and Uncle Juju's going to make you piss blood, just you wait and see!"

One, two, three ... the seconds dragged by interminably.

Suddenly, shouts and screams burst from the refectory. The convicts had revolted! Juju turned his head involuntarily and in that split second Maurice was across the hut and on him, with a spring like a wild cat. They rolled to the floor. Yann leapt forward and wrenched Juju's gun from him. Maurice unbuckled the heavy cartridge belt the man was wearing and handed it to his father.

"You're coming too!" Yann hissed. "They won't dare shoot if you're with us. Now, come on, stand up and get moving, quick!"

The other guards stood huddled together near the refectory, not daring to intervene. The convicts were leaning out of the windows, hooting and cheering like people watching a play.

"Don't shoot, don't shoot!" Juju begged, as he felt the shotgun muzzle pressed into his belly. He had to walk backwards with little shuffling steps, like a sheep driven by a wolf, and his ashen, terrified face gazed imploringly at Yann, Maurice and a confused Stephanie.

Just then Stephanie caught sight of Lafaye at the window, miming excitedly. From her signs and gestures, Stephanie realised that she had heard the commotion from inside the refectory, created a diversion and got all the other convicts to join in. She had saved their lives.

"I'll be back," Stephanie shouted at the top of her voice, flinging back her head like a herald on the ramparts. "I swear to you all . . . I'll be back!"

They were making good progress now. In a moment they would have reached the shelter of the rocks, and from there they could see the forest, the banyans, the lagoon—Yann's boat. They were just drawing level with the screen of rocks and boulders when Yann suddenly reversed the gun, seizing it by the barrel and smashed the butt against Juju's head. He flung the gun away as the man collapsed unconscious.

'What's he doing? He must be mad . . . that's our only weapon . . . the other guards will shoot!' She stared at him in bewilderment. As if confirming her fears a group of kanakas suddenly appeared through the trees and encircled them.

"Yann!" she cried, flinging herself into his arms, eager for one taste of his lips before they dragged her away again, separated them ... killed them!

He clasped her to him, straining her close in a passion of protectiveness.

"What's wrong, my beloved? This is the crew from my boat ... they're all armed. I'm taking you away with me now!" His arm tightened round her waist. "My darling, my life, my own—you're coming away with me!"

Nothing mattered now, with his hand in hers, his body pressed against hers, his arm round her ... she was sixteen, twenty, discovering love for the first time, a whole new world was opening up. A quiver ran through her, and her flesh tingled, warmly expectant, all its aches and pains forgotten ... because he was there, next to her, whispering a litany of passion to her in a breathless, urgent, disjointed voice ... "My woman ... my wife ... my beloved ... you're coming away with me, I'm carrying you off!"

He was abducting her!

For her sake he had stormed the convict camp, and assaulted two men ... he was a man who would risk anything for the woman he loved, *his* woman, beside whom no others existed!

They raced hand-in-hand under the canopy of banyans. Suddenly the trees thinned and a bay opened before them, like a blue silk fan. A boat lay at anchor on the still water.

"The *Maraamu*!" Stephanie cried, catching her breath.

The *Maraamu*! The ship the Kerdelecs had had built to their own design, three times the tonnage of the lateen-rigged craft of the Mediterranean which it resembled. With her tall mast, bowsprit and jigger sail, and fully decked, the *Maraamu* was the most beautiful of *tartanes*. Stephanie stepped quickly into the dinghy.

No sooner were they on board than Yann led her straight to the companion-ladder, and down to a small cabin furnished with two bunks ... he was a man, he could wait no longer, he had to have her, his prey, his woman!

He tore the rough convict smock off her as forcefully as he had ripped through every obstruction that had stood between them.

"Your body! Oh, your poor body, my beloved!"

He caressed the bruises, now turning to yellow and mauve, and pressed his lips against them one by one as if he wanted to drink them in, make her pains his.

"I can't live without your body, without you. Oh, Stephanie my love, take me, keep me . . . !"

"I love you, Yann," she murmured, startled by the despair in his voice.

"I shall keep you with me! In spite of everything!"

The last sentence broke from him in a defiant cry.

"I love you too much, Stephanie . . . you've done what I never thought a woman could do, you've enslaved me, bewitched me!"

'Bewitched!' The word Maurice had used.

Yann's violence alarmed her. It was the violence of a jealous man, goaded by suffering. To reassure and calm him, she put all her love and desire for him into her voice.

"Yann . . . I love you . . . I . . ."

"Be quiet! I want you to know what you've done to me! I thought I was going to die when you disappeared, I howled in the night like a dog which scents death. You are my woman, my wife, I want you to stay here, with me! You are the star I have sought all my life! We will be happy together, I swear it . . . I'll give you everything I have and you shall bear me a son. We'll call him Stephen and we'll live together far from the world, just the two of us, alone together . . ."

His rising excitement was frightening. He was like a madman, raving about their future, an impossible future . . .

"My love . . ." she murmured tenderly.

"You're already married, yes, I know . . . I don't want to know anything about the man, do you hear, I've wiped him from my mind, he doesn't exist . . . the only real thing is *us,* Stephanie ... I'm here with you ... that's all that counts ..."

"Yann ..."

"What? You aren't going to tell me you love *him*?"

In his present state he looked as if he could easily have broken her neck.

"I did love him, Yann ... life ..."

"*I'm* your life!"

She said nothing for a moment, hoping that he would quieten down. Then she whispered, "I've got children, they're waiting for me, I can't ..."

"They're twenty thousand miles away!" he raged, with all the egotism of a male to whom nothing matters but the body of the woman he desires.

"But one day I'll have to ..."

"They can come here! All right, they're a part of you —but you're part of *me,* do you hear, flesh of my flesh! I know that every time I make love to you."

Another long, heavy, agonising silence. Why couldn't he make love to her now?

"Yann, I want you, make love to me, take me, I love you ... Later we'll ..."

"No!"

He drew back, towering above her, eyes blazing. Then he cried, in a voice hoarse with pain, "Promise me! Now! Swear to me that you are mine! No matter what bonds tie you to that land I've never seen, you're *mine*!"

"Please, I beg you ..."

"I'm begging *you*! You know what my love is, Stephanie, you know ... Stephanie ... Stephanie ..."

He came down on to her again, murmuring her name like a spell, an invocation, as he kissed her hair, face, shoulders, breasts ... His voice was husky with passion, it claimed her, bewitched her, filtered through her every pore. His supple loins bestrode her as he possessed her with a slow deliberation which set her swooning ... he was carrying her away with him now ... they were one, one flesh, she was in him and he in her, lost in the total, utter consummation of a man and a woman dying to the world, reborn in love . . .

Several hours later, the *Maraamu* headed out to the open sea from the calm lagoon. The boat tossed and rocked violently for a few minutes as the sheltered waters gave way to a long swell which caught her amidships, but in a moment she had veered round with the wind behind her and boat and sea were harmoniously one.

Stephanie stood wrapped in Yann's arms at the bows, quity dizzy and drunk with love.

"You're carrying me off," she whispered.

"That's it—in a nutshell!"

"We're on our way to Noumea?" she queried, wanting to be sure.

"No, I'm keeping you with me this time!"

For a few seconds she began to wonder whether he was bearing her away to some uninhabited island where they could be alone together.

"But what about your father?" she murmured, trying to recall Yann to the present. After all, the old man had forfeited his freedom in exchange for hers.

"He's safe. Atai is his friend."

"But . . . Aimé?"

"Don't worry about him, he's getting fatter every day!"

"You're disgusting!" she protested, trying to free herself from the inflexible arm riveting her to his side.

"Don't think about him, he'll come to no harm, think of us! I want you and I'm going to have you. For a fortnight you belong to me. I'm the master of this ship; there's nothing you can do about it. I found you, and I'm keeping you, do you hear? I want you with me day and night, your body waiting, ready for me. I want to feel your body yielding to mine. I want you to seek the lips which caress your breasts and thighs before I plunge into you. I want you to belong to me so deeply you can never forget . . . For two weeks of love, two weeks at sea, you shall be *mine*. Afterwards everyday life can take over again, business, timber shipments, the mines. But now, Stephanie, forget the world—forget it exists, there's only you and me afloat in a nutshell on the sea! I'd like to die like this! When we have loved I wish our boat would gently founder and sink down to the sea bed with us both, so that our love could continue through all eternity ... Stephanie ... Stephanie ..."

She nestled her head deeper into the hollow of his shoulder and murmured "Go on talking, Yann, tell me you love me ... tell me ..."

Stephanie's story will be continued in *The Price of Freedom.*